THE BODY OF A GIRL

Books available in Perennial Library by
Michael Gilbert:

After the Fine Weather
Be Shot for Sixpence
Blood and Judgment
The Body of a Girl
Close Quarters
The Country-House Burglar
The Danger Within
Death Has Deep Roots
Fear to Tread
He Didn't Mind Danger
The Night of the Twelfth
Petrella at Q
Trouble

THE
BODY OF
A GIRL

Michael Gilbert

PERENNIAL LIBRARY

HARPER & ROW, PUBLISHERS, NEW YORK

Grand Rapids, Philadelphia, St. Louis, San Francisco
London, Singapore, Sydney, Tokyo, Toronto

First PERENNIAL LIBRARY edition published 1989.

LIBRARY OF CONGRESS CATALOG CARD NUMBER 76-175153

ISBN 0-06-081015-7

89 90 91 92 93 WB/OPM 10 9 8 7 6 5 4 3 2 1

THE BODY OF A GIRL

1

SEPTEMBER 7 THAT YEAR fell on a Tuesday. On that day three things happened, none of them of any apparent importance. Later they were to combine, as certain chemicals, harmless in themselves, may do, to produce violent results.

Michael Drake-Pelley, age fourteen, and his younger cousin, Frank, planned an early morning swim, to mark the last day of an enjoyable summer holiday on the river.

Detective Inspector William Mercer received by first post confirmation of his promotion to chief inspector and of his appointment in charge of the CID at Stoneferry on Thames, which is one of the larger upriver stations of Q Division of the Metropolitan Police.

Later that morning in No. 1 Court at the Old Bailey, Mr. Justice Arbuthnot sentenced Samuel Lewis, Daniel Evans, and Raymond Oxley to fifteen years penal servitude each for robbery with violence. "This was a brutal and greedy crime," he said. "In the course of it you beat to the ground a young girl and smashed in the face of a man who sought to prevent your snatching the money which belonged to their firm. You can count yourselves fortunate that neither of them died. Had they done so I should have sentenced you to imprisonment for life and made a recommendation to the Home Secretary that the sentence was not to be reviewed for at least twenty-five years."

The three men received the homily and the sentence without a flicker of interest.

When Scotland Yard moved to Petty France, the police retained a block of offices next door to their old headquarters. They found them useful for informal meetings, since there is a subway entrance from Cannon Row police station. The building belongs to the Statistics Department of the Board of Trade and they actually occupy the ground and the first floor, but if you wander, by mistake, into the upper stories you will be politely sent about your business by a uniformed policeman.

In a front room, overlooking the Thames, three men discussed the Lewis case.

At the head of the table was Deputy Commander Laidlaw, thin, dedicated, and already showing the signs of the disease which was to destroy him. It was Laidlaw who had conceived the idea of the Regional Crime Squads and he was now in charge of all twelve of them. On his right was the CID boss of No. 1 District, Chief Superintendent Morrissey, a large, white-faced cockney Jew who looked as formidable now as when, twenty years before, he had climbed into the ring to box for the Metropolitan Police. The third man, who would have passed unnoticed in any bowler-hatted crowd of commuters, was in his own way the most distinguished of the three. He was Sir Henry Hartfield, seconded from the Home Office as standing adviser to the Clearing House Banks. He said, "You can congratulate yourselves, I think, on getting rid of that little lot."

"We'd congratulate ourselves," said Laidlaw, "if we thought they were the last of their kind."

"Or the worst," said Morrissey.

2

"You've put away three major gangs in the last two years."

"All due to Dibox," said Morrissey. Adding, "That sounds like a TV commercial, dunnit?"

"The Dibox system has certainly proved its worth," agreed Sir Henry. "Do you think the opposition might be beginning to tumble to it?"

"I imagine they must be starting to put two and two together," said Laidlaw. "They're not fools. They must wonder how we got onto Oxley within twenty-four hours. Particularly since he was only driving the getaway car and no one identified him on the job and he had very little form. They must guess it was something to do with the notes themselves, even if they weren't able to work out the answer."

"Suppose they *did* work it out," said Sir Henry. "What could they do about it? You can't remove the mark. You can't even decipher it, except with proper apparatus."

"What they'd do," said Morrissey, "they wouldn't be in any hurry to spend the money. They'd set up a stocking. The stuff from today's job goes into the top of the stocking. The pay-out for it comes from the bottom. From a job done maybe two years before."

"On a mixed lot of notes from a number of different jobs," said Laidlaw.

"If they operated on that scale there'd be a lot of money involved. It's curiously bulky stuff. Where do you suggest they'd keep it?"

Morrissey said, with a grin which exposed two gold-capped teeth, "When we put out the buzz that the big boys might be stocking up, you'd be surprised at the ideas our favorite little grasses came in with. Everything from a blasted oak in Epping Forest to the third lavatory from the left at Waterloo."

"Neither of those sounds very promising," said Sir Henry primly. "More likely they keep it in a safe, in a

3

private house, or some legitimate-looking business. Or maybe in a strong room or a safe deposit."

"Agreed," said Morrissey. "The trouble is, our informers don't move in such select circles. They hang round in pubs, picking up gossip. Most of it's untrue, and what isn't dead lies is twisted."

"It's a fact," said Laidlaw. "We've never been able to get a man on the inside of any of the really important outfits. They're too careful. They pick their own recruits, from prison or Borstal mostly. And they check them, and their families and backgrounds, very thoroughly before they even approach them. Then they're given small jobs to start with, to try them out. It might be years before they graduate to a real operation. And they know that if they do get caught, their families will be looked after. There's not much inducement to split."

"And plenty of bloody good reasons not to," said Morrissey. "Anyone who gets ambitious in that direction gets reminded about Cobbet, and then he thinks again."

"Cobbet?"

"It was the Crows. They're just about the biggest outfit left. They'll be bigger still, now that Sam Lewis has gone, because they'll pick up the minor characters from his lot. Cobbet was a fringer. He did small jobs for them. He was never on the inside. He got the idea he wasn't being treated right. Then there was some trouble about a girl. What with one thing and another, he offered to squeak. We handled him dead careful, I can tell you. Outside telephones, third-party contacts, different meeting places each time. But they found out."

Sir Henry said, as if he hardly liked to ask the question, "What did they do to him?"

"They had a full-scale trial, judge and counsel for the prosecution and counsel for the defense and 'Yes, me lud,' and 'No, me lud,' and they found him guilty and executed him. What they actually did was they popped him headfirst into a barrel—alive, I gather—and filled it up with wet cement. You could just see the tops of his legs sticking out. It was stood, like that, in a garage work-shop the gang used, with a canary in a cage hung on the left foot. The only one who thought that touch real fun was the canary. He chirruped away like anything for forty-eight hours, I'm told."

"You mean they kept it there, openly, for two days?"

"That's right, and all the boys were brought in to see it, in turn. Then it was put into a van, driven to Grays in Essex, and dropped into the river."

"How did you find all this out?"

"Find it out? We didn't have to find it out. The story was round the whole of South London. They meant it to be. They didn't even mind people knowing where they'd dumped the barrel. It went into thirty foot of water with a tidal scour running at five knots. It'll have rolled some-where out into the North Sea by now."

"They've learned two lessons from America," said Laidlaw. "The power of money, and the power of fear. A man who knows how to handle those two weapons can become very powerful. He can laugh at the law for a long time."

"But not forever," said Sir Henry.

"I hope not. Although there have been times and places when crime has got on top. It goes in waves. And it can't last forever. But it's very unpleasant while it does last."

A slight and quickly controlled tightening of the lips signaled the pain which had unexpectedly reached out and gripped him.

"And things are happening here, under our noses, that I don't like. I don't only mean the crime figures, though they're frightening enough. I mean the sort of general breaking loose and kicking over the traces that's going on in all classes. It may sound an odd thing for a policeman to say, but I believe the real reason is the breakdown of religion. If people aren't afraid of going to hell in the next world, they don't see any reason why they shouldn't have the best time possible in this one. And if your idea of a good time is drink or drugs or girls or boys, and they cost money, and you haven't got any money—the answer's obvious, isn't it?"

"There's a difference," said Sir Henry, "between a lowering of moral standards and a breakdown in law and order."

"One leads to the other," said Morrissey. "I don't suppose you heard what happened at Kings Cross Station just before Easter. It was kept under hatches. This was the Crows, too. They'd joined up for the occasion with two local outfits. There were more than thirty of them involved, and they were most of them armed. They were aiming to lift a very big consignment of used notes that was coming up for pulping. It was guarded, of course. Two of the boys from the Birmingham force came up with it and there were two railway policemen to meet it. We got a last minute tip-off, realized it was going to be a nasty party, put in six carloads of our own, *and* called out the heavy mob from Wellington barracks. In a way, we overdid it, because they saw what was coming and scarpered. Total casualties, one of our men with shotgun pellets in his leg, and one getaway car caught in a side street. And all we could charge *him* with was obstruction. All right. But just suppose for a moment that we *hadn't* been tipped off. What do you think the score would've been then? Four dead policemen, plus any outsiders who happened to get in the way."

"All the same," said Sir Henry, and he said it in the tones of a man who needs reassurance, "you are not suggesting a total breakdown of law and order. The men would have been caught and punished eventually."

"If the police all did their job," said Laidlaw.

"Are you questioning the morale of the police?"

"I'm not questioning their morale. I think it's pretty high at the moment. But policemen are human. Their training makes them less susceptible to bribery and fear. But there must be one or two of them who can still be bought—or frightened."

Outside, a police launch was coming down against the flood tide. The man in the bow held a boat hook. He signaled with his free hand, and the boat sidled across toward a long black bundle that was drifting upstream. He reached over, drew the flotsam toward the boat, then lost interest and pushed it away. The boat shot off downstream, the bundle continued to drift, bobbing slightly in a ruffle of wind as it passed under Westminster Bridge.

Morrissey said, "Even one bent policeman can give criminals a lot of help. The higher he is, the more he can give them."

Detective Chief Inspector Mercer was finishing his packing. He was a man in his late twenties or early thirties, with a lot of dark hair, worn rather long, and a thick, sensual face. His appearance was not improved by a puckered white scar which started at the cheekbone and gathered up the corner of the left eye so that it seemed permanently half closed. He had thick shoulders, a barrel of a chest, and legs disproportionately long for such a body.

The furnished room in Southwark which had been his home for the last two years held a bed, an armchair, a wardrobe and a chest of drawers, and not much else. Emptying one of the small drawers, he pulled out a battered diary and thumbed through the pages. In the section headed "Useful Notes" there were half a dozen entries, each containing a girl's name followed by a telephone number. Mercer tore out the pages, dropped them into an ashtray, set fire to them, and watched them burn.

They had all been useful to him, and some of them had been fun, too. He hoped he would be as lucky in Stoneferry, but he rather doubted it.

That evening, as they did every Monday, business permitting, Superintendent Bob Clark, the head of the uniformed branch at Stoneferry, and his wife, Pat, drove round after dinner to play bridge with Lionel Talbot and his wife, Margaret. Lionel Talbot was a JP and chairman of the local bench, and before the game started, while Margaret was cutting sandwiches and Pat was helping her with the coffee, the two men sometimes talked business.

Bob Clark said, "The new man starts tomorrow. Name of Mercer. Youngish, I'm told. Probably a bit of a new broom."

"No harm in that," said Talbot. "I liked Watkyn well enough. We all did. But he was a sick man toward the end. He may have slipped a bit."

"If he did," said Bob Clark, "it wasn't reflected in the crime statistics. Do you realize that this station has the highest average in the division for indictable crimes cleared up?"

"Good show. I expect you'll get a medal when you retire next year. If they decide to give you a gold watch, I'll open the subscription list."

The words were spoken flippantly, but the sincerity behind them pleased the superintendent. He was saved the trouble of answering by the return of the ladies.

It was half past six and the sun, which showed blood red through the early morning mist, had no warmth in it. Michael Drake-Pelley and Frank, naked as the day they were born, hauled themselves out of the black and smoking waters of the Thames by means of an overhanging bough, and stood on the narrow strip of shingle which formed the upriver point of Westhaugh Island.

8

"That was fun," said Michael.

"L-l-l-lovely," said Frank.

Their towels were in the punt, which was hitched to a willow. As they went to fetch them Michael caught his foot in something, tumbled forward onto his knees, and uttered a word which, at fourteen, should not have been in his vocabulary.

"What is it?" said Frank.

"Some bloody picnicker has buried a—" He stopped.

"B-buried w-what? Do come on. I'm freezing."

But Michael took no notice. Kneeling on the shingle, he scraped with his hands. It was a layer of stones which the river had been eating into. The wash of the current had nibbled away the lower stones and now the top covering had fallen in.

From the edge something white was sticking out. Michael who had touched it, got up, went across, and washed his hands in the river. It was a ritual gesture.

He said, "I think we'd better tell someone about this, don't you?"

2

"It's a quiet town," said Superintendent Clark, "and I'm aiming to keep it that way."

"I hope so," said Mercer.

The two men were in the superintendent's office, overlooking the roundabout at the east end of the town where the first feeder from the bypass came in. Mercer had reported his arrival at nine o'clock that morning and the two men were taking stock of each other.

"I hope your digs are all right. We fixed you up temporarily in Cray Avenue. It's a fair step from the station, but I imagine you'll be getting a car."

"The bed's a bit hard," said Mercer. "No other complaints so far."

"Mrs. Marchant will look after you all right. She's a good soul. When you've been here a week or so, if you find something you like better we can fix it up for you. Now the summer's nearly over there'll be plenty of places to choose from."

"Seasonal population?"

"Mixed bag. A hard core of commuters. And a lot of retired folk. But we do get a bit of a population explosion in the summer, when people crowd down here and fill up the bungalows and houseboats and barges—or just pitch

10

tents alongside the river. They don't give a lot of trouble, particularly if the weather's hot. They spend all their time in and on the water."

"Compared with Southwark," said Mercer, "it sounds like a rest cure."

"We've got a few problems. There was a bit of trouble with a gang of boys who used to hang round the public lavatory under the railway arch. We got the Council to shut it down, and open another one in the square. That's more in the public eye. It cleared the trouble. Lately we've had a run of shop-breaking. Transistors, tape recorders, typewriters. Tom Rye thinks it's the same man. You'll find Tom very sound. Toward the end he was really holding up Watkyn."

"How is Watkyn?"

"In Slough Infirmary." The superintendent made a face. "Exploratory surgery. *He* thinks it's ulcers. Oh, come in, Tom. Have you two met?"

"We arrived at the same moment and nodded to each other," said Rye. "And I'll wager you've been telling him what you told me when I first came here. That it's a nice quiet manor where nothing ever happens."

"Near enough."

"Well, it's happened. Two boys found a body on Westhaugh Island this morning."

There was a moment of silence. Then the superintendent said, "That's just below the weir. Could have been an accident."

"Not unless the corpse buried itself."

"Oh, I see."

"One of the boys—name of Michael Drake-Pelley—is a smart kid. He and his friend have been bathing off the island a lot this last two months. He says they noticed that when the new sluice was opened a lot more water came through on that side, and it's been steadily eating away the island. The body was a good three foot down. If

11

it hadn't been for that sluice being opened it'd be there still."

"Drake-Pelley," said Mercer. "It's an uncommon name. He isn't by any chance . . .?"

"Yes," said Rye. "That's just it. He is."

"What are you talking about?" said Clark.

"Michael's father is Sir Richard Drake-Pelley, the Director of Public Prosecutions. And, like I said, Michael's a smart boy. As soon as he'd finished telephoning us, he got onto the *Daily Mirror*. Gave them an exclusive. Just the sort of thing which would appeal to them. 'Headache for the Director. Unearthed by his own son.'"

"Damn," said the superintendent. "Better get the place sealed off before Central gets here. They won't be pleased if a lot of sightseers have been trampling over it."

"I've sent Sergeant Gwilliam down there," said Rye. "I'm not sure we're going to get anyone from Central."

Both men stared.

"I had a word with Superintendent Wakefield at Division. I thought we'd better alert him straightaway. He said he didn't think C1 had anyone on tap. They've got two men in Pakistan on this forged-passport lark, one in Jamaica and one in Lagos. The rest are already booked. Greig was the last, and he went up to Cumberland on that child murder last week."

"I'll have a word with Division myself," said Clark.

He was back in five minutes, looking grim. He said, "I had Morrissey on the phone. He wants us to do it ourselves. He said we can have a sergeant from Central to help if we want him."

Mercer and Rye looked at each other. Their reactions were identical.

"We don't want to be lumbered with him if we don't have to," said Rye. "I know these boys from Central. He'll be round our necks while we do the real work, and he'll grab all the credit at the end."

12

"What about facilities?" said Mercer. "Forensic Laboratory, Central Teletype, CRO."

"They'll give you any help you need on the technical side. Morrissey promised that."

"Then we'd better get moving, hadn't we," said Mercer. "Who takes photographs round here?"

"Len Prothero."

"Put him in the back of your car, and you can drive us both out."

When the Romans came they found a ford on the bend of the river, where the water ran deep and slow, and used it to transport stones across, from Brittlesham quarry, to make up the start of their great road to the north. They called it, in their own language, the Ferry of the Stones, and the name has remained in Anglicized form to this day. There is not much of the old town left. A group of rather nice Georgian houses round the church. An outer ring of standard commuter residences, and a belt of riverside bungalows, barges, boathouses and pubs.

As the car squeezed its way between the market stalls which were already blocking either side of the High Street, Mercer said, "The old man didn't seem very pleased at the high compliment which was being paid to the efficiency of his force."

"He's a year off retirement," said Rye. "*If* this case makes a splash *and* it isn't tidied up quick and neat, he'd like someone else to blame."

"Reasonable," said Mercer. "Wouldn't the traffic get up this street a bit easier if you shifted the market somewhere else?"

"We tried. to. Couldn't do it. Six-hundred-year-old charter. Would have needed an act of Parliament. Mind you, it's not so bad now they've built the bypass. When I first came here it really was a mess."

13

At the head of the High Street the road divided. The left turn went over the high humped bridge which had been built in the year of Agincourt, and joined the bypass road to Staines at the roundabout on the other side. They took the minor road to the right, turning left again down a small road which was sign-posted WESTHAUGH WEIR. NO THROUGH ROAD. The built-up area was behind them now. There was a scattering of smaller houses, and market gardens, then open country.

After half a mile the car slowed, and turned into a track which led gently downhill, winding between a fuzz of alders, thorn trees, and scrub oak. When Tom Rye stopped the car and said, "Now we walk," Mercer thought how quiet it was. The dominating sound was the lazy roar of the waters pouring through the half-open sluices of the weir.

A footpath between high nettles took them to a plank bridge which spanned the arm of the backwater. As they crossed it, the burly figure of Sergeant Gwilliam rose out of the bushes which crowned the backbone of the island. It was no more than a spit of sand and gravel a hundred yards long and nowhere more than twenty yards wide thrown up in times past by a freak of the river.

"Any visitors yet?" said Rye.

"Only swans," said Gwilliam. He was a big Welshman, with the build of a rugby forward. "A pair of them. Very inhospitable. They didn't like me being here at all. Hissed at me, they did."

"There's probably a nest on the island somewhere. Lucky the cygnets are hatched, or they would have gone for you. Introduce the new skipper."

"Pleased to meet you, I'm sure," said Gwilliam.

Mercer nodded briefly. He was staring down into the excavation which Gwilliam had started. He said, "We'll have some photographs before you do any more. When the pathologist has had a look at it, finish the digging carefully down each side. Disturb things as little as possible. You'll have to scrape away the last of the earth by hand. We'll have another set of photographs when you've got that far. Right?"

Detective Leonard Prothero nodded, and started to unstrap the stand for his camera. He was thin, and sad-looking; in fact, a noted mimic, and much in demand at police concerts for his impersonations of senior officers.

Mercer said to Rye, "There was a small house opposite where we turned. We'll see if we can borrow some planks. When the pathologist's finished he'll want to get that body up with as little disturbance as possible. And put a police notice at the end of the lane—No Entrance."

"It's a public footpath," said Rye doubtfully. "This is about the favorite snogging place in Stoneferry; we'll have to give some reason."

"Suspected foot and mouth disease," said Mercer.

Dr. Champion, the county pathologist, was an old man. He was also a tired man. He had spent a large part of his professional life looking at bodies and pieces of bodies and in the first flush of youth had written a treatise on bruises which had brought him professional kudos. Now he was looking forward to a peaceful retirement, when the only dead body he would have to cut up would be the Sunday joint.

"Judging by the pelvis," he said, "it was a woman. And not a very old one. She's been dead at least a year, maybe two."

"As little as that?" said Mercer, staring down at the assembly of clean white bones which had now been laid out on the mortuary table.

"Quick work, I agree. Three reasons for it. First, she was buried in loose sand and shingle, not packed down in loam or clay. Second, in winter the grave would have been near enough to the river for the water to seep through it. Under those conditions it wouldn't take long to sieve away the hair and flesh and tissue. There's some gristle left." He poked a long forefinger into the space between the hipbones. "It takes a long time to dissolve gristle. But everything else has gone."

"You said three reasons."

"Yes," said the doctor. "And the third reason's the most important. She was stripped before she was buried. She went into the grave naked."

"You're sure of that?"

"Quite certain. Clothing doesn't disappear as quickly as that. There's metal in most clothing. And leather and plastic. They last longer than human tissues. I've known even a cotton sheet to come out after three years, with an identifiable laundry mark on it."

"Any idea how she died?"

"I can give a good guess. Come and look at this." He picked up a pencil torch and shone it into the cavity under the jaw. "You see that small bone?"

"The one shaped like a U?"

"That's the one. Called the hyoid bone. Touch it with the tip of your finger. Very gently."

Mercer did so. He felt the bone give under the light pressure.

"It's been snapped," he said. "So what does that prove?"

"If you find the hyoid bone with a clean fracture, it's odds on the deceased was strangled. Manually strangled. Probably from in front. That way you naturally put your thumbs on the carotid artery." He demonstrated, and Mercer felt two surprisingly strong thumbs dig into the top of his windpipe.

"All right, all right," he said. "No need to snap *my* hyoid bone. I take your point. Can you give us anything to help with identity?"

16

Dr. Champion consulted the notes he had made. He said, "Age, I should guess, anywhere between eighteen and twenty-five, give or take a year either end. The height we can check two ways. By measuring the cadaver —but that can be quite inaccurate, particularly after it's been disturbed. But since we have all the major bones intact, the humerus, the clavicle and the femur, we can use Trotter and Gleser's tables or Rollet's formula." Dr. Champion peered at his notes again. "Both of which confirm a height of between five foot three and five foot four."

"That's something, I suppose."

"I can't invent facts to suit you, Inspector. Science is no man's handmaid. But I've noticed one unusual thing about the young lady. She's got no fillings in her teeth. None at all."

He shut his notebook with a snap. He thought he might just manage to get home in time for lunch.

"Wouldn't that be a bit unusual if she was as much as twenty-five? Most people have been to the dentist by that time."

"If we looked after our teeth properly," said Dr. Champion, "if we abandoned the foolish habit of brushing them first thing in the morning and last thing at night and brushed them after every meal, *and* ate the right sort of foods, there'd be no need for us to trouble dentists at all."

It was a favorite fad of his.

Back at the police station Mercer made his first report to the superintendent. He said, "We can't keep that island sealed off indefinitely. There was quite a crowd there already when I went back. Gwilliam's going to need help."

"I'll send a man down from the afternoon off-duty squad."

"We shan't need one man. We shall need six."

"Six?"

"I want them to go through the whole island, inch by inch, to see what they can pick up. And they ought to do it before anyone else gets onto it."

"I admire your zeal," said Clark. "But don't you think you're overdoing it? You tell me the body's been there a year, maybe two. There are times in the winter when the whole island's under water. Isn't it a bit late to start looking for clues?"

"It seems to me something that ought to be done," said Mercer. "If you authorize me to skip it, O.K."

"Certainly not. You're in charge. You said six men."

"With sticks or spikes. And a couple of scythes. They're to clear the island first. Then walk up and down it, prodding."

"I take it you'll be there? You can give them their instructions."

"At my last station," said Mercer, "if a plainclothesman gave a man in uniform a suggestion, let alone an instruction, all he got was a dirty look."

The superintendent said, "You'll find that discipline is better here."

The opening moves in a murder investigation have been as carefully thought out and are as stereotyped as the Sicilian defense in chess. At nine o'clock that evening, as the light was beginning to go, Mercer sat in the CID room wondering what he had forgotten.

Area sealed off. Coroner's officer alerted. Statement for the press, cleared on the telephone with the Press Office at Scotland Yard. Copies of the pathologist's report to the coroner and to Division. Two sets of photographs from the scene of the crime and one from the mortuary. Provisional description circulated to Missing Persons. Arrangements made for custody of the body.

What had he left out? The Forensic Science Laboratory. But he had absolutely nothing to send them. Not a hair, not a stain, not a scrap of tissue or rag of clothing. Just a parcel of bones, picked clean by the industrious ants, scoured by sand and water. All the same, they should have a copy of the pathologist's report; and since he had been given freedom of choice, it should go to Guy's, who had given him much friendly assistance when he was in Southwark.

Tom Rye and Gwilliam came in. They were carrying a wicker basket between them, and dumped it on the table.

"One island, contents of," said Rye. "Five hundred fascinating relics. Would you like to list them now, or shall we do it tomorrow?"

"Anything interesting?"

"It depends what you call interesting. How many French letters did we find?"

"Twenty-five," said Gwilliam.

"I don't believe it," said Mercer. "There isn't a square foot of that island that's level, and most of it's covered with nettles."

"The youth of Stoneferry are a hardy lot," said Rye. He started to extract articles from the basket. "One sardine tin, recent, with remnants of fish still adhering. One shoe, decrepit—"

Mercer got up abruptly. He said, "That girl's been there for a year or more. Another twelve hours won't make any difference. Let's knock off. I need a drink. What's the best place round here for picking up form?"

Tom Rye considered. He said, "There's the Chough, over there on the other side of the square, but that's really a lunch-time pub. At this time of night your best bet would be the Angler's Rest. Signboard, a gent holding his arms wide apart. Locally known as the 'Tall Story.' Down the steps by the war memorial, along the towpath, and it's on your left just before you come to the railway bridge."

The Angler's Rest was an old, dark place. It smelled of

19

stale beer, varnish, and what might have been fish but was probably dry rot. It had uneven brick floors, yellowing ceilings, and walls covered with cases containing glassy-eyed pike and barbel, who glared down at the drinkers, like the oldest members of the club disapproving of the rising generation.

When Mercer went into the public bar he attracted as much, and as little, attention as any stranger does when he goes into a pub. That is to say, nobody looked at him and everyone wondered who he was. He ordered a pint of bitter, and retired to an uncomfortable oak settee in the corner. The beer was all right. It was a good brand, and had been carefully looked after.

About ten minutes later an inner door opened, and a barrel of a man with sun-reddened face and close-cropped gray hair came out and rolled across to the bar. He ordered a light ale, a brandy and ginger ale, and two scotch and sodas. As he paid for them Mercer noticed that he had only one arm.

The barman said, "All right, Mr. Bull. I'll bring them in for you," and his eyes flickered very briefly in Mercer's direction. The newcomer moved over and perched on the arm of the settee beside Mercer. He said, "You the new skipper?"

"The local intelligence system must be very good."

"We all knew Watkyn was going, poor old sod. Soon as we saw you in a car with Tom Rye we had a good guess. My name's Bull—Jack Bull. That's my garage in the High Street. I used to look after Watkyn's car for him. Do the same for you if you like."

"When I get one."

"You looking for one?"

"About two years old," said Mercer. "Guaranteed to stand up to hard use. And must have a big boot."

"To bring bodies back in?"

Mercer looked up, studied Bull for a few moments,

20

and then said, "That's right. Bodies, and other things. Does everybody know all about that, too?"

"There's a bit in the *Standard*."

Bull handed him the folded paper that was sticking out of his right-hand jacket pocket. It occurred to Mercer that people with only one arm must quickly get into the habit of arranging things like that. It was only a short paragraph, mentioning that two boys had discovered a body while bathing. There were no names or details. Presumably the real story would be in the *Mirror* in the morning.

The landlord came past with the four drinks on a tray. Bull said, "Why don't you join us? It's quieter in the small bar. Put a pint of bitter with these, Bob."

The small bar was just large enough to hold two tables and six chairs. Three of them were occupied. A small, monkey-like man who was addressed as Johnno was given one of the glasses of Scotch. The brandy and ginger ale went to a gray-faced character wearing heavy horn-rimmed glasses, with untidy hair and untidy clothes, whose hand trembled very slightly as he picked up the drink.

The light ale was for the girl. She had a head of blond hair which could have been natural, blue and green shadow over the eyes, and an impertinent nose. Mercer was not in the least surprised to be told that her name was Vikki. She looked every inch a Vikki, down to her last pink-tinted toenail.

"What you see in front of you," said Bull, "is what you might call the brains of my establishment. The brawn is off drinking beer and playing darts somewhere else. Johnno looks after petrol sales, and tries not to swindle the oil company too noticeably. Mr. Rainey looks after our accounts, and Vikki looks after me."

"You haven't introduced your friend," said Vikki.

"Detective Chief Inspector . . . ?"

"Bill Mercer."

21

"You do pick up the oddest people," said Vikki.

The smile that went with it just prevented the words from being rude.

"You mind your manners, Vikki," said Johnno. "He looks as though he could eat you for dinner, and two more like you."

"I'm sure I hope he'd enjoy the taste," said Vikki. Her light-blue eyes were weighing and measuring him.

"I'll tell you what," said Mercer. "They'll be throwing us out soon. Why don't I order another round while the going's good?"

Johnno said, "Bob won't throw us out. Not while we've got the law here." No one resisted the idea of another round, least of all Mr. Rainey, who had already got outside his brandy and ginger ale. With the arrival of the new drinks the atmosphere warmed up. Jack Bull said, "You'll enjoy Stoneferry. Some people call it Sinferry. So many men living with other people's wives. Or little bits of fluff tucked away in bungalows down the river."

"You're a fine one to talk," said Vikki.

"I'm a bachelor," said Bull. "I can please myself. It's these married men who make me laugh. Come sneaking down here on the midday train on Saturday, with lust in their eyes, and crawl back to their wives on Sunday evening, telling them what a tiring time they've had at the reps' conference at Birmingham. What *they* don't know is that their wives have already rung up the area manager, just to check that there *isn't* a conference at Birmingham, and tooled off down to Brighton with their boyfriend from up the road. I suppose it's one way of staying happily married."

"I think you men are horrible," said Vikki.

Two drinks later Mr. Rainey got up and drifted off. He hadn't opened his mouth except to say "Cheers" each time a drink was put into his hand.

"Suffers from ulcers," said Bull.

"I thought if you had ulcers you weren't supposed to drink," said Vikki.

"You think too much," said Bull.

Mercer said, "There's only one thing wrong with your petrol station that I could see. It's in the wrong place. Bang in the middle of the High Street. If we'd wanted to stop for a refill this morning we'd have caused a traffic block just trying to turn in."

"That's because it was market day. Other days it's not so bad."

"Not so long ago," said Johnno, "there were *three* bloody great garages in the High Street."

"It's time you ordered a drink," said Bull.

While he was out of the room, Mercer nodded at the flap of sleeve stuck into Bull's left pocket and said, "War?"

"Arnhem. And that was a bloody shambles, if you like."

"So I'd heard. *Not* one of our brighter bits of planning."

"If some of those characters in scarlet hats who were running the war had been put in charge of a launderette they'd have been bankrupt inside the year."

"Well!" said Vikki. "That wasn't what you told me."

"About what?"

"About how you lost your arm. You said you ran off with a Frenchman's wife, and he challenged you to a duel, and cut it off with his sword."

They were still laughing when Johnno came back with the drinks.

"Bob says this definitely is the last round."

"That means we shan't get more than two more," said Bull.

"Not tonight," said Mercer. "Can't break the law on my first night."

As he walked home along the towpath, he was wondering about them. Rainey was clearly an alcoholic. Not a very safe man to have keeping your accounts. Johnno was sharp. He had the look and build of a jockey. Mercer thought that he would enjoy swindling his enemies but would probably be loyal to his friends. Bull was in a different class altogether. A capable dangerous man. Someone you might find yourself liking very much, though.

But it wasn't the men themselves that he was really thinking about. Mercer was a man whose trade had taught him to be interested in small things. It was the moment when Johnno said, "Not so long ago there were *three* garages." When he said it, Mercer had been admiring the nine-pound trout in the glass case over the fireplace. And, mirrored in that glass, he had seen, so fleetingly that it might have been his imagination, only he knew that it wasn't, the look which Bull had given his subordinate. It was a look which said, in clear black print, "Shut your mouth, you bloody fool." *And* he had packed him off to order a round of drinks before he could say any more.

Mercer stowed it away in the rag bag of odds and ends, pieces of information, and impressions which he had picked up in his first twenty-four hours at Stoneferry.

Somewhere below him, in the dimness a punt was moored to a landing stage, Mercer could see the two figures, a man and a girl, stretched full length on the cushions. He heard the girl laugh. He wished he was down in the boat with a girl who could laugh like that, instead of going home to a bed like a rockery, in Cray Avenue.

3

MERCER BOUGHT HIS COPY of the *Daily Mirror* on his way to the station. It was the second lead story on the back page. There was the usual efficient spread. A picture of Michael, grinning all over his face, and next to it one of his father, looking angry. The second picture had actually been taken several months earlier, but the juxtaposition was effective. There was a shot of the island taken with a good telephoto lens from the opposite bank of the river. It didn't show much, because screens had been put up round the excavation. The story was based on some pretty thorough footwork. It was clear that, among other people, the reporter had talked to Dr. Champion.

Tom Rye and Prothero were busy spreading the contents of the basket onto two trestle tables.

"It's a funny thing," said Rye. "Do you know we've found three shoes, and they're all right foot? You could build up quite a theory on that. The murderer with no left foot."

Mercer inspected the flotsam and jetsam. He said, "That red plastic handbag. That was an odd thing to dump."

"Odder still," said Rye, "it wasn't empty. I put the stuff out of it over there."

"If a girl left her handbag behind you'd think she'd take the trouble to come back and look for it. It wouldn't be hard to spot that color. Where was it?"

"In the opening of an old water-rat burrow," said Prothero. "It might have dropped there, or it might have been dropped somewhere else, floated downstream, and been washed into it."

Mercer was trying to separate the contents, which had rusted together into a lump. There were two or three coins, a small bunch of keys, what might have been a lipstick container, and what was clearly a powder compact. Mercer got out a penknife and, after a bit of fiddling, succeeded in opening it.

The airtight lid had preserved the contents surprisingly well.

"Suntan dusting powder," said Rye, who was a married man.

"There's a shopman's mark scratched inside the lid," said Mercer. "Bit of luck if it was bought locally. We should be able to identify it."

"We might," said Rye, "but what I was thinking was, if this girl came from London or somewhere down for the day for a picnic, and it wasn't till she got home she found she'd lost her bag, she might let it go; but if it belonged to a local girl, when she found she'd lost it why didn't she go back and look for it?"

"Perhaps she wasn't in any position to go back and look for anything."

"Ah," said Rye. "You mean it might belong to the girl we found?"

"It's possible, isn't it? The murderer strips her, and takes the clothes away with him. But he doesn't notice the bag. It's slipped down into this hole."

"Could be," said Rye. "Try it round the jewelers and fancy goods shops, Len. You can leave the rest of the junk for now."

Mercer said, "I suppose I ought to be getting down to the island to see how they're getting on." He made no immediate attempt to move, but sat on the edge of the table watching Rye trying to disentangle a sodden lump of newspaper which had apparently been used to wrap up the remains of a meal. He said, "Is it right there used to be three garages in the High Street?"

"That's right."

"What happened to the other two?"

"One of them was shut some time ago. A couple of years before I came here. Run by a man called Mike Murray. He was a naughty boy."

"How naughty?"

"They found a hot car in his yard and another one in his garage. He couldn't think *how* they got there."

Mercer laughed. "What about the other?"

"That was what you might call an entanglement with the law, too. The other sort of law. They took on a repair job, on the brakes of a doctor's car, and did it so bloody badly that the brakes failed and the car hit a woman with a pram. Didn't actually kill either of them but hurt them both pretty badly."

"Claim for damages?"

"That's right. Particularly when it came out that the job had been done by a temporary mechanic, probably unqualified, who'd scarpered."

"And that was the end of the garage."

"That's right. Like all those little places, there wasn't much in the way of capital behind them. The costs and damages finished them. To say nothing of the fact that no one was going to be very happy entrusting their car repairs to a place which made such a mess of them."

When Mercer made no comment, Rye said, "So what's it all about? Are you thinking of starting a garage yourself? I'd say there was room for another one."

Mercer smiled. It was a curious secretive smile which

suggested that he was amused more by his own thoughts than by what he had heard.

"I might do that," he said. "Mr. Bull struck me as a sound sort of businessman. If he offered me a partnership I might consider putting some capital into it."

Rye looked at him to see if he was joking and then said, "When did you meet him?"

"Last night, at that pub. With his pump man he calls Johnno."

"Johnny Johnson. Looks like a jockey."

"Right. And his accountant, who looks like a dipso, and his secretary, who looks like every middle-aged businessman's dream secretary. Incidentally, who *was* the second man?"

It took Rye a moment to work out what Mercer was talking about. Then he said, "You mean the second garage that went bust?"

"Correct."

"It called itself the Stoneferry Central Garage. It was run by a man called—hold it—Church ... Bishop ... Prior. That's right. Henry Prior."

"Where is he now?"

"I've no idea. Weathermans would tell you. They acted for him."

"Weathermans?"

"Solicitors. Far end of Fore Street. Second on your left as you go up the High Street. What's all this about, anyway?"

"Do you ever stay awake at nights worrying about names you can't remember?"

"Funny you should say that. Only last night, just as we were going to sleep, my wife said to me, 'Who was it gave us those beer mugs as a wedding present? Name beginning with *B*.' We both knew perfectly well, but we couldn't put our tongues to it. We were at it for hours."

"Well, I'm like that about things," said Mercer. "If

some little thing crops up that I can't understand, I have to worry away at it until I do understand it. Forty-nine times out of fifty, it turns out to be nothing at all. Sometimes fifty out of fifty." He got off the table and made for the door.

"The old man was asking for you," said Rye.

"What does he want?"

"He's been reading the *Mirror*, too."

"Tell him I'm on the job," said Mercer. "No time for idle gossip."

"It was Woods, actually."

"Who was?"

"The people who gave us the beer mugs."

Mercer found a crowd at the end of the path leading to the island, and a bored-looking policeman standing at the entrance to it.

"There's another lot down the other end," said the policeman. "I couldn't stop 'em. They came along the riverbank. Christ knows what they think they're going to see."

The crowd on the riverbank was mostly boys. They were gazing hopefully at the barricade of canvas screens. The island looked strangely different. It looked naked. The nettles had been scythed, thorn bushes and scrub alder pulled out, and the shingle raked over. Mercer pushed his way through the crowd, crossed the plank bridge, and found Sergeant Gwilliam and Detective Massey at work in their shirt sleeves behind the screen.

"We've gone down two foot below where the body was lying," said Gwilliam. "Can't go any further, the water's coming in. We shan't find anything else now."

There was a crowd on the other bank, too. And a number of boats were dawdling past so that the people in them could stare. One of them was a punt handled by a girl. She was clearly adept at that ancient and difficult method of propulsion. She was wearing a pair of faded blue jeans and an open-necked, short-sleeved, dark-blue shirt. Her head and her feet were bare. Her hair was drawn back into a short plait which somehow failed to look schoolgirlish. Her only ornament was a gold bracelet on one sun-browned wrist, which glinted in the sun as she dropped the pole, expertly close to the side of the punt, and leaned her weight against it.

"Eyes front, skipper," said Gwilliam. "You're looking at the local aristocracy."

"And boy, is she worth looking at," breathed Mercer. "Who is she?"

"She's the daughter of the late Lieutenant General Sir Somebody-Something. They've got the house on Chertsey Road, over the old bridge."

"I don't believe she's wearing anything under that shirt. Look, when she bends forward to put the pole in—there—see what I mean?"

Gwilliam grinned, and was about to say something when it all happened very quickly. The wash of a passing launch caught the punt and rocked it. The girl had her feet braced against the sides and was in no danger, but as she let go of the pole with her right hand the bracelet slipped off and dropped into the water. In what seemed to be a single movement the girl had shipped the punt pole and dropped into the water. Mercer took a step towards the bank. Gwilliam said, "I wouldn't bother, skipper. She can swim a lot better than you or me." A dark head reappeared. The girl made her way quickly to the punt, and pulled herself in over the end with one economical heave. Mercer saw that she had recovered the bracelet. Then she turned the head of the boat and started to move off downstream. The wet vest was clinging to her exciting body, and the water was running in streams from the hair plastered to her head. She seemed unconcerned about her appearance.

"They're a real pair of water babies, her and her

brother," said Gwilliam. "Brought up in and on the river. Win all the prizes at the local regatta."

Mercer, who was still staring at the boat as it disappeared downstream, said nothing. He was wondering if she was the girl he had heard laughing as he walked home the night before. He thought it was unlikely. If what Gwilliam had said was true, she was probably an inhibited upper-class dolly. All the same, it would be fun to find out.

"All right," he said. "We'll pack it up here. You can shift those screens. We'll let the public in."

When they left, the public was standing, three deep, round the excavation. One small girl had already fallen into it.

"We might be onto something with that powder compact," said Rye. "It came from Benson's. It's a stationer's shop really. They stock a few fancy goods for the summer trade. Benson remembers the compacts; they were a bit more pricey than his usual line of stuff, and he was afraid he wasn't going to get rid of them. There were only six all told. He's busy turning up his records and trying to remember who bought them."

"Good," said Mercer. "What's the name of the local paper?"

"The *Stoneferry Times and Gazette*. In South Street. Very sound for local digs, if that's what you're thinking of."

"That's what I was thinking of," agreed Mercer.

The *Gazette* was a weekly paper. Its back-numbers department produced copies of that year's production. It was in the number which had come out in the last week of July that Mercer found an account of the Stoneferry Annual Regatta and Water Sports. The sun had shone throughout the day ("a change from the year before," said the *Gazette*), and a large and appreciative crowd had watched the traditional aquatic contests and races, fol-

31

lowed by a display of lifesaving by the Boy Scouts and Girl Guides. Which had saved which? Mercer wondered. Lower down the page, results were given. The double punting had been won, for the third year in succession, by Venetia and Willoughby Slade. They had also scored a second in the fancy dress canoe contest, and Venetia had won the ladies' springboard free-style diving.

He thought about that athletic body dressed, he was sure, in the scantiest of permissible bathing costumes, running to the end of the springboard, bouncing upward in a perfect jackknife and straightening out to hit the water, one rigid line from fingertips to toes. He was still thinking about it when he got back to the station and found Rye talking to a worried man and a stout gray-haired woman.

"Mr. and Mrs. Benson," he said. "They recognized that compact. It's some stock they had about three years ago."

"That's right," said Mr. Benson. "A traveler from Hollingshed's sold us six of them. I thought, at the time, they weren't quite our line. But as a matter of fact, we sold three of them almost immediately to summer visitors. Then we never made another sale for twelve months or more. I remember saying to the wife, 'We'll never get our money back on those things—'"

"Which was nonsense," said his wife placidly. "Because we sold two more that same summer. The last one never went. So I thought, as we'd got our money back on the other five, I'd use it myself." She opened her bag and pulled out a compact. It was clearly twin to the one they had found. Mr. Benson pointed out the tiny mark which he had scratched inside the lid, an inverted B.

"I do that with anything valuable," said Mr. Benson. "In case there's a question of identifying it afterwards."

"Quite right," said Rye. "I only wish everyone was as methodical. Now about those other two . . . ?"

"They were cash sales, you understand, so there wouldn't be any actual record. But one of them we can remember. It was Captain Barrington's daughter, the older one who lives with him. The other one has quite gone out of my mind."

"Well, it hasn't gone out of mine," said Mrs. Benson. "I recollected as we came along. We were going past the cinema, and that brought it back to me in a flash."

"Of course," said Mr. Benson. "You're right. It was Mr. Skeffington."

"The cinema manager?"

"That's right. He's a bachelor, too, and I remember thinking he must have bought that for one of the usherettes. A leaving present, perhaps. It's just the sort of thing he would do. He's a very kindhearted man."

"Well, we can easily check up on those two," said Rye. "I don't suppose you can give us any lead to the earlier sales?"

"I can tell you one thing," said Mrs. Benson. "None of the women who bought the first three compacts would be seen dead carrying a handbag like that red plastic thing. They were ladies. Alligator or real leather was their style."

"We'll check up on the two local ones first," said Rye when he had got rid of the Bensons. "But you can bet your bottom dollar it won't be either of them. Life isn't like that. It'll be one of the first three. She didn't buy it for herself, she bought it for her daily, and when she gave it to her she said, 'I got it at Stoneferry. Pretty little place on the river. You ought to run down there for a picnic one day.'"

"You're probably right," said Mercer. He looked in to report progress to Superintendent Clark, who said, "Good work. If we can identify the girl we're more than halfway there."

As Mercer stepped out into the street he was reflecting that this common-sense diagnosis was probably correct.

Where a woman was murdered it was nearly always her husband or her boyfriend who had done it. Once they identified the body, the field would narrow dramatically.

The place he was making for was a Georgian house, converted into an office and wrecked in the process. The lower half of the bow windows on either side of the porch was obscured with the sort of wire netting which used to keep flies out of pantries before refrigerators were invented. The name WEATHERMANS was painted, in faded gold letters with curly corners, across the glass at the top, further blocking out the light of day from what must, originally, have been two pleasant rooms.

The front hall was a reception office and a girl with a face like an intelligent Cairn terrier took his name, brightened perceptibly when she found out he was a policeman, and dialed a number on the internal telephone. It appeared that Mr. Weatherman was in, and that Mercer was lucky to catch him because he always went out to lunch early on Thursdays; it was his day for the Rotary Club.

"I could show you up," said the girl, shaking the hair out of her eyes, "but I'm not really supposed to leave the front office until Mrs. Hall gets back from lunch."

"Lend me a map and a compass," said Mercer, "and I'll probably make it."

The girl smiled, and said, "It's not all that difficult. You go straight up the stairs, turn right, and Mr. Weatherman has the room on the right of the landing in front. The one on the left is Mr. Slade."

Mercer stopped for a moment, with one foot on the bottom stair. He said, "Would that by any chance be Willoughby Slade?"

"That's right," said the girl. "Do you know him?"

"By reputation," said Mercer. "I gather he's a very accomplished water man."

34

"Oh, he is," said the girl. "He's very good at everything on the river."

Chatting up girls in punts, thought Mercer.

"Tennis, too." It was clear that Willoughby was the sun and the moon.

Mercer's first impression of Mr. Weatherman was a black coat and a pair of striped trousers. After that you saw a pair of horn-rimmed spectacles, a Rotary Club badge, and a platinum key chain. It was only when you looked very closely that you could see that there was anything human behind the facade at all. Eyes so pale that they were almost colorless, a beaky nose dominating a thin mouth. A *shrewd operator,* thought Mercer. The sort of man you might have looked to find in Norfolk Street or Bedford Row, but unexpected in a quiet backwater like Stoneferry. A pike in a trout stream.

"And how can I help you, Inspector?"

"I was told that you acted for Mr. Prior in the case which was brought against his garage some years ago."

"Would it be indiscreet to inquire who told you?"

"Not at all. It was a client of yours. Name of Jack Bull. I ran into him last night."

"Ah," said Mr. Weatherman.

Mercer could visualize Jack Bull getting his knuckles rapped next time he met his solicitor.

"I should not normally discuss the affairs of a client with a third party. But I imagine you have a good and proper reason for your inquiry."

"I'll be honest with you," said Mercer. "I've no reason which would stand up to cross-examination. I was just following up a hunch."

"The matter can hardly be sub judice now. And in any event you could look it up in the files of our local paper. It was fully reported. I have no objection to giving you the facts as I remember them. I must put you right on one point, though. You said that the case was brought

35

against the garage. Unfortunately that was not so. The case was brought against Mr. Prior personally."

"Because he wasn't a limited company, you mean?"

"That is so. And it was not for want of my advice on the perils of personal trading."

"I'm sure it wasn't."

"The case rested, at law, on the proposition that a man is responsible for the acts of his servants. That he must select employees of adequate skill, or supervise them with reasonable care."

"Which he failed to do."

"Completely, I'm afraid. The man who attended to Dr. Simpson's car had been less than a month in the garage and there was no evidence, beyond his own say-so, that he was a trained mechanic at all."

"What was his name?"

"The mechanic? I think it was Taylor. Some name like that. He disappeared on the day of the accident and hasn't been heard of since."

"You tried to trace him?"

"Certainly. But you will appreciate, Inspector, that a firm of solicitors has very little machinery for a search of that sort."

"The police could have helped."

"Yes," said Mr. Weatherman. "They could have helped." The innuendo was so clear that Mercer started to say something, and then, meeting a glance from the lawyer's eyes, changed his mind.

"What happened to Prior?"

"He sold his stock and premises. I believe he got quite a good price. Enough to clear his debts."

"Where is he now?"

"After the case was over, I lost touch with him. I believe he left the district."

Mr. Weatherman's eyes strayed toward the watch on his left wrist and Mercer said, "Well, I mustn't keep you anymore. Thank you very much."

When he reached the front hall the Cairn terrier had gone and the seat behind the reception desk was occupied by a gray-haired woman. Mrs. Hall, he supposed. She was talking to a young man, who looked up as Mercer went past.

Chalk-stripe flannel suit, reversed calf shoes, white collar, regimental tie. A sun-tanned face and dancing blue eyes. The family resemblance was quite unmistakable.

As Mercer went past, Mrs. Hall was saying, "I'm sorry, Mr. Slade, you'll have to do your own shopping. I've got the books to write up before the auditors come in."

Mercer filed away the information that the two female members of Weatherman's staff seemed to have different ideas about Willoughby Slade.

4

Tom Rye had the operational part of the telephone balanced on his right shoulder and held in position by his chin. It was an arrangement which left both hands free. With one of them he was scribbling something on a piece of paper, with the other he was squeezing mustard out of a plastic container onto an open ham sandwich.

"Fine," he said. "That's good. The skipper's just turned up. I'll tell him. Better hang on. He'll probably want to come over himself." He rang off and said, "That was Len. He's over at the cinema. Old Skeffington bought that compact, all right. But he didn't buy it for one of the usherettes. No, sir! He bought it for Sweetie Sowthistle."

Sergeant Gwilliam, who was typing a report, using one finger of each hand, gave a long low whistle. Mercer looked blank. Tom Rye said what sounded like "Eez-oh-ow-is-orter." He then swallowed the large chunk of bread and ham which was obstructing him, apologized, and said, "What I said was, she's old Sowthistle's daughter. He's quite a local character. He lives in a barge on Easthaugh Island. That's about a quarter of a mile downstream from where they found the body.

"Then we'd better have a word with his daughter quick."

"There's an objection to that. She disappeared. When was it, Taffy?"

"More than two years ago," said Sergeant Gwilliam.

Mercer said, "Oh, I see. More than two years ago." His heavy face was thoughtful. "Well, it looks as though we might be able to short-circuit this one, doesn't it?"

"The only thing is," said Rye, "that if you're thinking that the next step will be to rope in Sweetie's boyfriend of two years ago and put him through the pulper, you're going to have your work cut out. She wasn't much more than seventeen when she disappeared, but she'd been laid by half the males in Stoneferry."

"Quite a girl," said Mercer.

"She was a trollop," said Sergeant Gwilliam. His upbringing had been chapel, and strict.

Mr. Skeffington turned out to be a smallish man with thick-lensed glasses and a mop of untidy hair. He greeted Mercer with a cheerful smile, and seemed unembarrassed by the circumstances which had brought him to the attention of the police.

"That's quite right," he said. "I knew Sweetie. She applied for a job here once. I'd have liked to give it to her, but I couldn't see my way of doing it."

"Why not?"

"I couldn't have trusted her, Inspector. You know what a cinema's like in the afternoon. Pitch dark. Practically no one there. You'd be surprised what we pick up in the back row of the stalls after the performance is over."

"You knew her yourself quite well?"

"What makes you think that?"

"You gave her this compact."

"I'm always giving things to girls. I've got a generous nature."

"Weren't you overdoing it a bit, sir? I mean, if your acquaintance with her was confined to one occasion, when she asked for a job and you weren't able to offer her one—"

"That wasn't the only time. I'd met her several times before that."

"Socially?"

"You might call it socially, I suppose," said Mr. Skeffington blandly. "She was a very popular girl. Everyone liked Sweetie. Sad to think she should have ended like that."

'Ended like what, Mr. Skeffington?"

"Murdered, Inspector. Murdered and buried on Westhaugh Island. At least, I think it must have been her, or you wouldn't be asking me all these questions."

"We have reason to think that it might be," said Mercer stiffly. He found Mr. Skeffington disconcerting. "When did you give her this compact?"

"Your sergeant was asking me that. I was able to tell him almost exactly." Mr. Skeffington consulted a desk diary. "It was in the third week of September, two years ago. One of the usherettes, a Miss Williams that was, had given in her notice to go and get married. I really bought the compact as a present for her. Then I found the other girls were collecting money for a fitted handbag and a compact, and since there didn't seem to be much point in giving her two compacts, I added my contribution to that, and kept the compact. Then Sweetie turned up asking for the job, and seeing that I had to disappoint her, I gave it to her."

"Do you give presents to all applicants for jobs that you have to refuse?"

"Not to all girls, but Sweetie was an exception."

"Why?"

"Because I was sorry for her."

"Why particularly?"

"It's clear, Inspector," said Mr. Skeffington, "that you're new here. You've never met her father."

40

"He's a filthy old sod," said Rye. "Real name is Hedges. It was the boys who called him Sowthistle. It used to be a dare among them to slip over to his island, crawl through the undergrowth, and peep in at one of the portholes to see what he was up to. You can imagine what sort of a kick they got out of doing that."

"Where did he come from?"

"Nobody knows. He landed up here after the war, and took possession of that derelict barge. He fitted it up, after a fashion, and started to live there with a woman who was charitably referred to as his wife. She walked out on him when Sweetie was about ten. I don't blame her. He used to beat her when he was drunk and he was drunk pretty often."

"Why didn't the authorities take the girl away from him?"

"They tried to. Sowthistle kicked up a fuss. The great heart of the British public was stirred. A fund was got up. Counsel was briefed. It was in all the papers. Poor lonely old man, deserted by his wife! Now they try to rob him of his daughter! His sole prop and stay! Yards of sentiment. Buckets of tears. Two years later she applied to us for protection. He'd tried to rape her."

"What did the great British public think of that?"

"They didn't want to hear about that bit. We put her into a local authority home at Slough and she stayed there until she was fourteen. Then she elected to go back and look after Dad. Maybe she thought she was old enough to manage him. Maybe she thought it was a good base of operations. She was quite a good-looking girl in a healthy animal sort of way."

Mercer cocked an eye at him, and Rye had the grace to blush. "I wouldn't have said no," he agreed. "But I wasn't her cup of tea. The men she went for were middle-aged men with money. When she disappeared we made a full list of 'em—just in case."

41

Rye extracted a paper from the file and pushed it across. Mercer saw that there had originally been about twenty names on it, but a lot of them had been crossed through.

"Died, or left the district," said Rye. "Or we couldn't prove they'd had anything to do with Sweetie at all. They were names other people had suggested, but they didn't come to anything. You know how people talk."

"I know how people talk," agreed Mercer. "Who are the ones that are left? Skeffington I know."

"Camberley—he's a commercial gent. He was one of her regulars. Barrington's a retired naval PO. Got a houseboat downriver. Henniker's a turf accountant. Jeejeeboy's a Pakistani. He runs the restaurant next to the Old Bridge."

"No color bar?"

"Certainly not. One of her regular ex-boyfriends was a Chinaman."

"And what about this one?" said Mercer.

It was the last name on the list.

"Rainey. He works for Jack Bull. Keeps his books for him."

"I've met him," said Mercer. "He's a dipso."

"I've heard he was a bit of a drinker."

"He's not just a heavy drinker. He's an alcoholic. When you've met one or two of them you can't miss it." Mercer was standing with the list in his hand. Rye had noticed that he had a habit of talking about one thing and thinking about something quite different. Now he said, "What was the official reaction when she disappeared?"

"We didn't treat it as a murder case, if that's what you mean."

"What did you do?"

"Had a word with her known boyfriends. They all said much the same thing. They all admitted they'd paid her money for favors received. But they all said they'd had

42

nothing to do with her for at least a month."

"What did they make of that?"

"The same as we did. That she'd picked up with a professional. Someone who saw she was worth more than small-town money. And he'd taken her off and she set up in London. That was our first idea, anyway."

"The first?"

"And the last, officially. All the same, there were some odd points about it. For instance, she had a lot of quite nice clothes. She didn't keep them at home. Her father would have pawned them. Mr. Jeejeeboy let her keep them in a locker, in a room behind his restaurant. She had some jewelry, too. Not worth more than a few pounds, but the sort of thing a girl gets attached to. She left it all behind."

"It's the sort of thing a girl might do," said Mercer slowly, "if she was starting a new life. Or thought she was. She wouldn't want the old stuff to remind her of what she was leaving behind. It was trash. It was devalued. It stank."

"Maybe," said Rye. "But there's one thing she left behind which would have been worth the same in London as in Stoneferry. We found this among the clothes."

Mercer took it. It was a Post Office Savings Book. The last figure in it showed a credit balance of £27.15.0.

"What did our revered superintendent say when you told him about this? Did he still rule out foul play?"

"He said she must have forgotten about it."

"When did she disappear?"

Rye referred again to his file.

"She was last seen in Stoneferry late afternoon on a Wednesday in March. Father Walcot spoke to her."

Mercer was examining the book. He said, "The last entry is five pounds drawn out on March seventh. She must have had a very short memory."

"I don't think the old man wanted it to be a murder.

He likes to keep his statistics healthy. If it was a disappearance, it wasn't a crime. Not even a suspected one."

"That's one way of keeping your sheet clean," said Mercer. "We'd better get after these six and put 'em through it again. Who've we got?"

"This is one of those moments," said Rye, "when we'd like a real detective force. Half a dozen clean-limbed youngsters sitting round, straining like greyhounds on the leash, waiting for the word *go*."

"Who *have* we got?"

"You and me. And Massey. Sergeant Gwilliam's starting his leave and Prothero's up in London, where he'll be for the best part of three days."

"What the hell's he doing there?"

"Waiting to produce some photographs and give five minutes' evidence about nothing at all. You know, skipper, I've often wondered why they bother to try people. Why don't they just say, 'The police have arrested them. They must be guilty. Send 'em to prison'?"

"You do Camberley and Barrington. Massey can take the bookie and the Pakistani."

"That leaves Rainey for you."

"Yes," said Mercer. "And by the way. That chap Prior. *Did* he leave the district?"

"Prior?"

"Owner of the Stoneferry Central Garage."

"Oh, him. No. I don't think so. I've got an idea he lives in one of those bungalows above Westhaugh Lock. Why?"

"Weatherman said after Prior went bust he left the district. I'm going to have a word with Rainey now. Be back in half an hour."

"Extraordinary chap," said Rye to himself. "Doesn't seem able to keep his mind on one thing at a time."

As Mercer was passing the superintendent's office the door opened and Clark came out. He said, "Oh, Mercer.

I understand you're making a bit of headway with the case of that girl."

"That's right, sir."

The superintendent was blocking the passage. Short of pushing, he couldn't get past him.

"I'd like to be kept in the picture about it. Fully in the picture."

"I'll see you're kept in the picture."

"Do I understand you've identified her?"

"We've got a tentative identification. Nothing definite yet."

"I see. Well, keep me posted." He made a half move, and Mercer slid past him. "You realize that if we clear this up without any help from Central this will be a feather in our caps."

"A feather in your cap, you crafty old bastard," said Mercer as he went out into the street.

"Wojjer say?" said Station Sergeant Rix.

"Nothing. Just talking to myself."

"Daft," said Station Sergeant Rix to Station Officer Tovey, who happened to come in at that moment.

"Who's daft?"

"The new CID man. Talking to himself."

"Those plainclothes characters are all cracked," said Tovey.

Bull's Garage and Motor Mart occupied what had been two shops in the High Street, and the yard behind both of them. The site had not been designed as a garage, and as a result the driveway in front was not as deep as it should have been and the four petrol pumps were squashed against the office frontage. All the same, it looked a pretty prosperous sort of outfit.

Johnno found time to grin at Mercer between finishing filling the tank of an old Bentley with high-octane petrol and starting to sell a quart tin of oil to a youngster in a Mini Cooper. Mercer wandered through into the office, where he found Vikki frowning over a pile of bills. The tip of her pink tongue was sticking out of the side of her mouth. When she saw Mercer she cheered up, and said, "Hullo, Sunshine. What can we do for you?"

"Where's the boss?"

"In the yard. What do you want?"

"That," said Mercer, "is absolutely nothing to do with you."

"Oh, I'm just the dogsbody," agreed Vikki with a grin. She looked as happy as a kitten that has found a warm spot to curl up in.

Mercer walked through the office and out into the yard. This was more spacious than the frontage had suggested. There was a row of four lock-up garages down each side, and an open-fronted workshop at the end with two inspection pits and some quite elaborate overhead gadgetry. Jack Bull was working with one of the mechanics underneath a van which had been hoisted on hydraulic stilts. Seeing him stripped confirmed Mercer's first impression. He was a man of formidable physique which was only just beginning to run to seed. He had the barrel chest and rounded shoulders of an old-style wrestler, and his one good arm was thick with muscle.

Seeing Mercer, he climbed out of the pit, wiped his right hand on the side of his denims, and said, "Don't tell me. Let me guess. You've come to buy a car."

"Five out of ten," said Mercer. "That's one of the things I've come for."

"I've got just the job. An MG. Not quite three years old. Done only fifteen thousand. New tires all round. Yours for two-fifty."

"What's the catch?"

"No catch. I like to see the force properly equipped. She's in the end garage. Come and have a look at her."

Mercer didn't need to look twice. Unless there was

46

something seriously wrong with it the car was worth four hundred pounds of anyone's money. "You realize," he said, "that if a back wheel falls off or the gear box seizes up first time I use it, you're going to have to put it right."

"The motto of Bull's Garage is service after sales. And until you find somewhere better, you can keep it here. All you'll need is a key to the yard gate, then you can get it out any time you like."

"That sounds fine," said Mercer. "The only thing is, they might want me to keep it at the station."

"You can't. They've only got two lockups there. Bob Clark's got one and Bill Medmenham's got the other. Of course, you *could* keep your car in the open yard at the back of the station. That'd be all right as long as the weather keeps fine."

"No need to twist my arm," said Mercer. "I accept your offer, till further notice. It's very kind of you."

"You won't be the first copper I've helped," said Bull. "Tom Rye used to keep his jalopy here, until they found him a house with a garage. And so did Sergeant Rollo. That's fixed then. What's your other bit of business?"

"I want to have a word with Rainey."

"And if I ask you what it's all about, I suppose you wouldn't tell me."

"I can't see why not, seeing that he'll tell you all about it as soon as I've gone. I want to ask him about a girl called Mavis Hedges, otherwise Sweetie Sowthistle."

Bull made a noise in his throat. It might have been the "Oh" of incredulity or the "Ah" of enlightenment, or it might have been a mixture of both.

"So that's who you dug up, was it?" he said.

"It's a possibility."

"And was Rainey one of hers?"

"A suggestion has been made to that effect."

"You'd better have a word with him then. He operates in a room behind the workshop."

Mercer said thanks and moved off. As he turned the corner he looked back. Jack Bull was standing watching him. When other pictures had faded, Mercer was to remember that particular one. The man, massive and unmoving, dressed only in an undershirt and denim trousers. The army surgeon had taken the left arm off neatly at the elbow. The end of the stump was puckered and seamed.

Most men hide their wounds, thought Mercer. But not Jack Bull.

5

"DID YOU GET anything out of him?" asked Rye.

"I got what you always get out of a dipso," said Mercer. "I got a load of old crap. First he couldn't remember the girl at all. Then he did remember her very vaguely. 'Time passes so quickly, Inspector. There've been other girls. I couldn't tell you their names, Inspector. That wouldn't be right, would it?'"

Rye laughed, and said, "You'll find Stoneferry is a permissive place. It's something to do with being on the river, I expect. Romantic."

"What you mean is that a punt is more convenient than the back seat of a car."

"Something in that," said Rye. "Talking of cars, is she yours?"

They were standing at the window of the CID room overlooking the yard.

"Do you like her?"

"Quite a nice-looking bus," said Rye. "What did Jack Bull sting you?"

"Two-fifty, and unlimited time to pay."

"It's a gift."

"That's what I thought."

"All the same," said Rye, "I wouldn't have done it myself."

"Oh. Why?"

"It makes it a bit awkward if you owe local people money."

"Oddly enough," said Mercer, "I've never found that to be so." He was smiling again the smile which Rye found disconcerting. "All my life I've owed people things. It was usually them who found it awkward, not me. Who *is* Bull?"

"Lived here all his life. Went off to the war. Lost an arm at Arnhem. Came back. Bought the garage with his annuity and a mortgage. Did all right. Paid off the mortgage."

"Any record?"

"Good heavens, no," said Rye. He sounded genuinely shocked. "He was on the Council for ten years. Member of the Rotary. Past chairman of the Chamber of Commerce. President of the Ex-Service Organization. You might call him the unofficial mayor of Stoneferry."

"A solid citizen."

"Solid as they come. Why? You don't think . . . ?"

"I don't think anything," said Mercer. "It's just that he seems to be on the Christian-name terms with an awful lot of senior policemen."

"He's a friendly sort of chap. He let me keep my car in one of his lockups."

"Free?"

"Practically. I think I paid him a bob a week."

"Did Sergeant Rollo have the same arrangement?"

Rye looked up quickly. Mercer had his back to him and was staring out the window. Rye said, "Has someone been talking to you about Sergeant Rollo?"

"The name cropped up. He ran into a bit of trouble, didn't he?"

"Dick Rollo was a damn nice boy," said Rye.

When that seemed to be all he was going to say, Mercer swung round. He wasn't smiling. He said, "Cough it up, Tom. I've got to know about it sometime."

"He had a warning that disciplinary proceedings might be taken. They sent two men down from Central to look into it. Preliminary investigation."

"What charge?"

"Accepting payments to compound an offense."

"Did they peg him?"

"They didn't peg him. There were no proceedings. He opted out."

"How?"

"Since you're so bloody interested, he ran a length of hose-pipe from the exhaust into the back of his car and switched the engine on."

"Did he leave any message?"

"No."

"Wife or children?"

"Wife. No kids."

There was a long silence. Mercer seemed disinclined to break it. He was staring out of the window again. It had started to rain, and fat drops were running down the glass, leaving tracks in the summer dust which had accumulated on the outside.

Massey came in. He was carrying a brown paper parcel, which he put down on the table.

"You been shopping?" said Rye. He seemed glad of the interruption.

"I saw that Jeejeeboy," said Massey. He was a big serious youngster with light hair, blue eyes, and the build of a campus athlete. "He gave me these."

He opened the parcel and spread out the contents.

"They were things he was looking after for Sweetie. When she disappeared, he thought he'd hang onto them until she turned up again. Now that it looks as if it might

51

be—well—it might be sort of permanent, he thought he ought to hand them over."

There was a knee-length coat, trimmed at the cuffs and hem with fur, a fawn-colored skirt, a lemon-colored sweater, and a pair of lizard-skin shoes. The coat was old, and the moths had got into the fur. The other items were newish and looked as if they had cost money. Massey put his hand into his coat pocket and pulled out a paper bag with JEEJEEBOY'S STONES printed on it. He tilted it up and a pile of trinkets fell out. There were two bracelets, an elaborate costume-jewelry brooch, a slave-girl anklet, a necklace of soapstones, a few rings, and finally, as Massey gave the bag a shake, a thin mesh chain with a small golden cross on it.

The three men stood, for a moment, looking down at the pile on the table. Outside the rain was coming down harder. It was beginning to wash away some of the grime.

Mercer said, "I'm going visiting. You can come with me, Massey. Parcel that stuff up. We'll take it along."

Massey started to say something, but Mercer was already out of the door. He looked at Rye. Rye said, "You heard, boy. Get weaving."

Mercer drove his new car carefully, getting the feel of it. They had cleared the High Street before he spoke. He said, "You'd better guide me. I've never been there before."

"I don't know where we're going."

"And you call yourself a detective. What do you suppose we've brought this stuff with us for? To give it an airing?"

"I imagine we're going to ask Hedges to identify it," said Massey. "If that's right we've gone past the turning."

Mercer stamped on the brake so suddenly that Massey nearly hit his head on the windshield. Then he reversed the car nearly into a gateway.

"I just wanted to test the brakes," he said. "They're pretty good, aren't they?"

"Very," said Massey. "Turn down here to the right. You can take the car as far as that clump of alders. Then we have to walk."

Easthaugh Island was a bigger version of Westhaugh, covered by the same ragged growth, divided from the bank of the river by a deeper backwater, which was spanned by a rather more permanent-looking bridge on cement piles. Sowthistle's barge had been grounded on the island side, and had subsided so solidly into the mud that it looked like an extension of the island.

"God, what a hole," said Mercer.

The place stank of stagnant water, rank vegetation, and slime. He thought of Sweetie tripping home at night over the bridge. No wonder she had left her gear behind in Mr. Jeejeeboy's store.

"How do we get in?"

"The door's round the other side."

A sloping plank led up to an opening cut in the side of the barge. Knocking produced no answer. Massey said, "He's probably at the boozer. They won't throw him out till two o'clock. Not if he's got any money left."

"Where does he get his money from?"

"It's a mystery. He never shows up at the labor exchange, and so far as anyone knows he doesn't draw an old-age pension."

Mercer said, "The pubs don't shut till two. That gives us half an hour."

Balancing on one leg, he swung the sole of his heavy shoe flat against the door, just under the catch. It burst inward.

"Oughtn't we to have a warrant?" said Massey.

Mercer looked at him curiously. He said, "I'd heard of people like you. I didn't believe they existed outside of books."

Massey flushed scarlet, and then muttered, "All right, all right. It's your responsibility, skipper."

"As long as we're clear on that point," said Mercer. They stepped down into the barge.

Inside was worse than outside. Much worse. Outside the smells had been rank and vegetable. Inside they were animal. Massey turned round abruptly and made for the opening.

"If you're going to be sick, be sick outside," said Mercer. "We may have to make a chemical analysis of this muck. Don't let's complicate it."

"I'm all right," muttered Massey.

"Hold the torch then."

It was a heavy double-power inspection lamp, and its white light showed up the disastrous squalor of Sowthistle's living arrangements. There was an old iron bedstead with a leaking feather mattress, blankets which had once been white and were now gray, and an old army overcoat. In one corner a paraffin stove was almost hidden behind a pile of unwashed saucepans and crockery.

"If he cooks his food in those, and eats it off these," said Mercer, "he must have a bloody wonderful inside. You or I, we'd be dead of food poisoning inside twenty-four hours." He lifted up a saucepan and peered into it. "What do you think that is?"

Massey sniffed delicately and said, "It smells like kidneys. Do you mind—"

"Sorry," said Mercer. "I thought it'd be a nice change from the other smells. Let's have a look in that cupboard."

The cupboard was padlocked. Mercer found a poker, put the point through the staples, and twisted them out of the woodwork. The shelves were so tightly crammed that when the doors came open the contents started to cascade onto the floor. There were piles of books and magazines. Mostly foreign and all featuring naked or near naked girls with enormously inflated bosoms and behinds. There were photographs, single and in sets. There were sheets of typewritten, handwritten, and mimeographed paper. Mercer picked up one of them and started to read it.

After a minute he said, "Well, well," put it down, and started on another.

"What's it all about?" said Massey.

"Sexual intercourse," said Mercer. "This one's entitled, 'The Ballad of Shooters Hill.' It's hot stuff. Rhymes, too. Hold that torch steady."

"What *is* all this?"

"I guess it's Sowthistle's personal collection of pornography. Phew! Look at that photograph. On second thoughts you'd better not. You're too young."

"Dirty old man."

"I don't think," said Mercer, turning the photograph over and examining the back of it, "that it's all for his own edification. I think what we've stumbled on is a Licentious Lending Library. You see those crosses and dates?"

"Yes."

"I'd guess each one represents a loan. The lads of the village come over here and he lets them read these, or maybe borrow them. For a shilling a time, or whatever the going rate for filth is round here. Judging from the number of crosses, he must be making a bloody good living out of it. Tax free, into the bargain."

They heard the gangplank creak, and the opening was darkened for a moment as Sowthistle came through it.

Massey turned the torch on him.

"Who is it?" The voice was high-pitched and querulous. "Who are you? What do you want? You've got no right in there. Clear out, the lot of you."

"You got a lamp?" said Mercer.

"Wassat?"

"I said, have you got a lamp? You must have some light in this hole."

"Who are you?"

"We're police."

"Police?" The old man was swaying on his feet, and each time he opened his mouth the sour smell of whiskey was added to the other elements in the atmosphere. "You busted open my door, didn't you? You've got no right to do that. And my cupboard."

"If you don't get that lamp lit, grandpa, I'll bust you, too," said Mercer.

"All right, all right."

"Get a move on."

The pale, smoky light of a paraffin lamp showed up the interior of the barge. It also illuminated its owner. He would have looked a lot less unpleasant, thought Mercer, if he had been dressed in the traditional rags of a tramp, with his toes sticking out of holes in his boots. In fact, he had assembled an outfit which, in different circumstances, might have looked almost respectable. He was wearing a blue suit, two sizes too large for him and shiny at the corners, a flannel shirt and a made-up bow tie which had twisted on its stud and was now pointing north and south, rather than east and west. On his feet, a pair of brown lace-up boots. Red-rimmed, watery eyes and a stubble of gray beard completed the picture.

Mercer said, "All right. Sit down."

"I want to know what right you've got—"

Mercer took two quick steps up to him. Sowthistle retreated from the menace, the backs of his legs touched an old armchair, and he folded back into it.

"That's better," said Mercer. He perched on the edge of the table beside him. "Let's have that stuff."

Massey opened the bag he was carrying and took out the clothes and trinkets one by one. Sowthistle made no pretense of examining them. He simply nodded his head at each item.

"You identify these as her property?" said Mercer.

"I wouldn't say identify. I knew she had some things. Kept them down in town. Wouldn't bring them home."

"Why not?"

Sowthistle waved a vague hand round the dirt and shambles of his home.

"Answer the question," said Mercer. "Do you mean she was afraid of the dirt? Or was she afraid you'd take 'em off her?"

"I don't follow you, Inspector. Are you suggesting I'd rob my own flesh and blood?"

"You could read that into it," said Mercer, "or take it the other way if you like. Did you ever take her clothes off her?"

This got a reaction. Sowthistle started to come out of his chair. Mercer raised his leg, planted his foot in the old man's chest, and pushed him back.

"All you've got to do," he said, "is sit still and answer questions. Are any of those photographs in the cupboard photographs of your daughter in the next to nothing?"

"Of course they aren't. I bought 'em."

"We shall see when we've had a chance to look through them." Mercer sat swinging one leg and looking down at the old man. "You're on a spot. You know that, don't you."

"What do you mean? I've done nothing wrong."

"No? What about all that filth?"

"Like I told you. I bought 'em for myself. There's no law against that."

"Try and get the court to believe you. I'll put up half a dozen witnesses who'll say you charged them to look at it. Young boys, some of them. There'll be other charges, too. Indecent behavior—"

The old man opened his mouth to say something, and then shut it again. He seemed to be fascinated by Mercer's leg swinging within inches of his face.

"There's a lot of people in this town have been waiting

57

a chance to run you out. You'll get four years, I'd guess. Maybe seven, when all the charges have been added up. And as soon as you're safe inside we'll get a clearance order and burn this place down. I'll be happy to light the first match. I don't like people like you. Not one little tiny bit, I don't. And I think it's time someone taught you a lesson."

He slid further round the edge of the table, until he was sitting almost on top of the old man, who cringed back in his chair.

Mercer said to Massey, "I think you'd better step outside, son, and keep your eyes open. We don't want anyone butting in."

"Don't you go. Don't leave me alone with him."

Massey hesitated.

Mercer said, "Outside, son. I'm not going to touch him."

"Anything you say, skipper," said Massey. He went out, and they heard the gangplank creaking as he went down it. Then silence. Mercer let it hang for a full ten seconds while Sowthistle crouched in his chair, his eyes ablink.

Then Mercer leaned forward, crooked a hand into the old man's coat, pulled him forward until their heads were no more than a few inches apart, and spoke, very quietly.

"You're in bad trouble, gran'pa." He gave the coat a little shake and Sowthistle's head seemed to nod in agreement. "And a sensible man, when he sees trouble coming, the first thing he thinks about is how he can sidestep it. Right?" Again a little shake. "And I'm going to show you how to do it. I'll let you buy your way out of this, if you like."

"Buy?"

"Not with money. With a piece of information. Just one piece."

"Anything I can do to help, Inspector. You know I'd do it."

"Fine. Then here's what I want to know. During the last month of her life your girl had picked up a new boyfriend. She was meeting him secretly. No one seems to know who he was. But you'd know, wouldn't you?"

"She never told me anything, Inspector."

"You're lying. There's nothing she did you wouldn't know about, or couldn't find out."

"I swear to God—"

"Just the name. That's all I want."

There was a moment's silence. Then Sowthistle said, in a different, sharper voice, "There's someone outside. I heard him."

"It's only Massey."

"There's someone out there, listening. I can't talk to you."

"You've got to talk. You've got no option."

"Not now."

"What are you frightened of?"

With a sudden jerk the old man freed himself, tearing the lapel of the coat right off. He wriggled out of the chair and scuttled round to the end of the bed.

Then he started to scream.

"Stop that," said Mercer. "It won't do you any good."

Massey came back through the opening. He looked curiously at the old man, who was holding onto the end of the bed. He had stopped screaming, and was shaking violently.

"Anything I can do, skipper?"

"Not just now," said Mercer. He put down the torn piece of coat on the table and led the way out. They made their way back to the car in silence.

When they got back into the town, Mercer said, "Who's the next man on your list?"

It took Massey, whose mind was on other things, a

moment to work this out. Then he said, "It's Henniker. He's a bookie. Betting shop at the top of the High Street."

"I'll drop you there. I've got another visit to make."

Massey said, "O.K., skipper," got out, and stood on the pavement looking down at the car. There was clearly something he wanted to say and Mercer waited for him to say it.

"Did you get anything out of the old coot?"

"It depends what you mean by anything. Information, no. One fact, yes. He does know something, and he's frightened to talk."

"Frightened of who?"

"If we knew that, son," said Mercer, "we'd be a long way on."

6

THE NOTICE, in sun-blistered white letters on a black board, read: BRATTLES BOAT HOUSE. PUNTS DINGHIES SKIFFS CANOES. BY HOUR, DAY, WEEK OR MONTH.

Mr. Brattle was at work on the sloping plankway in front of his boathouse. He had a punt upside down on two wooden trestles, and was replacing a cracked bottom plank.

"How did that happen?" said Mercer.

"Some silly kids, skylarking," said Mr. Brattle. "Ran her onto the parapet of the bridge." He didn't sound upset about it. He didn't look the sort of man who would upset easily. His thick bare forearms were almost as brown as the teak he was shaping. Mercer had been watching him with pleasure for some minutes before he spoke to him. He thought that he had rarely seen a more relaxed character.

"You were asking about Mr. Prior," said Mr. Brattle. He held the plank up, decided that it could do with a fraction more off the left-hand side, and walked over with it to his workbench to position it in the vise. Mercer followed him.

"There's two different ways you could get to his place. One is, you could go right back into the town, cross the bridge, take the turning to the left—not the first one, the second—go as far as the cemetery, and turn down the small road opposite the cemetery gate. That'd bring you back, you see—to there."

Mr. Brattle pointed with his spokeshave across the river.

"You mean that's his bungalow I can see."

"That's right."

"And I'm on the wrong bank."

"That's right."

"Damn," said Mercer.

Mr. Brattle removed a sliver of wood from the plank, and said, "The second way is, I could run you across in the boat."

"Well," said Mercer. "If it isn't taking up too much of your time."

"Time," said Mr. Brattle, "is meant to be took up."

He led the way down to the landing stage, unhitched the chain with one large hand, picked up the pole with the other, motioned Mercer aboard, and drove the punt out into the river, performing every action with an economy of movement and effort that was poetry in action.

It was very peaceful on the river. The weir lay downstream, hidden by a bend, and they could hear it grumbling to itself. The water slapped against the bow of the punt. A moorhen scuttled out of one patch of reeds and disappeared into another.

"There you are, Inspector. If you're not going to be too long, I'll wait for you."

"Might be ten minutes."

"Time for a pipe," said Mr. Brattle. Mercer walked up the path between two gardens. The bungalow on the left belonged to the Priors. The one on the right looked empty. There was no other building in sight. The service road seemed to have been built for them alone.

Henry Prior answered the doorbell. He was a thin man

with a lot of untidy gray hair and glasses. He seemed surprised. He said, "I didn't hear anyone drive up."

"That's because I didn't drive," said Mercer. "I was ferried." He showed him his card.

"Police?" said Mr. Prior. "Not Mabel..."

"Your wife?"

"She's in town, shopping. She hasn't..."

"Nothing to do with your wife, sir."

"Silly of me. Every time she takes the car out I think something's going to happen to her. Actually she's a much better driver than I am. Come in."

A room with French windows opening onto a strip of lawn which dipped down to the river. Shabby furniture, which had been good once. Photographs of children and grandchildren. A lot of books. If you had to sit down somewhere and wait for death, it wasn't a bad spot to sit in.

"It's about your garage," said Mercer.

"Oh, that." Mr. Prior made a face. "That's over and done with, or so I'd hoped."

"As far as you're concerned, sir, that's right. Not an agreeable topic, I expect, and I apologize for raising it. The fact is, we're interested in that mechanic. The one who caused all the trouble."

"Taylor."

"Was that his name?"

"That was the name he gave. I understand now that it wasn't his real name. He was a shocking mechanic. I ought to have checked up on him, I suppose. But mechanics are very hard to get."

"I don't think he was just a bad mechanic. I think he was a crook."

"Whatever makes you think that, Inspector?"

"Bad mechanics don't operate under false names. And when they get into trouble they don't disappear. They haven't got the facilities."

"I see," said Mr. Prior. He didn't sound very interested. "Well, if he was a criminal, and has got into more
trouble, I can't be expected to have much sympathy for
him."

"Naturally not," said Mercer. "Did it ever occur to you
that he might have been planted on you?"

"What on earth do you mean?"

"Deliberately planted on you. With the idea of running you out of business."

Mr. Prior sat very still. Then he said, "Who would
have done such a thing? And why? I haven't got any
enemies that I know of."

"It would have been to Jack Bull's advantage to have
you out of business."

"I'm quite certain he wouldn't do a thing like that.
Besides—"

He stopped. Then added, "This didn't come out at the
time, but he was very good to me. When a business goes
bust you usually have to sell the fixed equipment at scrap
prices. He bought it all from me at its full balance sheet
value. But as for someone planting that mechanic on me,
I did think about it. But it didn't seem possible to prove
anything. It'd be more difficult still by now."

"If we could find him, we might prove it."

"My solicitors tried to find him. That was three years
ago. If they couldn't do it—"

"We're better than solicitors at finding people. If we
give our minds to it. What I was wondering was whether
you had any old records. For instance, Taylor could
change his name, but he couldn't change his National
Insurance number."

"The solicitors thought of that. The cards had gone.
He must have taken them out of the office."

"Were there any other sort of papers? Did he give any
references? Or mention any other job he'd been in?"

"References? No. I'm pretty certain there was nothing in writing. My wife looked after all that sort of thing—and here she is."

There was a sound of badly adjusted brakes squeaking and of a car door slamming. Mr. Prior trotted out of the room and came back, shepherding in his wife, and looking like a dog who has done something rather clever.

Mrs. Prior had gray hair like her husband, but there the resemblance ceased. She was a rounded cheerful person and was clearly the driving end of the Prior axis. She listened carefully to what Mercer had to say, and shook her head.

"The lawyers went over all that. There wasn't a scrap of paper in the office belonging to him or referring to him."

"When you sign on a new man and take over his National Insurance cards there's a form which gives the name of his last employer. You couldn't possibly remember what the name was?"

"I could, and did. It was the Crescent Garage, at an address in Southwark."

"Which was duly investigated, I imagine, and found to be nonexistent?"

"Correct."

"I see," said Mercer, and was silent for a moment, staring out of the window. A launch went slowly past upstream. A man in a panama hat was seated at the wheel. He was smoking a cigar.

Mrs. Prior said, "I did think of one thing. After it was all over. Too late to be any use. Taylor was very thick with our other mechanic, Beardoe. They used to go out drinking in the evenings. He might have let slip something, talking to Len."

"It's a possibility," said Mercer. "Where's Beardoe now?"

"What brought it into my mind was that I ran into him in Staines a few weeks ago. He's got a job there. It's not a garage. It's a light engineering works. Carcroft was the name."

"My wife has a marvelous memory," said Mr. Prior. "I'm getting terrible. Not long ago I woke up in the night and I couldn't remember my own middle name."

Mercer found Mr. Brattle knocking out his pipe. He offered Mercer the punt pole. He said, "Like to try your hand on the way back?"

"I'll have a shot."

"Can you swim?"

"Well enough," said Mercer. "But I hope it won't come to that."

He didn't fall overboard, but it was almost the only mistake he didn't make. He put the pole in too far back, and got no propulsion. He put it in too far ahead, and stopped the boat altogether. He put it too far out, and turned in a solemn circle, until he was facing the landing stage again.

"Want to give up?" said Mr. Brattle.

"I'm going to get this bloody thing across if it kills me," said Mercer.

"You don't want to lift the pole quite so high," said Mr. Brattle. "When you raise it up like that the water runs down your sleeve."

"I had noticed."

In midstream he turned another complete circle, nearly running down a canoe. The girl who was in it took prompt evasive action, shouted, "Port to port, you oaf," and shot off upstream. Mercer gritted his teeth.

Five minutes later, damp but exhilarated, he rammed the bank only a yard above the landing stage, and Mr. Brattle, who had been watching his moment, jumped nimbly ashore with the painter.

"I hope I haven't damaged her."

"A well-built punt," said Mr. Brattle, "will stand up to almost anything. You didn't do too bad. A few years' practice and you might be good. You've got the shoulders for it."

"I'll bear it in mind," said Mercer.

"You want someone to teach you, you could do a lot worse than take lessons from that girl in the canoe you nearly hit. Miss Slade, her name is."

"I recognized her," said Mercer.

"You know them, perhaps."

"I know of them."

"Her brother now, he thinks he's good. But he's all brawn and no brain. She's got the better head of the two. Handle any sort of craft. The only thing I've never seen her bother with is one of them things."

He jerked a contemptuous thumb at the motor launch which was coming downstream. Mercer noticed that it was being steered by a man wearing a panama hat and smoking a cigar.

Mr. Brattle refused to take any payment for the trip. Mercer drove home, changed his shirt, and made his way back to the station, where he found an air of subdued excitement in the CID room.

"Guess what?" said Rye. "Tell him, Bob."

Massey said, "I talked to that Henniker. He was one of Sweetie's real steadies. He recognized the bits and pieces. But that's not all. He said there was one missing. It sounded like the only really valuable piece. A twisted gold filigree ring with three small but quite nice diamonds in it."

"Is he sure about that?"

"He gave it to her himself. He said it set him back sixty quid."

"It looks as though Mr. Jeejeeboy must have hocked it."

"Which raises a question, dunnit?" said Mercer. "How did he know Sweetie wasn't coming back to claim it? Get a proper description of the ring from the shop that sold it to Henniker and put it on the pawnbrokers' list. I'll go and have a word with that Pakistani prune peddler."

7

"But I assure you, Inspector," said Mr. Jeejeeboy earnestly, "that what I am telling you is entirely the truth. I know the ring well. It never left her finger."

"It wasn't on her finger when we found her," said Mercer.

"Pray don't say that."

"Why not?"

"It is so dreadful. I cannot bear to think of her in the grave. She was so vital. Just a child, Inspector, but a vital child."

Mercer looked at him. He was either genuinely moved or he was a very good actor. There were tears in his eyes.

"Was this where she kept her stuff?"

"I allowed her to do so. She could not take it back to that—that den where her father lived. I will show you."

They were in the room behind the shop. It was crammed with cartons, crates, boxes, and bottles, and smelled pleasantly of coffee and spice and sawdust. They threaded their way down a narrow passageway among the clutter to the far end, where there was a closet. Mr. Jeejeeboy opened it with a flourish. Except for a couple of wire coat hangers, it was quite empty.

"That was her very own cupboard," he said. "The only

private place she had in the world."

The tears were coming down fast now.

"I suppose she kept it locked."

"Of course. My assistants are frequently in this room. I know them to be trustworthy, but you cannot blame her for being careful."

"Who had keys?"

"She had one, and I had another."

"One of these?"

Mercer took out of his pocket the keys they had found in the red plastic bag. Hard work with emery paper and a nailfile had got most of the rust out of the wards.

"Yes. That is the one. The long one."

Mercer tried it in the lock. It was stiff, but it worked. He said, "The afternoon she disappeared. That's to say, the last afternoon anyone saw her. Was she in here?"

"That afternoon, she could not have been in here. Because it was the early closing day."

"How do you know?"

Mr. Jeejeeboy looked surprised. "Wednesday is always the early closing day."

"How did you know she was last seen on a Wednesday?"

"How did I know? Of course I knew."

"How?"

"Everyone was talking about it."

"Talking about what?"

Mr. Jeejeeboy started to look harassed.

"When she did not appear, Inspector, her friends started to ask themselves, 'When did we see her last?' Someone said, 'I saw her on Monday.' Another said, 'Tuesday.' Then it was remembered that she had been seen in the town, walking down the street, on the late afternoon of Wednesday speaking to a clergyman. After that, nothing."

Mercer listened critically. He had long ago concluded

that it was not so much what witnesses said, but the way they said it. He thought that the thin brown anxious little man might be telling the truth.

He thought about it as he drove the five miles along the new bypass to Staines.

The Carcroft Engineering Works was a small place, out on the Chertsey Road. He had a word with the manager, and Beardoe was brought into the office. He was a middle-aged man, who hid his apprehensions about life behind a large moustache and a gruff manner. He thawed a little when he found what the inspector wanted.

"Taylor? I wooden say I knew him all that well. We got on all right. Tell you the truth, I was a bit surprised Mr. Prior took him on. He didn't seem to have had much experience."

"That was the point I was interested in," said Mercer. "He must have talked sometimes about other jobs he'd done. It'd be a natural thing to do. Where he'd been before. That sort of thing."

"He may have done, but it was a good time ago, Inspector. Three years and more. I do seem to recollect he told me he'd worked at a place in Southwark."

"The Crescent Garage."

"That sounds right."

"He didn't mention any other place?"

Beardoe ran a black-ingrained fingernail down the flank of his moustache and started to say something and then stopped and thought about it again. "I do recollect," he said, "one night. He must have been pissed at the time or he'd never have said it, but we were talking about stolen cars. He said, if ever you were lumbered with a hot job, the place to take it was to—"

"Was what?"

"I'm damned if I can remember. It was a foreign name. Sounded like Italian or Greek. He gave me the address, too. I wasn't very interested, you understand."

71

"I quite understand. But if you could remember it—either the name or the address—it would be very helpful."

"You know how it is," said Beardoe. "When you try to remember a thing, you can't. When you're not trying, it comes back to you."

"If it should come back to you," said Mercer, "ring me at this number at once."

He drove back to Stoneferry in the dusk, devoting only a quarter of his attention to the road and the rest to a consideration of the question of whether he might not be chasing a wild goose. Possibly it was this preoccupation that prevented him from noticing a small black sedan, which had kept two cars behind him on the way out and was maintaining the same respectful distance on the return journey.

At about this time, Mrs. Prior had a shock. She had come back from an afternoon of shopping and gossiping, had parked the car and opened the front door. Her husband was standing in the hall. She saw at once that something was wrong. His face was unnaturally white, and when he stretched his hand out and put it on her arm, she saw that it was shaking. "Henry, my dear!" she said. "You're ill. I'll put you straight to bed."

It was the effort he made to control his voice which told her that something really serious had happened.

He said, "You remember that man who came this morning."

"The police inspector?"

"Yes."

"Has he been here again?"

"He hasn't been here again. And listen to me. If he does come here again, he's not to be allowed inside the house. If he rings up, you don't answer the telephone."

His voice was rising. She took him by the arm and led him back into the sitting room. She said, "Sit down there. By the fire. I'll get you a drink."

She took as much time as possible in pouring out the drink, and by the time she came back with it, her husband had recovered some of his self-possession. As she handed him the glass, her hand brushed his hair. She said, "Your hair's quite wet. What on earth have you been doing? Bathing?"

Mr. Prior started shivering again.

On the following Monday morning the formal inquest was opened on what the newspapers now referred to as "The Body on the Island." The coroner, Mr. Byfold, a sleepy-looking man with three chins and a dimple, said, "I take it, Inspector, that you will ask for an adjournment. We appreciate your difficulties in this case. How long would you like?"

"The police would ask for an adjournment of seven days."

"I'd be happy to give you longer than that."

"It seems probable that we should be able to offer evidence of identification within that period."

"Very well, Inspector. Adjourned until September twentieth."

"Weren't you sticking your neck out a bit?" said Superintendent Clark.

"I don't think so," said Mercer. "We've got a prima facie identification already. There's no doubt the handbag was hers. The powder compact made it pretty certain and the keys clinched it. She disappeared two years ago. And we'll get Dr. Champion to say that's about the time he estimates the body had been buried. And another thing, it's only negative evidence, but as far as I can make out Sweetie had never been near a dentist."

"We'd better warn Champion that we shall be relying on his evidence. Well, what's happened now, Tom?

You're looking damned pleased with yourself."

Inspector Rye, who had come in without knocking, said, "We've got an answer about that ring. In fact, we've got the object itself. Turned over to us by a pawnbroker at Slough."

He put the ring on Clark's desk and the three men looked at it curiously. It was a pretty thing, and clearly quite valuable.

"Has he got a record of the deposit?"

"He certainly has," said Rye. "He was so suspicious of the whole transaction that he made a note, in his own handwriting, in the margin of the ledger. 'Calls himself Smith. Old man. Dressed like a respectable tramp.'"

"Sowthistle." Mercer and Clark said it together.

"Get us a positive identification," said Clark, "and we'll pull him in."

"I've done it, sir. You remember when there was all that fuss with the local authority. Hedges' picture was in all the papers. I took the pawnbroker straight down to the *Slough Gazette* office and showed him some of the photographs."

"And he identified him?"

"Not a shadow of doubt."

"He's an unmistakable sort of character," said Mercer.

"All right. We can organize a proper identification parade afterward. If it comes to that. Meanwhile, I imagine you'll pull him in and charge him."

"With theft? Or murder?"

"I must leave that to your judgment *after* you've questioned him."

"We shall have to make our minds up which horse we're backing before we charge him."

"I am acquainted with judges' rules," said Clark. "I also believe that any detective officer worth his salt knows how to get round them."

74

Mercer said equably, "You wouldn't care to give me that in writing, sir?"

"No. I would not."

"Because we really are in a bit of a cleft stick. If we charge him with theft, he'll put up some story. Sweetie was going away and gave him the ring. Why? To pay for board and lodging, or because she loved the old bastard, or for any other reason he puts forward. The point being that if Sweetie isn't here, she can't deny it."

Clark said, "Mmm." He didn't sound pleased.

"On the other hand, if we go the whole hog and charge him with murder, it could misfire badly. There's a lot of suggestive evidence. He wouldn't have dared to sell the ring unless he was sure she wasn't coming back. But it's not direct evidence. We may get there in time, but if we go off at half cock, the whole thing may blow up in our faces. You remember what a lot of sympathy he got out of the papers last time. We don't want a second campaign of that sort, do we?"

The superintendent was spared the trouble of answering by Detective Massey, who put his head round and said, "Sorry to interrupt. But we've had a message from the box out on the Staines Road. They've pulled in Hedges."

"Pulled him in. What for?"

"Assault, sir."

"What happened?"

"From what I gather, he was walking along the road and he flagged a lorry. He had a big knapsack on his back, and the driver thought at first he was a hiker, and stopped. When he saw Hedges—"

"Smelled him, you mean."

"Yes. Well, anyway, he said no. Hedges was pretty tight, and he got mad and tried to clamber on board, and there was a bit of a fight, and in the middle of it one of

75

our patrol cars came along. Then Hedges hit the police-man."

"That solves one of our difficulties, doesn't it?" said Mercer. "By the way, what was in the knapsack?"

"All his clothes and things."

"You mean he was scarpering?"

"It certainly looked like that. He told the lorry driver he was heading for the West Country."

The superintendent said, "Well, I think that's very satisfactory. You'll take over, Mercer."

"I'll take over," said Mercer. The scar on the side of his face showed up red for a moment.

Sowthistle was brought in at midday. The events of the morning had not improved his appearance. He was taken straight up to the CID room. Coming in from the street at about three o'clock, Inspector Medmenham stopped and said to Station Officer Tovey, "What on earth's all that noise? Where's it coming from?"

"Up in the CID room," said Tovey with a wooden face. "They're questioning that old man they brought in for clocking Peters."

"Has it been going on for long?"

"About an hour."

Medmenham said, "Oh!" and walked upstairs and along the corridor. He was making for the superinten-dent's office.

At four o'clock Tom Rye came into the CID room with three cups of tea on a tray. He looked curiously at Sowthistle, who was crouched on a chair, his face in his hands, and his whole body shaking.

Rye said, very quietly, "The chief's getting worried."

Mercer said, "Then tell him from me to stop worry-ing. I haven't laid a finger on the old sod, and I've had Massey here all the time to watch me not doing it. Right, son?"

Massey, who was sitting in a corner with a notebook

balanced on his knee, nodded.

"Then what's he been screaming about?"

"It's a defensive mechanism. When I ask him a question he can't answer, he opens his mouth and screams."

"Do you think he knows something?"

"He knows something, and we're going to get it out of him if we sit here all night asking questions. And all tomorrow, and the day after."

"Would you like me to give you a spell?"

"Not right now," said Mercer. "We're just beginning to get to know each other."

The ragbag in the chair showed no sign of hearing what was said. Now he looked up and Rye could see two eyes, startlingly alive within their red circumferences, and spittle at each corner of the loose mouth.

"He's not having a fit, is he?"

"If you want my honest opinion," said Mercer, "it's ninety percent put-on. He knows bloody well what we want, don't you, gran'pa?"

Sowthistle snarled at them.

"That's more like it," said Mercer. "Stop playing the idiot boy. Just be your own filthy self. Then we shall get on. Let's start again. When did you say you saw Sweetie last?"

Rye went back again at six o'clock with tea and at eight o'clock with yet more tea. At half past nine Mercer came out and walked along to the superintendent's office. Clark was still at his desk. He looked as if he was feeling the strain more than Mercer.

Rye said, "How's it going?"

"We've got a confession. Of a sort."

"Written?"

"Written out, but not signed. He says he'll think about signing it tomorrow. When he's not so tired."

"Which means he'll repudiate the whole thing."

"Very likely. But it was made in the presence of two

77

police officers. It's enough to hold him. When he comes up tomorrow, we can oppose bail on the grounds that there are more serious charges pending. They'll give us that, won't they?"

"Treat Lionel Talbot right," said Clark, "and he will give you all the help you want. Get that confession signed and we'll charge him straightaway."

"I'm not all that happy about the confession. Not as it stands right now."

"What does he say?"

"He's told us at least six different stories. The one I've got down is the last one he told us. That Sweetie came home pretty high herself one evening. They had a real set-to, she fell and hit her head. He found she was dead, and pushed her into the river. When I said, 'Then how did she end up three foot down in a grave on Westhaugh Island,' he said he supposed he must have buried her."

"Do you believe a word of that?"

"Frankly," said Mercer, "no. Whatever happened to her, it wasn't that. It was something a lot more cold-blooded. And anyway, she wasn't killed by a blow on the head. She was strangled. But he was involved in her death. I'm sure of it. She's on his conscience. She's at the back of his mind. She's walking in his sleep."

"You'll be walking in your sleep if you don't get to bed soon," said Clark.

Mercer started back to his lodgings in Cray Avenue, but halfway there, changed his mind and turned down to the river. He had an unpleasant taste in his mouth and he thought that a pint of beer might wash it out.

Mercer took his beer into the back room at the Angler's Rest and found Jack Bull and Rainey in front of the fire, drinking whiskey.

He said, "Where's the supporting cast?"

"Johnno's just pushed off," said Bull. "Vikki wouldn't come out tonight. She's sulking."

"That young madam wants slapping down," said Rainey.

"I wouldn't advise you to try it," said Bull. "She packs a fast right hook, with a lot of weight behind it."

"Speaking from experience?" said Mercer.

"Am I not." Bull rubbed the point of his jaw with a big finger.

"You ought never to have taken her on," said Rainey. Whiskey seemed to have loosened his tongue. "She's got no head for figures."

"As long as her own figure's right, I don't give a damn about her head."

"Don't say I didn't warn you."

"My dear old Percival," said Bull with sudden ferocious good humor, "you must know that I'm far too old and far too evil to be warned. I'm beyond redemption. And you're tight. Go home to bed."

There was no doubting the tense of the last sentence. It was in the imperative affirmative. Rainey finished his drink and shambled to his feet.

"Maybe you're right," he said. He made for a point to the right of the door, tacked at the last moment, and made contact with the door handle.

"And while you're passing the bar, see if you can remember to order a couple of whiskeys. Doubles."

"Is his name really Percival?"

"Gospel truth. Perce the Purse, the boys call him. He's a highly qualified accountant and a bloody marvelous mathematician. When he's sober."

"Is he often?"

Bull laughed, and said, "He's mostly sober from ten till six. If he wasn't, he'd be out on his ear."

"It's your business, but I should have thought there might be danger in having a man like that in charge of the cash."

"Yes and no. He'd swindle me if he dared. But he

79

knows I know that, and I'm watching for it, so he doesn't do it. Also he knows if I caught him fiddling I wouldn't only sack him, I'd break his bloody neck."

The drinks arrived. Bull paid with a pound note and waved away the change. "Water or soda?"

"I never touch the stuff," said Mercer.

On top of the beer the whiskey slid down smoothly. Bull let a companionable minute tick by before he said, "And how are you finding Sinferry?"

"It's an interesting sort of place," said Mercer. "Full of characters."

"Like Sowthistle Hedges?"

"No. Not like Sowthistle. He's unique, I should say."

"He's a freewheeler," said Bull. "Do you know, when he first came here—must have been more than thirty years ago, before he sank up to his neck into the shit—he was quite a boy. When the local Council tried to make him pay rates he fought them through the Rating Tribunal and the high court. Conducted his own case and won it. I believe it's still the leading case on the difference between a house and a houseboat."

Mercer tried to visualize Sowthistle addressing the high court and failed. He said, "Talking of characters, I met a real one today. Mr. Brattle."

"Charlie Brattle. One of the best. A warm man, too. That boathouse and the land round it has been in the Brattle family for a hundred years. I'm told that a firm of property developers offered him twenty thousand for it. They wanted to put up a river club complete with chalets. When he said no they upped the offer to thirty thousand. He told them to go and jump in the river."

The landlord put his head round the door to say, "Any more orders?"

"Two more large whiskeys," said Mercer.

"Make it four," said Bull. "Save your legs. What were

you talking to Brattle about? Don't tell me he'd broken the law."

"Certainly not. I was looking for Prior's place. He took me across in the punt."

"Henry Prior?"

"That's right. Used to keep the Stoneferry Garage. Before he ran into that bit of trouble."

"Henry was all right," said Bull. "We may have been cutting each other's throats in business, but that didn't stop me liking him personally."

"So he told me."

"Oh?"

"About you buying his fixed equipment."

"It was good stuff. More useful to me than the scrap dealers. If I'm just being bloody inquisitive, tell me to keep my trap shut, but why would old Henry Prior interest the police?"

"As a matter of fact, it's something you might be able to help me on. Being in the same line of business. You remember the mechanic who caused all the trouble?"

"Taylor."

"That's what he called himself. Did you, or any of your chaps, ever talk to him?"

"I didn't. They might have. Why?"

"I'd be very interested to know where he came from. In fact, I'd be interested in anything about his past at all. He's such a shadowy figure. Comes from nowhere, wrecks the Stoneferry Central Garage, departs to nowhere."

"I could ask my boys. They're bound to ask me why I want to know."

"Tell them I'm a nosy bastard," said Mercer. He sank back still more comfortably into the padded armchair.

"I'd be telling 'em nothing but the truth at that," said Bull with a grin which showed a set of sharp white teeth. "You *are* a nosy bastard."

"I'm interested in people," said Mercer. The second whiskey had followed the first, and his voice had a very slight slur to it. "In where they come from, and where they're going to, and what makes them tick. And I'm interested in things that happen. When a lot of different things seem to be happening at the same place and the same time, I want to know whether it's blind chance, or whether it's cause and effect. Once, in London, I wanted to find out why a boy was late for school some mornings and not on others. He always set out from home at the same time. It was worrying his mother."

The outer bar was very quiet now. The landlord had got rid of the other customers and must have departed to organize his own supper.

"Go on," said Bull sleepily. "Tell me."

"He'd been put on by his older brother to watch the bank manager and report what time he arrived at the bank. Sometimes the manager was punctual. Then the boy got to school in time. Sometimes he wasn't. Then the boy was late. It was as simple as that."

"Let's have the punch line," said Bull. "The older brother was a bank robber and you caught him."

"He was working for a crowd who organized wage snatches. I stopped that particular snatch, and I caught this." His finger caressed the scar on the left side of his face. "It's a memento from a very undesirable character called Liston."

There was a long silence after this. A casual observer might have supposed that the big men stretched out in chairs in front of the fire were asleep.

8

"WHO WAS MRS. TYLER?" said Mercer.

"Never heard of her," said Tom Rye.

"Mrs. Agatha Mainwaring Tyler of the Thatched Cottage, Stoneferry Common. Where's Stoneferry Common?"

"South of the river between Chertsey and Laleham. Highclass district. The Thatched Cottage is probably a little place with twenty bedrooms standing in its own park."

"No," said Mercer. He was turning over the pages of a dusty office docket, one of a dozen he had unearthed from a cabinet and spread over his table. "Judging from the evidence available, Mrs. Tyler may have been a gentlewoman—but she was a depressed gentlewoman. Depressed, and oppressed."

"Who by?"

"According to her, by Bull's Garage."

"What would they do that for?"

"It's an interesting story. Like all these dockets. All interesting stories. Some with beginnings and some with middles, but very few with endings."

"The ones in that cabinet were all Dick Rollo's cases. I don't think I've looked at them since he—"

"Since he went."

"That's right," said Rye. "Since he went." Mercer had noticed that talking about Sergeant Rollo always made him edgy. "What's so interesting about Mrs. Tyler?"

"It's a very human story. Mrs. Tyler was seventy-seven years old. She had long outlasted Mr. Tyler and she lived, in modest but declining widowhood, in the Thatched Cottage, which stands"—Mercer consulted the docket—"three miles from the nearest railway station and half a mile from the nearest bus stop."

"She can't have got about much."

"That's where you're wrong. The old duck possessed a motorcar. *And* a driving license."

"At seventy-seven."

"Old ladies of seventy-seven cause less trouble on the road than kids of seventeen."

"True," said Rye. "So what happened?"

"Her car went in to Bull's Garage for its three-year road test. Since it had been driven by Mrs. Tyler alone, and maintained with scrupulous care, she had no reason to anticipate trouble and was therefore horrified when she was told that the differential was in such a bad state that it would have to be removed and replaced. At a cost of eighty-five pounds."

"Lousy workmanship. I'm told one car in ten that comes out of the factory has something radically wrong with it."

"You may be right. But that's not the point. The point is, there was nothing wrong with the differential at all."

Rye stared at him.

"Mrs. Tyler had a grandson, who was a friend of Sergeant Rollo. They'd been at school together. They were both mad about cars. Not just mad about driving them. They loved taking them to pieces to see what made them tick."

"That's right," said Rye. "Dick Rollo was never happier than when he was lying under some piece of machinery up to his elbows in black grease."

"The two of them spent a whole weekend dismantling granny's differential. They couldn't find a blind thing wrong with it, and what's more, they came to the conclusion that *it hadn't even been looked at*. Some of the bolts on the casing were rusted in so tight it was clear they hadn't been shifted for years."

"Well?" said Rye. "What happened?"

Mercer was silent. He seemed to have lost the train of his thoughts. Possibly he was seeing Sergeant Rollo, crouched behind his own car wiring a piece of rubber tubing to the exhaust pipe. Finally he said, "Nothing happened. Bull apologized. He said that two reports had got switched. Mrs. Tyler's car had a clean bill of health." He had started leafing through the other dockets. He said, "All the same, I don't think he was quite happy about it. He seems to have started an unofficial inquiry, all on his own. Finding out the names of other people—particularly people who lived outside the town, elderly people who depended absolutely on their cars but knew damn little about them. I think he was looking for a few other cases where the same sort of 'mistake' might have been made."

"He didn't say anything to me about it."

"If he had said something to you—*before* he'd collected some other evidence—would you have believed him?"

"Believed that Bull was on the crook? No, I don't think I should have. I should have thought he could make all the money he wanted honestly."

"It depends how much he wants," said Mercer. "Don't you think it's time you told me about him?"

"About Jack Bull?"

"No, no," said Mercer gently. "About Rollo. I'll have to know sometime."

85

"I suppose so," said Rye. He didn't sound happy. "We'd been having a run of cases of thefts of portable typewriters and tape recorders. Wireless sets, television sets, hi-fi gear, that sort of stuff. Not one big bust, but a steady trickle. Rollo was put onto it."

"Who did Rollo think was doing it?"

"He didn't seem to get very far with that job. I didn't bother him. It was just one of a lot of jobs. If a lead turned up, he'd follow it. You know how it is. The next thing was we got a note."

"Anonymous, naturally."

"Naturally. Written in block capitals on a piece of toilet paper. It just said that Rollo had taken one of the stolen color TV sets as a payoff. We'd find it at his house. If the note had come to me, I'd have put it where it belonged and pulled the plug."

"Who did get it?"

"The old man. I don't think he liked it much, but orders are orders. Any complaint, however trivial—you know the form. As a first step we got a man from the next division to drop in on Mrs. Rollo. The set was there. In the parlor, as large as life. When she was out of the room, he got a sight of the serial number. It was one of the stolen sets. No question."

"Out in the open? In the middle of the room?"

"That's right. When Rollo was asked about it later he told us how he got it. Apparently a man had called at the house one morning about three weeks before, when Mrs. Rollo was alone, produced his card, and said he was an area representative of the Starlight supermarket chain, and wasn't Mrs. Rollo a lucky girl! She was the millionth customer to make a purchase at one of their shops since the chain had started operating, and she was going to be presented with a handsome new television set. There'd be a proper presentation later, with the press in attendance, and all that jazz. But they didn't see why she shouldn't use it meanwhile."

"Did she tell anyone about this at the time?"

"No. The man said to keep quiet about it until the presentation or it'd spoil the surprise."

"Clever," said Mercer. "Plausible, too. What happened next?"

"The old man asked Rollo about the set as soon as he came off duty. He told us what I've just told you. And we believed him. It was an obvious fix. We told him we didn't intend to take any further step in the matter. Only the man who'd been put on the job was a sticker. We didn't know it, but for the next few evenings he kept up a watch on Rollo's house, from a car parked over the way. On the third evening he saw Rollo come out, quite late, and drive off. He followed him. Rollo drove out of town, upriver, toward Westhaugh Island, stopped on a lonely stretch, get something out of the boot—it was pretty heavy by the way he handled it—heaved it into the bushes, and drove off."

"Let me guess," said Mercer. "It was an unopened sales carton with a brand-new record player in it."

"A typewriter actually."

"And what did he say about that one? That he'd won it in a raffle?"

"He said he'd found it in the boot of his car when he got home that evening. He wanted to tell us. His wife talked him out of it. She said no one would believe it. She said just go and dump it. So he did."

"He must have been worried stupid," said Mercer. "I don't mean pulling a silly stunt like that; I mean doing it so bloody inefficiently. He was a trained detective, and he allowed himself to be followed, at night, on a little-used road, and didn't spot the tail."

"He was worried, all right," said Rye. "He took it very hard. After what happened we had to go on with the

87

investigation. This time they sent two senior men down from Central. They started asking a lot of questions. Then Rollo took the short way out."

"Which everyone assumed to be an admission of guilt."

"I suppose so."

"Did you?"

Rye took time out to answer this. Then he said, "It's hard to say. His wife didn't help. She was a bit of a bitch and apt to get hysterical. All the same, taken by itself it didn't seem to me to be enough. All he had to do was to say that the whole thing was a plant, and stick to it. Agreed he behaved stupidly. Agreed it would have left a black mark. He might have got booted out. If he'd been near the end of the line, with his pension gone and nothing much to live for—but hell! He was twenty-four."

Mercer said, "Before I went to Southwark, when I was attached to West End Central, I learned a lot about framing. The villains round those parts made quite a specialty of it, and the police had studied it, too. One thing I found was they very rarely tried to frame an absolutely straight man. There had to be a crack in the fabric first. Just wide enough to get the point of a knife into. And the person most likely to be framed was one who'd done them a few favors in the past and then had stopped. Maybe he saw the light, or maybe he didn't think the game was worth the candle. Those were the ones they'd really put the hook on."

"I'm not sure that I follow you," said Rye stiffly. "Are you suggesting that Rollo *was* guilty?"

"Not of the things he was charged with. But I think it's possible that once or twice, in the past, he may have done a few small favors. It mayn't have seemed important at the time. It was probably for someone he liked. Someone who'd done favors for him. But when the crunch came, it was this little bit of rottenness inside that broke him up."

Rye said, "I've never listened to such utter balls in my life," and stormed out, slamming the door behind him.

Mercer returned to the pile of dockets on the table. He was grinning, but there was not a lot of mirth in it.

Rye's way out took him past the superintendent's office. The door was open and Clark beckoned him in.

He said, "Shut the door, Tom, and sit down. I've been wanting the chance of a word with you. You look worried. Something wrong?"

"I've just insulted my superior officer."

"This isn't the army. You won't be court-martialed. As a matter of fact, it was your superior officer I wanted to talk to you about. What do you make of him? It's all right. You're not giving evidence in court. This is completely unofficial and off the record."

"I'm damned if I know what to make of him," said Rye. "Usually, I can sum a man up quickly. I've been working with Mercer for nearly two weeks now, and I know less about him than when he arrived. He talks a lot, but he doesn't tell you anything. And he never seems to be thinking of less than three things at once. You'd think handling a murder investigation would be enough to occupy a man's mind. But when you think he's thinking about Sweetie and old Hedges, he's off on Prior."

"Prior?"

"Chap who owned the Stoneferry Garage that went bust three or four years ago."

"Oh, yes."

"Now he's started looking through all Sergeant Rollo's old cases."

"What on earth for?"

"I think he's got a bee in his bonnet about Jack Bull."

"And yet," said Clark, "he seems to be very friendly with him. Exceptionally friendly." He picked up a typewritten slip from his desk. "That was one of the things I wanted to talk to you about. Medmenham showed me this."

It was a report from the Station Occurrences Book, contributed by P.C. Harper. It said that he had seen two men come out of the side door of the Anglers Rest public house at twenty minutes after midnight. They were walking a little unsteadily but were not drunk, and had stopped under the railway arch to talk. There had been complaints about breaches of licensing regulations at the Angler's Rest and P.C. Harper had been curious to see who those late customers were. One was easily recognizable as Mr. Bull. As soon as he saw that the other man was Detective Chief Inspector Mercer he had broken off observation.

"I like 'broken off observation,'" said Rye. "What he means is, he pissed off bloody quick."

In the CID room the telephone rang. Mercer put down the docket he was examining and said, "Mercer here. Oh, hullo, Mrs. Prior. What can we do for you?" Then, "Where are you speaking from? A call box? Where?" And, "All right. I'll meet you there." He grabbed up his hat and went out.

The Dolly Varden Café was a quiet place opposite the end of Fore Street. Mrs. Prior was at a table at the back of the nearly empty room. She had ordered two cups of coffee, and was making a pretense of drinking one. Mercer sat down beside her.

"I thought it better not to come to the police station," she said. "You know what small towns are like for gossip. It would have got back to Henry, and he'd never have forgiven me."

"Why not?"

"He categorically forbade me to speak to you."

Like a breeze coming in at an open window, a tiny prickle of apprehension touched the back of Mercer's neck. He said, "That was high-handed of him. Funny, because he didn't strike me as a high-handed sort of person."

"He's not high-handed," said Mrs. Prior. "He was scared. Scared out of his wits. It took me a whole day to get it out of him. Even now I can hardly believe it. When I was out that afternoon two men called. They just said to Henry, 'We hear you've been talking to the police. You mustn't do it.' Henry blustered a bit, and said, 'You've got no right to come in here and say things like that to me.' And then"—Mrs. Prior's voice broke for a moment— "they frog-marched him into the kitchen, filled the sink with water, twisted his arms behind his back, and held him face down in it. They held him there for about a minute. Then they let him go and said, 'If you talk to the police again, we'll hold you down for five minutes.' Then they went."

"Could he describe the men?"

"He can't."

"Can't, or won't?"

"Does it matter which?"

"I suppose it comes to the same thing in the end," said Mercer. "Tell me, did you happen to notice a lush-looking character in a panama hat, smoking a big cigar, coming up your stretch of the river?"

Mrs. Prior said, slowly, "Yes. I think so. The day you came. I didn't notice the man particularly, but I noticed the boat. A twenty-footer with a diesel engine."

"That sounds like the one. Where would anyone hire a boat like that?"

"It's not a local boat. Upriver at Staines or Windsor. Or down at Teddington or Richmond. Or even further. It could have come up from London, or down from Henley."

Mercer said, "Thanks for coming to see me, Mrs. Prior. And will you give your husband a message? I shan't trouble either of you again. You've told me all you could tell me, and I guess these men know it."

"Then why did they do it?"

"It was an exercise in fancy brutality. It's their specialty. It was meant as a warning."

"I still don't understand. If there's nothing more he can tell you, and they knew that, what was the point of warning him?"

"It wasn't him they were warning," said Mercer. "It was me."

He stopped at the pay desk on the way out and asked the manageress if he could use her telephone. She said, "You're our new policeman, aren't you? I thought so. The phone's in my office. Help yourself."

Mercer dialed the number of the Carcroft factory at Staines and asked for the manager. The manager said, "I'm afraid you can't speak to Beardoe. He's in hospital."

"Nothing serious, I hope."

"Not too bad. He broke his wrist."

"How come?"

"He fell downstairs. Concussed himself. Messed his face up a bit, too. If you want him badly, he should be able to see you in a day or two."

"Well, thanks," said Mercer. He made a note of the name of the hospital, paid for the call, and walked out into the High Street. On his way back to the station he found himself doing things which had been second nature in Southwark, but had been left behind him when he came to Stoneferry. Like walking in the middle of the pavement, and taking an occasional look in a shop window to see whether anyone was crowding him.

The CID room was empty. There was a message, in Rye's vile handwriting, on a piece of paper pinned to the front of his table by a paper knife. It said, "The boss wants you. Panic stations."

Mercer looked at the message for a long minute, his

eyes abstracted, his thick body rocking gently, from heel to toe and back again. Then he drifted out, along the passage, and into Bob Clark's room. The superintendent said, "There you are. I've been looking for you. We're in a mess."

Mercer said, "Oh?"

"We've got the adjourned inquest on that girl coming up on Monday and we've lost our main witness."

"Lost?"

"Dr. Champion. He died this morning. He collapsed at home. Just after breakfast. He was dead before they could get him to hospital."

"Do they know what it was?"

"An acute coronary, they think. It wasn't entirely un-expected. He had high blood pressure, and he'd been overworking for years. He was due to retire next month, actually."

"Mercer said, "Poor old sod. Anyway, it was quick."

"Yes," said Clark. "And it's left us in a devil of a mess."

"I'm sorry," said Mercer. "But I don't see it. Naturally we can ask for a further adjournment now."

"Certainly. But what are we going to do with Hedges meanwhile?"

"Ah," said Mercer. "I take your point."

"If the inquest had gone as planned we'd have got a positive identification. That would have been enough to justify holding him. But if we're going to charge him with murder, we've got to do it next time he comes up. Other-wise we can't possibly oppose bail. There's a lot of feeling about that already. And once he's out, God knows if we shall ever see him again."

"I don't think we *should* see him again."

Clark looked at Mercer. He said, "And what exactly do you mean by that?"

"I've never believed that Hedges murdered Sweetie, but I think he knows something about it. Either he had a

93

hand in it, or he saw her being killed. Or being buried. Or thought he did. As long as he was taking the rap, as long as he was locked up here, he was safe. Let him out and I wouldn't give you sixpence for his chances."

"I think you're exaggerating," said Clark. But he didn't sound happy.

"Could we run him in for assault and put him inside for a month?"

"I might have a word with Lionel Talbot. He'd help us if he could. The trouble is, Hedges is something of a public character. The local paper has taken up his case. Did you see the article yesterday? Raking up all the old history."

"I saw it."

"There's talk of briefing counsel to defend him. If they put up a real fight, I wouldn't guarantee we could put him away. Throwing a punch at a policeman. It isn't as serious as all that."

And the last thing you want is a press crusade against you on the eve of your retirement, thought Mercer. Aloud, he said, "I've got a better idea. If you got a positive identification at the inquest, you think we could justify a charge?"

"Coupled with the sale of the girl's ring and what we've got by way of a confession, yes."

"All right. We'll ask Dr. Summerson to come down from Guy's. He's seen all the evidence. I sent him duplicates of everything, in case there was a laboratory angle to it. He's seen all the photographs, and Dr. Champion's notes."

"Summerson," said Clark. "Summerson. Yes. That should do the trick. Do you know, Mercer, I think that's rather a good idea."

9

"AND NOW, Dr. Summerson," said the coroner, "are there any points with regard to the sex, height, age, or physical condition of the victim which might help the jury to arrive at some firm conclusion as to her identity?"

"I'll deal with those points separately if I may, sir," said Dr. Summerson. The Home Office pathologist was a slight, spare, middle-aged man, nondescript at first sight, remarkable only when he began to speak.

Most of the spectators had recognized him from his appearances in the press. They were disappointed to see him step into the box without an assortment of gruesome anatomical specimens, and armed only with a single sheet of paper.

"I take it that there was no doubt as to sex?"

"None at all. I entirely agree with the very careful notes on the subject made by the late Dr. Champion. The light build of the skull with its feeble superciliary arches and thin orbital margins would have been almost conclusive in itself. Taken in conjunction with the measurements of the femur and the humerus—particularly the head of the humerus—they place the matter beyond any reasonable doubt."

"Does he mean," said the foreman of the jury, "that she was a woman?"

The coroner, who was hardened to the ways of juries, said, "That's right. She was a woman." The foreman made a note. The lady next to him had started feeling her forehead with the tips of her fingers. She was evidently worried about her orbital margins.

"As to height," said Dr. Summerson, "again I see no reason to differ from Dr. Champion. He refrained, quite rightly in my view, from any attempt to measure the skeletal remains as a whole, but applied Trotter and Gleser's tables to the respective lengths of the humerus, radius, tibia, and femur. When all four of these bones are present and in unbroken condition the results have usually proved remarkably accurate."

"Dr. Champion said, between five foot three and five foot four."

"I would myself put the standing height as nearer to the latter."

"Five feet four inches high," said the coroner, and the foreman wrote this down, too.

"Fortunately for her," said Dr. Summerson, "but unfortunately so far as the chances of identifying her are concerned, the body evidenced very few abnormalities or weaknesses. As you have heard, the teeth are in perfect order and show no sign of filling or capping. There is slight evidence that the two top incisors may at some time have been braced. However, there was one point which could assist. I observed that the first phalanx of the big toe of the right foot was deviated outward and there was considerable exostosis of the outer side of the head of the first metatarsal bone."

The foreman looked pathetically at the coroner, who said, "She had a bony lump on the outside of her big toe."

"Something like a bunion?"

"Not actually a bunion," said Dr. Summerson kindly. "But there might have been a bunion there, too. Very likely there was."

"Your point, I take it, doctor, is that this deformity might have been noticeable in her shoe sizes."

"I think so. It must have been very difficult for her to find a standard pair of shoes which fitted both feet. She could, of course, have had them specially made. But failing that, she would have been driven to buy a different fitting for her right foot."

Superintendent Clark passed a note across to Mercer. "Anything on this yet? Local shops?"

Mercer scribbled back, "I only got it from Summerson this morning. I'm sending a circular out today."

The coroner said, "Thank you, doctor. Was there anything else?"

The pathologist looked down deliberately at his notes. As he did so, Mercer, who was watching him closely, experienced an irrational feeling of alarm. Dr. Summerson had given evidence so often, before so many different tribunals, that he was, by now, a totally experienced performer, an expert witness, expert not only in his own field, but expert in the presentation of evidence, weighing the value of the flat statement, the full exposition, the one-word reply, and the throwaway line.

He said, "There *was* one other point, sir. And that was the age of the victim. I mention it because it is the only point at which I find myself at variance with Dr. Champion. He placed her age, you will remember, as between eighteen and twenty-five. His notes make it clear that he based this on the closing of the sutures in the skull. As I expect you know, the skull, in youth, does not present a continuous expanse of bone. It is divided into sections, and the gaps between the sections are filled with a comparatively soft, gristly substance."

The lady next to the foreman was now running the tip

of her finger across the top of her head. She thought she detected a soft spot, and missed a good deal of the evidence.

"As you grow older, these sutures close and calcify, and since the closing takes place in more or less regular sequence, it can be a good guide to the age of a body. But it is only a rough guide. An error of five or even seven years would not be impossible. Recently, however, the work of such a pioneer as Gustafson has enabled us to be a great deal more accurate. Particularly if the teeth are in good condition, as was the case here. An estimate can be made which is dependent on six separate dental factors, perhaps the most important being the closing of the root canal and the increasing translucency of the tooth root. I have prepared a full note, sir, in case the matter wants looking into further on another occasion, but I fear the jury might find some of the technical terms confusing."

The coroner said, "I fear the jury are somewhat out of their depth already, Dr. Summerson. We should be very happy if, for the moment, you would simply present us with your conclusions."

Dr. Summerson glanced down at his notes again, and then said, "I find it impossible to believe that this girl was less than twenty-three. I should be inclined to think that she was even older. Twenty-five or twenty-six at least."

10

"So what the hell," said Superintendent Clark, "do we do now?"

"We start again," said Mercer.

"I suppose there's no chance of upsetting Summerson. After all, it's only his opinion. Dr. Champion said eighteen to twenty-five."

Mercer looked at him curiously. One of the tricks which growing older played on you was to make you less flexible. It stiffened up your mind as well as your joints. You couldn't turn about as quickly as you used to. He said, "What good would it do? No one would believe it. We shouldn't believe it ourselves. Besides, I've had a word with the shoeshop. Sweetie had perfect feet. She took a narrow fitting in number five shoes."

"So all the work we've done so far is wasted?"

"I wouldn't say wasted. It's been aimed at the wrong target, that's all. I'd still very much like to know who was dating Sweetie during the last three months of her life."

"What the hell does it matter who was dating Sweetie? It's not her murder we're investigating."

"Aren't we?"

Clark stared at him. His face was an ugly mottled color. Frustration and anger fought with curiosity. Before he could say anything, Mercer added, "You haven't forgotten that we found her handbag, half buried, on the island."

"I suppose it *was* her handbag."

"It's been identified half a dozen ways. The bag and the contents. When we thought the body was Sweetie, we thought about it one way. Now we've got to think about it another."

"You're paid to do the thinking round here."

"That's right," said Mercer, with his sudden mirthless smile. "*And* I've been doing some. You can work it out three different ways. It was an accident that the bag got left there. Let's say she was fooling round on the island and she dropped it, and she didn't bother to go back and look for it. Or to report its loss. Me, I don't believe a word of it. For a start, it had all her keys in it."

"So?"

"Second idea. She went into the river, higher up. Over the weir, perhaps. And the bag was washed up on the island."

"Then you think she's dead?"

"Oh, yes," said Mercer bleakly. "She's dead, all right. There's very little doubt about that. *And* her father knew it. That's why he wasn't afraid to sell the ring."

"When bodies go into the river, nine times out of ten they turn up again. They float to the top and someone sees them and pulls them out."

"Right. And that brings us to the third possibility. The man who killed Sweetie may have thought about that. He may not have wanted her body to turn up. If it had surfaced too soon it could have been identified. It might have shown how she was killed. It might have led back to him."

"Then what would he do?"

"What he did with the other one," said Mercer. "He'd bury her."

There was a long silence. When Clark spoke, his color and his voice were both back to normal. "You seem to have worked all this out very clearly," he said. "Have you got as far as thinking out where he'd put her?"

"Murderers haven't got a surprising lot of imagination. Look at Christie. He buried all his girl friends in the same garden."

"Meaning what?"

"Meaning I should start by digging up the island. Not just prodding it this time. Digging it right up."

"The whole island?"

"The whole island. Trench it across. Put half a dozen men onto it and we could do it in a day. Less than that if they worked intelligently. Stop digging as soon as they came to a layer of packed stone or hard earth. Concentrate on the soft parts."

"The press would have a field day."

"The whole thing would be over before they got there."

But the superintendent was pursuing a fresh line of thought. He said, "What are we going to do about Hedges?"

"Ask for an adjournment on the assault charge. Don't oppose bail. I suppose he can raise it."

"We've had three people come forward already offering bail."

"Fine. Let him go. But keep a careful eye on him."

"If we keep any sort of eye on him," said Clark, "we shall be accused of hounding him. He's a public figure."

When the knock came, Mr. Weatherman looked up with a frown from the complicated lease he was studying and growled, "Come in." When he saw it was Mrs. Hall the frown changed to a smile. He approved of Mrs. Hall. She had only been with the firm for six months, but she had already shown that she was capable of doing the work

101

which had been handled previously by a male cashier and an assistant. She worked hard, and talked very little; sovereign virtues in Mr. Weatherman's eyes.

"Well, well," he said. "I hope you haven't come to tell me that our client account is in the red."

"Nothing like that, sir. It was just that I was talking to young Jarvis."

"More likely he was talking to you."

Mrs. Hall smiled in turn, and said, "That's true. He does talk a good deal. What he said was that he had been reading about the inquest on that girl—the one they found on the island—and he was wondering if it might be Miss Dyson."

Mr. Weatherman considered the matter, drawing his upper lip down over his teeth as though he were preparing to shave it. Then he said, "What makes him think that?"

"It was her feet. Something she once told him. That she had to take a different shoe fitting on each foot."

"That's not uncommon."

"And she did disappear rather suddenly. And it was about two years ago, which was the time they thought—"

"I recall that we made a number of inquiries at the time. It seems she simply packed up her things and went off up to London. She certainly gave us no notice here."

"How did we know she went to London?"

"A policeman who knew her by sight saw her catching the evening train. She had her luggage with her. I can't think of any reason why she should come back here, in order to be murdered and buried. Can you?"

"It doesn't sound very likely," agreed Mrs. Hall. "Why did she walk out on us?"

"I telephoned her previous employer. He told me she had played the same trick on him. She was a bird of passage, Mrs. Hall. I imagine she has done it half a dozen times. And left bad debts behind her, as she did here."

"If she left bad debts behind," agreed Mrs. Hall, "she wouldn't be very likely to come back."

"I shouldn't give it another thought," said Mr. Weatherman.

Despite this good advice, after Mrs. Hall had gone he did not return at once to his lease. He lay back for a time in his chair, his long face abstracted.

At three o'clock that afternoon Hedges left the Stoneferry magistrates' court, temporarily a free man. He accepted the congratulations of the middle-aged lady, the retired colonel, and the Congregational minister who had among them organized his bail. But it was not congratulations he wanted. He wanted a drink. And the pubs were shut. He had a bottle at home. It had been carefully hidden, and might have escaped the attention of the policemen, pressmen, and Nosy Parkers who had, he suspected, been ransacking his barge.

When he reached the bridge which led to the island he was pleased to find that there was no one in sight. A light misty rain had started falling. Maybe that was discouraging sightseers. So much the better.

The police had put a new padlock on the door, and had supplied him with the key. He had it in his hand when he became aware that two men had materialized behind him. The shock this gave him made him drop the key. One of the men stooped down and picked it up, but made no move to hand it back.

"What do you want?" said Hedges, his voice squeaking oddly. The men both wore raincoats, the collars turned up and partly concealing their faces. He didn't like the look of them at all.

"Are you the man they call Sowthistle?"

"The kids made it up. It's just a bit of sauce."

"It's not made up," said the second man. "Sow thistle's

103

a real plant. It grows on sour and marshy soil."

"You give me back my key."

"Surely," said the first man, but made no move to hand it to him. "Would you like to give us a story?"

"Are you from the papers?"

"That's right."

"London papers?"

"That's right." He mentioned the name of the paper and Hedges smirked. He said, "You boys come inside. I'll tell you anything you want to know. Police brutality. Third degree. The lot."

"That's fine," said the first man, but still made no move. "Tell me, Mr. Sowthistle. That island where they found the body. My friend and me were just arguing. Can you actually see it from here?"

"Can you *see* it?"

"I said you can. He said it's impossible. Too many trees and bushes in the way."

A look of deep cunning appeared on Sowthistle's face. This was the sort of talk he understood. He said, "How much would it be worth to you to win your bet, mister?"

"I always like winning my bets. It could be worth a quid."

"Then you've won it. I'll show you." He led the way, following a path through the dripping, knee-high undergrowth, to a point at the upstream end of the island. Here there was an apparently unpregnable screen of overgrown elder, thorn, and matted growth with a single scrub oak in the middle of it. The three leaned out at an angle over the water, and the men could see that rough steps had been formed in it, and that there was a sort of platform near the top.

"Your private observation post, dad?"

"That's right."

"You're a dirty old voyeur. How much did you charge

to let your customers watch the boys and girls having fun together?"

"I'm not admitting anything, son. Not if you're going to put it in your paper."

The man looked at Sowthistle curiously. He was an experienced crime reporter, and had met, in the course of his duty, all sorts of criminals, perverts, and layabouts. He thought he had never encountered anyone quite as fantastic as the old man in the shiny blue suit who was jigging about in the mud beside him.

"Go on," said Sowthistle. "You climb up and have a peep. You can see the whole bloody island. Every bloody bit of it."

Treading carefully on the slippery trunk, and grabbing the handholds which presented themselves, the reporter hauled himself up onto the platform. He stood there for a moment, then came down a lot more quickly than he had gone up. He touched his companion on the arm, and doubled off up the path, slipping and stumbling, as he went.

Sowthistle stared, open-mouthed, after the departing figure. Then he turned and started to climb the tree. As he did so, a sound of which he had been vaguely aware became clearer. It was the clink of metal on stone. There were men on Westhaugh Island. They wore black waterproof capes, and they were digging.

Sowthistle watched them for a moment. Then he clapped his hand to his pocket.

"God rot him," he said, "he's gone off with my key. He never paid me that quid, either."

There were screens round the bed in the casualty ward. The sister said to Mercer, "We put them there because you asked us to. They're quite unnecessary really."

"How is Beardoe?"

"He's all right. It was concussion and a few bruises. If

105

it hadn't been for his wrist, we'd have treated him in Outpatients."

"We'd be obliged if you could keep the pretense up for a couple of days. Then we'll fix it to take him off your hands."

He edged past the screen and went in. Beardoe was sitting up in bed, reading a newspaper. There was a lurid bruise down the side of his face, and his left wrist was encased in plaster. He said, "Hullo," in an unfriendly voice.

Mercer said, "I'm sorry about all this. I ought to have warned you. I don't suppose it would have done much good, but you could have taken some simple precautions, like getting a pal to walk home with you, and not answering the door after dark."

"What I want to know is, what the hell's it all about? What am I supposed to have done?" His blue eyes were puzzled, angry.

Mercer sat down on the edge of the bed and talked for five minutes. At the end of it, Beardoe said, "I'm not going to say anything about what happened. To tell you the truth, I don't remember a lot about it. There were two men. I couldn't describe them, and I'm not sure I would if I could. I don't want to get mixed up in that sort of thing."

"Understood," said Mercer.

"They tell me I got concussion. That means the old brain box was shook up. Right?"

"Right," said Mercer, wondering what was coming.

"Then I'll tell you something funny. It shook me up so hard, I remembered something I thought I'd forgotten. The name of the garage that chap Taylor mentioned to me one night when he was pissed. You remember you were asking me about it?"

"Yes," said Mercer softly. "I remember."

"It was the Hexagon Garage in Baswell Street, Stepney."

"I'm much obliged," said Mercer. His heavy face was expressionless. Only the lips moved, as if he repeated something to himself. At last he said, "You'll get a bit of sick leave after this, won't you?"

"Can't go back to work with my wrist busted."

"Have you got any friends you could go and stay with?"

Beardoe considered. "I've got an old aunt in the Isle of Wight. She's always on at me to go and see her."

"Would she put you up for a fortnight?"

"I expect so."

"Telephone her now. The ward sister will fix it for you. I'll send a police car for you tomorrow evening. Stay away for two weeks. That's all. After that, I reckon everyone will have forgotten about you."

"I hope you're right," said Beardoe. He was still angry.

Mercer had left his car parked in the hospital forecourt, in a section labeled "Consultant Gynecologist." He backed it out carefully, and drove back toward Stoneferry with one eye on the driving mirror. The dashboard clock was showing a quarter after five and it was still light. Too light for what he had to do. He pulled in at a small transport café a mile short of the town and had a mug of unpleasant tea. When he came out, it was beginning to get dark. The cars going past mostly had sidelights on, but no headlights yet. Mercer got into his car, switched on his own sidelights, and started back the way he had come. A few hundred yards along, picking his moment, he swung across the traffic into a side road and immediately killed his sidelights. It was a long, straight road of semidetached houses and little shops. Near the end of it he turned into an even smaller road. Here he drew into the curb and stopped.

He sat for a full five minutes in the darkened car and

watched. No car crossed the end of the road. No one turned into it. Two or three householders coming home from work passed the car without a glance.

Mercer looked at the clock again. It was a few minutes before six. He got out quickly and crossed the road. The legend above the door said: M. BALDOCK. NEWS AGENT AND TOBACCONIST. PAPERS DELIVERED. A burly man, dressed in a gray cardigan, who could well have been Mr. M. Baldock himself, was pulling down the blind over the window.

"You're just in time," he said. "I was shutting up."

"Better late than never," said Mercer. He closed the door behind him. Then said, in quite a different tone of voice, "Got the doings?"

Mr. Baldock unlocked a drawer beside the till and took out a stout manila envelope.

"Want to count it?" he said.

"I'll count it when I get home," said Mercer. "If it's wrong, I'll come back and tell you all about it."

Mr. Baldock grinned, exposing a broken front tooth. "I bet you would," he said.

When Mercer got back to the station he found Rye waiting for him.

"The gov'nor wants to see you," he said. "He's flying storm pennants."

"What's eating him now?"

"Haven't you seen the evening papers?"

"No."

"Then take a butcher's."

It was on the front page. Maybe it wasn't as big, or as black, as a headline announcing the outbreak of war or a general strike, but it certainly hit the eye. It said: DEATH ISLAND. Underneath was a photograph. It had the blurred edges and foreshortened effect of a picture taken with a telephoto lens, and it showed a line of caped policemen, digging. Partly by luck, partly by professional judgment, the photographer had produced a very effective composition.

"Good picture," said Mercer.

"Try telling that to Bob Clark."

"What's wrong? It shows his men doing some work for a change."

"They were working, all right. They took that island to pieces. But the point is, they didn't turn anything up. Barring a few rusty cans and pieces of old iron. So what now? That's what the press of this country is clamoring to know. What were we looking for?"

Superintendent Clark said the same thing more forcibly. He was really angry this time.

"Look what you've let us in for," he said. "Death Island! They'll be running coach trips to it soon."

"It was just one of those things," said Mercer. "I found out what happened. A couple of newspapermen were talking to Sowthistle. He showed them a spot on Easthaugh from which you can get a good view of Westhaugh. He used to stand there and watch the boys and girls having fun among the nettles on a summer night. Probably charged his customers to use it."

"I'm not interested in Hedges. It's us I'm thinking about. You've made us look fools."

"I wouldn't say that."

"Well, I'm saying it. You've mishandled this case from beginning to end."

"Is that an official reprimand?"

"It's unofficial at the moment, but I'll make it official quickly enough if you don't pull your finger out. If you don't see the mess you've got into, it's time someone pointed out the facts to you. Everyone knew we thought the body we found was the Hedges girl."

"We never said so."

"If we didn't think so, why did we question all her boyfriends? It was obvious. It's now equally obvious that

109

we were wrong. Then we dig up the island. That means we still think she's dead, but we don't know where she is. Two girls missing. One we can't identify and the other we can't locate. I think it's time we had someone down from Central to show us how to do the job."

"They may not oblige. They're not too keen on picking other people's chestnuts out of the fire for them."

"I've already had Division asking for a report. And it didn't originate with them. It came down from District. What am I going to tell them?"

"Tell them the truth. That we turn up a two-year-old body, with very little identification. We think it may be a local girl who disappeared about that time. We were wrong. But we're still worried about her. Not only because she's disappeared, but because there's a murderer round these parts. And a man who's killed one girl and got away with it is twice as likely to do it again."

Before Clark could say anything, the internal telephone on his desk rang. He seemed to be glad of the interruption. He listened for a moment. Then he said, "I've got Mercer here. I'll tell him. It's the station officer's desk. They've had a message from a Mrs. Hall. She's a cashier at Weathermans', the solicitors. She thinks the body we dug up might be a Maureen Dyson, who worked there two years ago. If you got round there quickly, she says you could catch Mr. Weatherman before he goes."

11

"I HAVE FOUND Mrs. Hall to be a very sensible person," said Mr. Weatherman, "and a considerable asset to the firm. But I think, on this occasion, that she may have allowed her imagination to run away with her."

"What makes you think that?"

"I see that I had some correspondence with Miss Dyson's parents at the time of her departure. They were worried as to what had happened to her. It is curious, is it not, Inspector, how parents continue to think of their children as helpless and irresponsible creatures, even when they are in their mid-twenties and quite old enough to look after themselves."

"Very curious and very useful to us sometimes, sir. What happened next?"

"Oh, I made some inquiries. At her address here. It was a furnished flat. She seems to have packed her bags and walked out. She also left five weeks' rent owing. We paid it for her."

"That was very kind of you."

"I didn't regard it as a kindness. I regarded it as an investment. It was worth five weeks' rent, and a great deal more, not to have the name of this firm connected with fly-by-night tenants."

"One way of looking at it, I suppose."

"I also informed the police. It then came to light that one of them, who happened to know Miss Dyson by sight, had been coming back to Stoneferry and had seen her, on the other platform, with her bags, waiting for the train to London. I passed this information on to her parents, and I imagine they switched their inquiries to London."

Mercer thought about it. It seemed odd, but not unbelievable. A girl who was still unmarried at twenty-five was an unpredictable creature. And he could imagine an employee finding Mr. Weatherman a difficult man to work for.

As if reading his thoughts, the lawyer said, with a dry smile, "She did not do a great deal of work for me personally. She was mainly employed in the litigation department, and did a certain amount for my partner, Mr. Slade."

"Willoughby Slade?"

"Ah, you know him."

"You can hardly live in Stoneferry without hearing his name. He is one of your celebrities."

"Willoughby is an accomplished athlete," agreed Mr. Weatherman. He seemed to be in no hurry to terminate the interview, and it crossed Mercer's mind to wonder why. Possibly he was waiting for a very late client.

He said, "What sort of girl was she?"

"Do you mean personally, Inspector? Or in her work?"

"Both."

"She wasn't unpersonable, but she was not what I would call an attractive girl. At least, she did not attract me. She came from the Midlands, and had that hard, uncompromising character you sometimes find in those parts."

"Appearance?"

"It was two years ago, Inspector, and I am not very

112

adept at describing girls. I should have said that she had a sallowish complexion and dark hair and was of normal sort of build and medium height."

"And did you know that she wore different sized shoes?"

"She did not discuss her feet with me."

Talking to Mr. Weatherman, Mercer thought, was like playing checkers. You moved a piece. He moved a piece. And all the time you had an uneasy feeling that he was one move ahead of you, and might even be planning to jump over two of your pieces and promote a queen.

"If you want any sidelights on her work or character, I would suggest that you have a word with my partner."

"I'll do that," said Mercer. He got up.

"Would you mind letting yourself out? The front door is still on the latch."

Mercer was getting into his car when he heard the steps rapping sharply on the pavement, some way behind him. He turned his head to watch. There was a street lamp opposite Mr. Weatherman's front door, and he was able to identify the solicitor's late visitor.

It was Rainey, the alcoholic cashier from Bull's Garage. He seemed to be in a hurry. Mercer engaged gear and drove slowly out, along the Chertsey Road, thinking about this.

The Slade house was a surprise. It was little more than a villa, with an overworked patch of garden in front. As Mercer walked up the patch he readjusted his ideas. The father had been a regular soldier and was dead. The widow would have some of his pension and not much else. The son, as junior partner in a firm of solicitors, probably spent most of his money on himself. The daughter did nothing, and did it beautifully. It didn't add up to much. It was Venetia who opened the door. She said, "Hullo," in a neutral sort of voice. And then a second time, in a more interested way, as if she thought she recognized him.

Mercer said, "I'm Detective Inspector Mercer from your local station."

"Oh, God! Not parking again."

"We leave that to the uniformed branch. Actually I came out to have a word with your brother. Mr. Weatherman suggested he'd be home by now."

"He should be. But he isn't." A moment's hesitation, and then, "Would you like to come in and wait?"

"When do you expect him back?"

"Any time between now and midnight. It depends how many friends he meets when he drops in for a quick one at the Angler's."

"If I could wait for a few minutes."

"Of course." She led the way into the sitting room. Mercer's first impression of it was that it was too full of furniture and pictures, and that most of them had come from a better house.

"Mummy. This is Detective Inspector Mercer. He's looking for Willoughby."

Mrs. Slade had neat gray hair, a firm brown face, and a voice trained to command. It was clear that she was uncertain whether Mercer belonged in the officers' or the sergeants' mess.

She said, "If it's my son you want, you may have a long wait. Will you have a glass of beer?"

Sergeants' mess, clearly.

"Thank you," said Mercer, "but not just now."

"It's very tiresome of Willoughby. I particularly wanted him home punctually tonight. I'm making a fish pie. It needs the most accurate timing, and it's almost spoiled already. We'll give him five minutes more, and then we start."

This was over her shoulder as she departed for the kitchen. Venetia said, "Do take your coat off, and sit

114

down. When Mother says five minutes she means ten. And are you sure you won't have a drink? It doesn't have to be beer; we've got sherry. Or are you like those policeman on TV who say, 'I don't drink on duty, sir.'"

"I drink on duty and off," said Mercer. "It's just that I was afraid it was going to be bottled beer."

"I don't like bottled beer," agreed Venetia. "It blows me up like a balloon. Have some Cyprus sherry." She went across to a cupboard in the corner and gave Mercer an opportunity of admiring her legs. She had been wearing jeans on the two previous occasions. As she swung round he hastily averted his eyes and pretended to look at one of the huge pictures which dominated the wall. It was worth looking at. It was a portrait of an officer, in the uniform of a bygone age.

"That's my great-great-great grandfather. Known in the Mutiny as Mango Slade. I understand he was stupid even by Anglo-American standards."

"He really is extraordinarily like your brother."

"Not very tactfully put."

"The face, I mean, of course."

"Of course."

They both laughed, and things were easier.

He said, "I saw you go overboard after your bracelet the other day."

"Where were you? Oh, of course, You were one of the men on Death Island."

Mercer shuddered. "Please don't call it that. The police don't like it."

Mrs. Slade shouted from the kitchen, "Any sign of Willoughby yet?"

"Not a sign."

"I also nearly ran you down."

"That was you, wasn't it? I noticed old Brattle sitting solemnly in the back of the boat."

"It was my first time out. I got across. I also got very wet."

"If you're going to try experiments with a punt, it's safer to try them below the weir."

"It never occurred to me. If we'd been in any real danger I imagine Brattle would have taken over pretty quickly."

"I nearly went over it once," said Venetia. "I still dream about it sometimes." She put one hand up and brushed the lock of dark hair away from her eyes as if she were sweeping away a nightmare. "It was my own damned silly fault for taking a punt out with a pole but no paddles. I was about a hundred yards above the weir, and suddenly found there was no bottom. If I'd had an ounce of sense I'd have gone straight over the side and swum for the shore, but I thought I could save the boat, swinging the pole behind it, just like the gondoliers in Venice. Have some more sherry."

"No, thank you."

"It isn't very nice, is it?"

"You can't stop a story in the middle like that. What happened?"

"All I succeeded in doing was to turn the punt sideways. Not too far from the bank luckily. The sluices aren't very wide, so the boat simply got stuck. If it had been out in the middle of the river, I think the force of the water would have broken it in two. As it was, it simply tilted it sideways. I stepped up onto the superstructure and walked ashore. They winced the boat out afterward with hardly a scratch on it."

"As Brattle said, a well-made punt will stand up to a lot."

"I even rescued the things that were in the boat. Cushions and a shopping basket and things like that. They went over the weir, but all came safely to land on West-haugh Island. The only thing I lost was a stone jar full of ginger beer. That's probably still swirling round at the foot of the weir—"

The light had gone out of Mercer's eyes, leaving them blank. Venetia broke off. It was as though blinds had been drawn, shutting off the inside of his head.

"Have I said something I shouldn't?"

Mercer came back to the present with an effort. "No. On the contrary. What you've just told me was—look here, it'll take much too long to explain. Can you teach me to punt?"

Venetia stared at him. Then she said, "I expect I could. It's not very difficult really."

"Tomorrow afternoon."

Venetia thought about this, too. Then she said, "I don't see why not."

"I'll meet you at Brattle's boat house. Four o'clock."

Before she could change her mind, Mercer had jumped and was making for the door. He said, "Tell your brother I'll call at the office tomorrow morning and have a word with him." The next moment he was striding down the front path.

As he got into his own car, a smart little Mini Cooper pulled up and Willoughby Slade got out. Mercer made no move. He watched the boy disappear into the house. Then he started his own car and drove off. Possibly he was being kind to Mrs. Slade's fish pie.

He drove very slowly back to the station.

It was half past eight when he got there.

"The phantoms are working overtime," said Station Sergeant Rix to his deputy, Police Constable Lampier. Lampier said, "None of them spivs get up till nine, Sarge. They don't know what work is."

Mercer found Gwilliam in the CID room. He was on night duty for the Division and had two telephones on the table in front of him, six packets of potato crisps, and a bottle of nonalcoholic cider. He said, "What are you looking so bloody cheerful about? You look like a cat who's been at the cream."

"Nothing special," said Mercer. "Just a clear conscience and a good digestion."

"If I didn't know you better, I'd say you'd picked up a bit of skirt."

"You're wasted in the police," said Mercer. "You ought to be in the crystal ball department. Do you remember anything about a girl called Maureen Dyson?"

Gwilliam disposed of a mouthful of crisps. Then he said, "Girl who walked out on old Weatherman. November two years ago. Yes?"

"Yes."

"It didn't surprise anyone. He can't keep a secretary. He's a gorgon. He turns them into stone."

"The idea now is that the body we turned up might have been her."

Gwilliam pondered this through a further crackling mouthful. Then he said, "That can't be right. She was seen going up to London. Why would she come back here and be buried?"

"Who saw her?"

"It was two years ago."

"Would it be in any report?"

"I don't think anyone was asked for a report. Not an official report like. It wasn't a police matter. Not then."

"It would have been in the Occurrences Book."

"It should have been."

"Where are the O Books kept?"

"They'd be downstairs. The boys in blue look after them."

Station Sergeant Rix, on being appealed to, said that he thought the old O Books would be in a cabinet in the interview room. He produced a ring of keys and they went along together. The cabinet was unlocked, and a gap in the row of thick, leather-bound books showed that

118

the volume covering the October and November of two years earlier was missing.

"Now who'd have had that out?" said Rix.

"I can't guess," said Mercer.

He went upstairs to Superintendent Clark's room. The book was lying on a side table. There was a slip of paper marking the date November 16. He took it back with him to the CID room.

The page was full of the usual trivialities. P.C. Dring, on beat duty along the towpath, had noted that the couple who had been using the green trailer unlawfully parked at the north side of the trailer site had deserted it, and had apparently left the door unlocked. P.C. Philpott had heard the Alsatian in Dunroamin howling its head off for the second day running and had tried the doors of the bungalow but found them all locked. Note. Tell RSPCA. Detective Prothero had observed an old lady having an epileptic fit on a seat in Torrance Park recreation ground and had arranged for her transport to Outpatients. At the foot of the page, in a round, boyish handwriting, was the entry he was looking for. Detective Sergeant Rollo, returning from a visit to London to give evidence at the South London Quarter Sessions, had observed Maureen Dyson, known to him as a typist working for Messrs. Weathermans, standing on the up platform, evidently waiting for the seven-fifteen train to Waterloo. There were two large suitcases on the platform, one on either side of her. He had been surprised because he had been talking to her two days before, and she had not said anything about leaving.

Mercer sat staring at the entry for a long time. Shadows were forming in his mind, specters of old mistakes, past misdemeanors, stale passions, a misty, shifting kaleidoscope, forming first one pattern, then another, and behind it all, like a dim negative, with the blacks and whites reversed, like the ghost of a picture, a young man slumped in the back seat of a car, shaking slightly as the engine throbbed and the carbon monoxide gas poured in a steady stream from the end of a piece of rubber tubing wedged in the top of the nearly closed window.

Bob Clark was saying to his wife, "I'm afraid we're going to have trouble with that new man." He took off his tie and rolled it neatly into a ball.

"Mercer?"

"Chief Inspector William Mercer."

"What's wrong with him?"

"He's a troublemaker. Since he came down here we've had nothing but trouble, one way and another. First he thinks this body we find is one girl. Then he asks his pal Summerson down here, who blows the idea sky-high. Then he decides to dig up the whole island, and the press get in on the act. We shall have them round our necks now."

"If the press are in on the act and you solve the case, you'll all get a lot of credit, won't you?"

"If Mercer would keep his mind on one thing at a time, he might have a chance of solving it. You'd have thought that a murder investigation was a full-time job. But not for our Mr. Mercer. He seems to be far more interested"—the superintendent sat down and started to take his shoes off—"in something that happened in a garage two years ago."

"He sounds like an odd character."

"He's not only odd. He's queer."

"Queer?"

"No. I don't mean that exactly. I mean—look here, you mustn't repeat this to anyone."

"I'm not in the habit of repeating things you tell me."

"I know you're not." The superintendent removed his trousers. "But this really is confidential. It's something that happened in his last job. The one he had before he came back to London. He was in the Middle East. . . ."

Five minutes later, Mrs. Clark said, "If that's true, you've certainly got yourself a packet of trouble."

"I'm afraid it's true, all right."

"Get into bed and stop worrying about it."

Being a dutiful wife, she did her best to take his mind off his troubles.

Mercer walked back to his lodgings in Cray Avenue, treading softly in his rubber-soled shoes. He could hear the rumble of the traffic on the bypass over the other side of the river, but at that time of night the High Street was deserted. There were a few shops which kept their window lights blazing all night, reckoning that the advertisement was worth the extra electricity bill. After he had passed the station approach and walked under the railway viaduct he was in an area of small, dark houses and occasional street lamps.

A lovely place for an ambush.

Mercer grinned unpleasantly as the idea crossed his mind.

The house in Cray Avenue was in darkness. As he walked up the front path he started to put his hand in his trouser pocket to feel for his key. He took it out again quickly. Someone was standing in the darkest part, between the doorjamb and the side of the porch. Mercer slowed his pace, but did not stop. As he did so he felt in his left-hand jacket pocket, and found the small flashlight which he kept there. He snapped it on, held it for a moment, focused on the inside of the porch, said, "Well!" and turned it off again.

It was a girl.

She said, "I wanted to have a word with you."

121

12

"ROCKET," said Detective Prothero.

There was a slip of paper on the table in the CID room.

"What is it?" said Mercer.

"It's an official reprimand. A stately raspberry."

The note said, "Would CID personnel who remove books or documents from Superintendent Clark's room kindly have the courtesy to replace them after use."

Mercer read it and tore it into sixteen pieces, which he deposited in the ashtray. He said, "He must be hard up for something to do."

"What's it all about, anyway?"

"I borrowed an old O Book last night from his room."

"Doesn't seem enough to start a riot," agreed Prothero. "Mind you, if the boys in blue can get in a niggle at you, they will. You want to watch it when they start sending you notices calling you 'personnel.' Last station I was in, the station sergeant was nuts about personnel. 'Would CID personnel kindly wipe their shoes when coming into the canteen.' Shoes, you see. That's what really got him down. *They* had to wear boots."

Mercer wasn't listening. He was trying to decipher a scrawl which Sergeant Gwilliam had left for him. He gave up trying, and pushed it across to Prothero, who said, "I know about that. George Hopkins, from the Chough, rang up just before Taffy went off duty. He wants to see someone."

"About what?"

"He didn't say. Except it was something to do with Sweetie."

"Don't tell me," said Mercer. "I can guess. For the last two years Sweetie has been serving drinks in the saloon bar, and no one's recognized her."

"I don't think that can be right," said Prothero. "The woman who hands round drinks in the saloon bar is married to the head waiter in the snack bar. She's got a black moustache, too."

"Exactly. She was disguised."

He found the landlord of the Chough polishing glasses. George Hopkins had been an international water polo player and still looked like a muscular sea lion. He said, "It's what we've all been reading in the papers about that skeleton, Inspector. The one you thought might be the Hedges girl, only it wasn't. Would you care for a drink?"

"It's a bit early for beer."

"Make it a gin and peppermint and I might join you. It's settling to the stomach after breakfast. Like I was saying. Young Sweetie Hedges. I take it you're still interested in her, by the way?"

"Very much so."

"Well, I was talking to the wife, and it came to our minds that we might have been some of the last people to see her. They were saying March twelfth two years ago was the last time anyone saw her. Right?"

"As far as we know."

"That would be Wednesday. She was in here that evening, just after we opened. She came into the private bar, and she stayed almost an hour."

123

"How on earth would you remember a thing like that?"

"I didn't remember it. My wife did, when she mentioned it, I said the same thing to her. I said, 'How would you remember a thing like that?' Cheers."

"Cheers," said Mercer.

The hand in which the landlord held his glass was large, and rounded with muscle. A hand and wrist that could flick a heavy water polo ball the length of a swimming pool. A hand that could very easily choke the life out of a girl.

Mercer said, "All right. I'll buy it. Tell me how you did remember it."

"Two ways. Because the second Wednesday in March is always stock-taking day. The checker from the brewery comes down and goes through everything. And I'm always in a bloody bad temper by the end of it. Like I was that evening. Sweetie said something, and I snapped her head off. Then she looked so miserable, I was sorry for her, and like I said, I stopped for the best part of an hour talking to her. And that's the other thing that made me sure it was a Wednesday. It's only on early closing day we'd be as empty as that. Any other night I'd have been too busy to stop and talk."

"I see," said Mercer. It sounded plausible. "I suppose you can't remember what she talked about."

"Have a heart, Inspector. It was two years ago. But I'll tell you one thing. I think she had a date to meet someone."

"I see." Mercer tried to keep his voice level. If you showed you were too interested, a witness would often make things up to keep you happy. So take it steady. He said, "What made you think that?"

"It was the weather. It was one of those sort of days in March when one moment the sun's out, and the next moment someone's pulled the plug, and down it comes.

124

Real rain, by the bucket. She was wearing one of those very light mackintoshes. Things you can screw up and put in your pocket. They're convenient to carry round, but they won't keep out heavy rain. You know the sort of thing I mean?"

Mercer nodded.

"Well, once or twice she looked at her watch and looked out of the door, as if she was wondering whether she'd chance it, and I thought, she's got a date, but she doesn't want to arrive looking like a wet hen. As soon as it did stop, she pushed off quick, as if she'd been keeping someone waiting, and she knew he wouldn't be very pleased."

"What was the color of the mackintosh?"

Mr. Hopkins screwed up his eyes to assist thought. Then he said, "Dark. It might have been red."

"Had she her handbag with her?"

"I suppose so. She was paying for her own drinks. Brandy and ginger ale."

"You didn't feel so sorry for her you stood her the drinks?"

"Not as sorry as that. Buying drinks for customers is a mug's game. I don't mean you," he said hastily as Mercer felt in his pocket for some money. "You're here on official business. Call back whenever you like."

The Church of Saint John the Evangelist stood almost opposite the point where Cray Avenue joined the High Street. On the very rare occasions when he lay awake at night Mercer could hear the hour being chimed on its old-fashioned belfry clock. The rectory was behind the church. Father Philip Walcot opened the door himself, and led the way down a tiled passage into his study at the back.

Father Philip was small and unpretentious and homely. He looked like anything but a clergyman. He

125

reminded Mercer of one of Beatrix Potter's friendly animals. A gray squirrel? The likeness was enhanced by a certain nimbleness of movement and a pair of bright and inquisitive eyes.

"It's about Mavis Hedges."

"Mavis who?"

"Old Sowthistle Hedges' daughter."

"Oh, you mean Sweetie. Was her name Mavis? No one ever called her that."

"That's what her birth certificate called her. Mavis Paula."

"I'm surprised that Hedges bothered to register her birth. Well, now, Inspector. How can I be of assistance to you?"

"The last time the girl was seen was on March twelfth, two years ago. She came into town sometime in the late afternoon. It was a Wednesday and early closing day, so she couldn't have come for the shopping. One or two people have mentioned that they thought she came to see you."

"So she did, Inspector. So she did."

Mercer waited.

"She was a member of my congregation. Not a religious girl in the conventional sense of the word. But very simple and sincere in some ways."

Mercer said, "Would you be prepared to tell me what she talked to you about?"

"I'm not sure," said Father Philip.

There was something else there, besides unpretentious friendliness. There was authority.

"Tell me, Inspector. The body you found on Westhaugh Island. There was a theory that it was Sweetie. But now it's thought to be someone else. Is that right?"

"The medical evidence proved quite conclusively that it couldn't be Sweetie. She would have been barely eigh-

126

teen at the time of her death. This was a woman in her middle or late twenties.

"Is Sweetie dead?"

"I can't prove it. But I'm quite sure of it. And I think I know how she died. She went over the weir, from a point near the northern bank."

"How can you possibly know that?"

"Her handbag was washed up on Westhaugh Island. According to a young lady who happened to have a boating accident at the same spot, that is what would be likely to happen to any floatable object which went over the weir. The bag was washed into an old water-rat burrow and got silted over. That's what first made us think the body was hers."

"When you say that she went over the weir, do you imply that it was an accident? Or are you saying that she was pushed?"

"It could have been an accident. It was an evening of sudden violent rain. The planking would have been very slippery."

"But it might have been deliberate."

"Yes."

"And it is your honest opinion that if I tell you what she said to me that afternoon it will help you to arrive at the truth?"

"I can't answer the question until I know what she did say. It might turn out to be quite irrelevant."

"A Jesuitical answer," said Father Philip. "If it is irrelevant will you promise to forget about it?"

"Policemen aren't good at forgetting things. But I'll do my best."

"If you're to make any sense of what she said to me, you'll have to understand the sort of girl she was. You've seen her home?"

"Yes," said Mercer. "I've seen her home, and I've met her father."

127

"If you had been forced to live in that place, as the only alternative to an institution, what would you have done?"

"Got out of it damned quick."

"You're thinking of yourself as a boy. Boys have strength and skills to sell, even if they're totally uneducated. In the same position, all a girl has to sell is herself. But she wasn't wanton. She was doing it quite deliberately."

"For money."

"Oh, yes. For as much money as she could get. All of which she spent on herself. Buying proper clothes, eating proper food, keeping herself clean." The priest picked up Mercer's crooked smile, and said, "When we preach that cleanliness is next to godliness I think it's just that sort of external neatness which is meant. And it must have been very difficult, in the conditions she was living in. But she did it, because she kept her eye steadily on her main objective. Which was to find a husband. Not necessarily a very rich man, but someone with enough money, and the power that money brings, to rescue her from the pit into which fate had thrown her."

"And she found him," said Mercer softly.

"Yes. She had found him. And because she wanted to marry him, and she thought that he genuinely wanted to marry her, she had refused to have sexual intercourse with him. You can imagine the result."

"Very easily."

"A girl who had sold her body to men she did not love was refusing it to someone she did love. And it must have seemed to the man that she was using the refusal as a weapon. A piece of blackmail, if you like."

"Wasn't she?"

"Not entirely. She was a very odd girl, Inspector. Have you noticed something? Usually, when a girl carries on in the way she did, the men who have enjoyed her favors despise her. Loathe her, perhaps. Did you find any of that?"

Mercer shook his head. "I hadn't thought about it," he said. "But you're quite right. They were good friends to her."

"Loving, not loathing. The bleak wind of March made her tremble and shiver. But not the dark arch or the black flowing river."

"That sounds like poetry."

"Thomas Hood. 'The Bridge of Sighs.' A bit old-fashioned for modern taste, Inspector. But you should read it. It might give you ideas. 'Mad from life's history, Glad to death's mystery/Swift to be hurled—/Anywhere, anywhere/Out of the world.'"

"Do you mean she might have committed suicide?"

"It seems to me to be a possibility. She was going to meet him that evening. Did you know that?"

"Yes. I knew that she also had quite a few drinks to set her up for the meeting."

"The man would have a car. He would drive her out on the quiet road, along the north bank of the river. He would know that she had been drinking. Perhaps he had been drinking himself. What would happen?"

"He'd try to rape her," said Mercer. "There'd be no holding him."

"Then she realizes that he is just the same as any other man. That he had no intention of marrying her. She jumps out. Stumbles down the path onto the weir. Perhaps the man is coming after her. It is pitch dark. The planks are slippery. What does that make it? Accident, suicide, or murder?"

"That's for the lawyers," said Mercer. "Tell me, Father, who *was* the man?"

"If I knew, I wouldn't tell you," said Father Philip. "But I don't. She never mentioned his name."

*   *   *

129

On the way back to the station Mercer bought an early edition of the evening paper from the one-legged paper seller under the railway arch. "Death Island" had been replaced on the front page by "Balance of Payments," but it was still there, on the turn-over news page, and reading it Mercer had an uncomfortable feeling that the storm center was still ahead. It was clear that Sowthistle had been talking. The ominous words "allegations of brutality" were beginning to appear like harbingers of the storm.

He found a note on his desk summoning him to Clark's room. There was a man with him, and Mercer recongized him, although this was the first time they had met face to face. it was Detective Superintendent Wakefield, in charge of the CID of Q Division. He had a nose like the prow of a ship, prematurely white hair, and a reputation as a disciplinarian.

He said, "You seem to have been stirring things up down here, Mercer."

"I'm afraid so, sir."

"You know what we say about publicity. The only time we like it is when it comes from the judge, *after* the prisoner's been sentenced. Before that it's usually nothing but a pain in the arse."

"I couldn't agree more."

"Did you rough this man up?"

"Nobody touched him. I had Detective Massey with me, making notes. And I kept the door open. There were people going past and coming in and out the whole time. And I persuaded Hedges to take a bath that evening and took the opportunity of getting the police surgeon to give him the once-over. All he found was flea bites."

"I'm glad you had that much sense."

He looked at Clark, who said, with a suggestion of anger in his voice, "I didn't know about that."

Wakefield grunted and opened his briefcase. It was

crammed with papers and it took him some time to find what he wanted. Then he said, "I've got a report you were asking for. On the Hexagon Garage in Baswell Street. The local boys have had it under observation for some time, on and off. Thought to be handling stolen cars. Nothing proved yet."

Mercer was skimming through the report, reading between the lines of the cautious police shorthand. "They mention a man called Wheeler. One of the mechanics who works there. Thought to be a hanger-on of the Crows. Would the fact that he works there be the reason they think the place is bent?"

"One of them."

"Could they get a snap of him?"

"If you can give me a good reason for wanting it."

"I think he may be a man who called himself Taylor when he was down here, some years ago."

"What was he doing in a nice place like Stoneferry?"

"If it's the man I think it was, he was sent down here with the object of ruining a garage proprietor called Prior. He took a job at his place, made a deliberate mess of it, landed him with a lawsuit, and scarpered."

Clark said, "I think you're building sand castles. The whole thing could easily have been an accident. Where's the proof of a plot?"

"No proof," said Mercer. "Just a coincidence. Prior wasn't the only garage owner down here to be driven out of business. The same thing happened to Murray. In *his* case it was a hot car which was found in his workshop. I see from the records that we got an anonymous tip-off about it."

Wakefield was watching the two men closely. He seemed less interested in what they were saying than in the evident hostility sparking between them. He said, "Give me details of that car. If you can pin it *and* Taylor to the Hexagon Garage, and the Hexagon Garage to the

Crows, you might have something. But I'm not quite sure what. A crow's nest, or a mare's nest?"

When he had gone, Clark said to Mercer, "I think we should get on a lot better with a little more cooperation. I know the CID likes to work on its own, but you're not a private army. We happen to be part of the same organization. I'd be obliged if you'd remember it."

Mercer said nothing.

13

Mercer followed Mr. Brattle out along the catwalk which spanned the weir. There was a light handrail on the downstream side. Under his feet the river slid sedately through the half-open sluices in a blue-black arch.

"Not a lot of water going through now," shouted Mr. Brattle. "January and February. That's when they open up and let her rip."

"It would still be pretty high in March."

"High enough. Specially if we got any snow."

"The bleak wind of March/Made her tremble and shiver;/But not the dark arch,/Or the black flowing river."

"What's that?"

"I said, it's quite a river."

"So it is," said Mr. Brattle, with the pride of proprietorship in his voice. "So it is. Five years ago it flooded up to the main road. Washed away twelve trailers. And I'll tell you a funny thing about that. Old Birnie, who keeps the trailer site, had a donkey and it was drowned. Third day, when the water went down a bit, Birnie and me, we put our waders on, and went to look at him. Do you know what we found?"

Mercer shook his head. What could they have found? The donkey transformed into a mermaid? A rope of dia-

133

monds round his hairy neck?

"We found six or seven big eels. Inside the donkey. Birnie sold them in the market and reckoned he got more for 'em than the old moke was worth. There's a silver lining to every cloud, if you know where to look for it. Mind how you go round that stanchion. It's slippery."

They climbed back onto the flank of the lock, crossed the upstream lock gates, and made their way back onto the towpath.

Mercer said, "I imagine you get bodies coming down from time to time."

"Regular," said Mr. Brattle.

"When you spot one going past, I suppose you report it to the police."

Mr. Brattle looked at him as if he had said something particularly stupid. "Why would I do that?" he said.

"You mean you let them drift past and do nothing about it?"

"Certainly not. I get the old punt out quick, and I pull 'em ashore. On the Surrey side, naturally."

"What's wrong with Middlesex?"

"Attendance fee at the inquest, son. It's a guinea in Middlesex. Thirty bob in Surrey. You've got to think of things like that."

"I suppose so. How much did Birnie get for his eels?"

"I can't remember the precise figure. But it was more than five quid. Why?"

"Just a thought," said Mercer. "Tell me something, Mr. Brattle. How long does it take a body to surface?"

"Depends on a lot of things. Age. State of health. Sort of clothes he was wearing. I've known a heavy pair of boots keep a body down for a month. On the other hand" —Mr. Brattle paused to light his pipe—"I remember one which came up almost straightaway. Can you guess why?"

Mercer shook his head. Mr. Brattle's riddles were too hard for him.

"Wooden leg."

"Can you imagine any case where the body might not come up at all?"

"Why, yes," said Mr. Brattle. "I can. Mind you, this is just a theory of mine. And I can't see as how anyone's going to prove whether it's right or wrong. Do you know just what would happen to you if you went over that weir?"

"I don't like to think."

"I'll tell you. First you go straight down to the bottom. Then you'd scrape along the bottom. Then you'd come up, nearly to the surface but not quite. Then you'd be drawn back toward the face of the weir. That's what we call the backlash. Then you'd go down again."

"How long would that go on?"

"You can't tell. That's my point. Not long ago I happened to see an old petrol can go over the weir. It wasn't floating high. It must have had some liquid in it. It was one of the old-fashioned two-gallon sort. You don't see a lot of them about nowadays. It was painted bright green. I remember saying to myself, 'I wonder where that'll bob up?' And I stopped to watch."

Having reached this point in his story, Mr. Brattle stopped to relight his pipe, which had gone out.

Mercer said, "And where did it come up?"

"That's just it. It didn't. But—when I was going past about a week later, I'm blessed if it didn't pop up right under my nose, thirty or forty yards from where it had gone in. It had been working its way along, see. A few inches at a time. In the end it got into a cross eddy, and that brought it out."

"And it had been going round and round for a week."

"That's what I judged. Now take a dead body. What happens to it?"

135

"It sinks."

"Right. First it sinks down to the riverbed. And it lies quiet there for several days."

"Unless it has a wooden leg."

"Unless," agreed Mr. Brattle gravely, "it should happen to have a wooden leg. Next, it gets blown up. Distended, as you might say, by the gases of its own corruption. And that brings it to the surface. That's what you might call the normal proceedings. But suppose the body happens to fall over the weir. You get my point?"

"You mean," said Mercer slowly, "that the bashing it would get would drive all the gas out of it, and it might never surface at all."

"That's precisely my meaning."

"It would roll along the bottom, and finish up in the sea. What was left of it by that time."

"I've never seen it set down scientifically, but I remember explaining it to a doctor I was taking out in one of my boats, and he said he thought it was a very interesting theory."

"I think so, too," said Mercer.

They were in sight of the boathouse by now and they could see that Venetia had already run a punt out, and was unshipping the pole. She looked trim and workmanlike in jeans and sweater.

"Sensible girl," said Mr. Brattle. "She's left the cushions behind. Always soaks the cushions, someone learning to punt."

Two hours later, damp but happy, Mercer brought the punt slowly upstream to Mr. Brattle's landing stage. Venetia sat at the far end, paddle in hand.

"Don't use that," said Mercer. "Let me see if I can bring it in myself."

"Stick the pole in forrard if you want to stop the boat."

"O.K.?"

"O.K.," said Venetia. She jumped ashore with the painter and made fast. "What are you planning to do next? Have a hot bath and change?"

"I've got a better idea than that," said Mercer. "We'll have a hot drink."

Venetia said, "That's a good idea."

Mercer's receiving set picked up the fractional moment of hesitation before she said it, and he grinned to himself. He said, "We'll go in my car, shall we? I'll drop you here on the way back and you can pick up yours."

"Fine."

It was a few minutes after six when they got to the Angler's Rest. It had the nice fresh feel of a pub which has just opened for the evening and has had no time to start smelling of stale beer and cigarette smoke and people. They went into the private bar.

"Just because it's the first time you've come out with me," said Mercer, "there's no need for you to pretend you like beer. I'm going to have a whiskey and ginger wine. Technically known as a whiskey mack."

"That sounds terrific."

He went out to get the drinks, and Venetia watched him thoughtfully as he walked to the bar. A practiced hand at the game, she thought. Good technique, based on a lot of experience. Not an entirely agreeable face. A fighting body.

He came back with the drinks, put one down on the table in front of her, and stood with his back to the newly lighted fire.

"Tell me about yourself," she said. "The murderers you've caught, the armed robbers you've disarmed, the state secrets you've saved."

"Naught out of three."

"I don't believe it. All the real-life policemen I've read about have done things like that."

"They don't write their own memoirs. There's a little

man up in London who does it for them."

"There must be some truth in them."

"There's kidney in a steak and kidney pie. Sometimes."

"You're starting to steam. Sit down. Stop being modest. Talk."

"All right. But I'll get us another drink first. Put that one back."

"If you're planning to get me tight, I ought to warn you that I've got a terrific head for drink. The last man who tried it ran out of money, and I had to buy the last two rounds myself *and* drive him home."

"I'll bear it in mind," said Mercer.

The second drink went down smoothly.

"Go on," said Venetia.

"You really do want the story of my life."

"Every sordid detail."

"Well," said Mercer, "I hardly like to mention it in the presence of the Oldest Member, but I was only able to go to primary school."

"The Oldest Member—oh, you mean that stuffed pike. He does look a bit like the club bore, doesn't he? Was it fun?"

"I enjoyed it. I was stronger than most of the other kids and I used to give them hell. Then I got a scholarship to a grammar school. I didn't like that at all."

"Because the boys were bigger than you and gave you hell."

"It wasn't only that. There are good grammar schools and bad ones. This was a bad one. It tried to be like a public school. Houses and prefects and fagging and beating and all. I suppose your brother went to a public school."

"He went to Wellington. It nearly bust Daddy to send him there."

"Was it worth it?"

138

"I'm not sure. Go on. What did you do?"

"I quit. I don't mean I ran away. I just stopped going. I was nearly sixteen. There was nothing much anyone could do about it. Or that's what I thought. Then I found something out and I've never forgotten it. You can't buck the system. I couldn't get a job. The first thing they all asked was how many 0 levels? When I said, 'I haven't got any of those,' they said, 'Thanks very much; next, please!' So I joined the army. And that's where I had a bit of luck. The mob I was with were posted to the Gulf. It was a cushy life, with lots of spare time. I used it to learn Arabic. Mostly from Arab girls I was dating."

Mercer looked at Venetia out of the corner of his eye when he said this. She was grinning. She said, "I suppose they'd sleep with anything white in trousers."

"Mostly one took one's trousers off."

"You know perfectly well what I mean."

"Yes," said Mercer. "And you're wrong. Arab girls are far cleaner and far more choosy than most English girls I've met."

The landlord came in at this moment and Mercer ordered another drink. Venetia said, "I'll have soda in mine this time. Go on."

"I took to Arabic. It's a fine language, with lots of subtle shades of meaning. Did you know that there are a lot of words in Arabic which mean three different things according to the way you pronounce them?"

"In English, too," said Venetia.

"I got a few jobs as an interpreter. Even some elementary intelligence chores. I liked that. So I wangled a transfer to the military police. I learned a lot from them. I thought I knew something about dirty fighting. It took a broken arm and three cracked ribs to convince me how wrong I was. Then, just as I was really getting stuck in, we were moved, almost overnight, to BAOR in Germany."

139

"That sounds typical of the army," agreed Venetia.

"Well, I'd done my five, and arresting drunken squaddies in beer halls didn't appeal to me. So I got out and joined the Metropolitan Police. My time in the MPs helped. I got accelerated promotion. I was a sergeant by the time I was twenty-four. The police have got a lot more sense than the army. When *they* found I could speak Arabic, they used it. I joined K Division and worked down in the docks. There are a lot of Arabs and lascars and all such there. They speak their own lingua franca and are a very peaceful bunch, on the whole. When I got bored with that I volunteered for an attachment to help the ruler of M'qua. You won't have heard of it. It's south of Muscat. It's the size of Hampstead, and about as rich. My job was to organize the ruler's police force for him. I enjoyed that. I wouldn't have minded finishing my service there. I had the rank of inspector and was boss of my own show."

"Let me guess the next bit," said Venetia dreamily. "You made a pass at the ruler's favorite wife, and had to leave hurriedly."

"You think I'm making all this up, don't you?"

"Certainly not. I think it's fantastic."

"It wasn't the ruler's wife. It was his son."

"You made a pass at him?"

"No. He cut his old man's throat and took over. He didn't like me, so that was that, and I was back in England."

"Was that when you got that?" She leaned over and ran the tip of her finger down the side of his face.

"My dueling scar? No. That was in my next post. Dear old Southwark. I got savaged by Crows."

"Crows?"

"Not birds. Men. And in my opinion you can take the whole of the Middle East, Limehouse, the docks, Soho, the lot, and they're milk and water beside that little patch

140

of London due south of the City. For real savages, the Elephant and Castle beats darkest Africa into a cocked hat."

Venetia said, "You'd better take me home now." She said it regretfully. She looked warm and happy but not, Mercer thought, in the least bit intoxicated. The last drink had been a double. Perhaps she really had a hard head. He said, "When do I get my next lesson?"

"Do you need another one?"

"Certainly. It's that twiddle as you put the pole in that I haven't quite mastered yet."

They both laughed, and were still laughing as they came out into the public bar, and saw Willoughby Slade standing there talking to a fair-haired boy, who seemed to be upset about something. Willoughby saw his sister, and said, "Hallo," and then saw Mercer and said, "Hallo" again, in quite a different tone of voice. "Here comes the law. What have you been up to, Venetia?"

"Minding my own business."

"All right. Hint taken." He swung round on Mercer, a movement of studied grace, designed to demonstrate the width of his shoulders and the suppleness of his hips. "I hear you came to the house looking for me the other night."

"That's right. I must have missed you."

"Now you've found me."

"If you want to talk to your friends," said the fair-haired boy sulkily, "I'll be going."

"It'll keep," said Mercer.

He made for the door, held it open for Venetia, and followed her out quickly. When they were in the car he said, "I don't know about your capacity for alcohol, but I thought your brother was pretty well tanked up already. Does he always get like that so early in the evening?"

"Some evenings."

"And who was the friend?"

"A boy from the office."

"I see," said Mercer. They drove, in silence, back to Brattle's boathouse.

Detective Massey was sitting in the room over an empty shop opposite Bull's Garage. He had been there for two hours, and he was cold, and stiff, but he had no intention of quitting. He was watching Johnno.

The little man operated from a lighted kiosk behind the petrol pumps, where he sat, on a tilted wooden chair, studying the racing pages in two evening papers and occasionally making notes with a stub of pencil. There was a telephone in the kiosk, and there had been three calls, one in and two out. Massey had made a careful note of the times. He had no reason for doing this, except that he had been taught at detective training school that times were important. "At 2146 hours I was maintaining observation when—" Hullo! Another customer. Johnno popped out, had a word with the driver, took the keys to unlock the filler cap, and started to operate the petrol pump. The driver got out to stretch his legs. He walked round the car to watch Johnno, then strolled into the kiosk to pay for the petrol. More talk, then he came out and drove off. Only just in time, too. Johnno was shutting up shop. Pumps locked. Lights switched off. Kiosk locked.

By this time Massey was downstairs. He used the back entrance to the shop. His big motor bicycle was parked in the yard. Johnno, he knew, kept a showy little sports car in one of the sheds behind the garage. It was fast, too. But not as fast as Detective Massey's MV Augusta 700. Here he came. Sidelights on, but no headlights as yet. This suited Massey very well. He could keep his own lights off and be in no fear of losing Johnno's taillights.

Half an hour later they were on the outskirts of Slough. So far it had been easy, and Massey was pretty certain that he hadn't been spotted. But now it was going to get tricky. There was enough traffic in the streets to allow two cars and a van to get between him and Johnno. The trouble was the traffic lights. Slough seemed to be full of traffic lights. If they changed at an awkward moment—As he was thinking about it, it happened. The van ahead of him braked. The lights turned from amber to red. Johnno was over, and scooting away down the High Street.

Massey swung his bicycle to the right into a side street, then turned left into a long and nearly empty street parallel to the High Street, and went down it fast. After a couple of hundred yards he reckoned he must be level with Johnno again, or even ahead of him, and he swung left, back into the High Street.

Johnno's car had disappeared. To his left he could see the van and the cars, released by the lights, coming toward him. To the right he had a clear view, under the street lamps, for four or five blocks.

Massey did some quick thinking.

If Johnno had turned right he would have seen him. Therefore he had turned left. Therefore his destination was somewhere in the confused nest of streets which lay off the left-hand side of the High Street. He started to search.

After half an hour he gave it up, and started home. To relieve his feelings, he let the powerful machine out. Halfway back to Stoneferry he overtook Johnno jogging sedately homeward.

14

MERCER'S ALARM CLOCK called him at four. By half
past four he had picked up Detective Prothero, and his
car was heading north. At seven o'clock they stopped for
breakfast at a big hotel south of Banbury.

The sun was up now. It was a fine day of early autumn. Mercer said, "Have you got any idea where we're
going or what we're going to do when we get there?"

"No idea," said Prothero. "Never ask questions. Do
what I'm told. Simpler in the end." He belched comfortably and loosened his seat belt a couple of notches.

"I'll fill you in," said Mercer. "We're making for a
town in south Staffordshire, called Heckmonwith. We're
going to have a talk with the parents of a girl called
Maureen Dyson. And with anyone else who can tell us
anything about her."

Prothero digested this information, with his breakfast,
for some miles, and then said, "Was she the one we
found on the island?"

"I hope so," said Mercer.

Porson Street, Heckmonwith, was a row of neat, two-
story, semidetached houses, and the neatest of the lot was
number 23, which had a shingle with the name *The Nest*
painted on it in italic script. The front path was freshly

reddened, the stones on either side freshly whitened, and every flower in the geometrically shaped flower beds knew its place, and kept it.

There were two mats in front of the front door. Mercer wiped his feet on both of them, and was conducted into the front parlor by Mr. Dyson, introduced to Mrs. Dyson, and invited to take a chair.

"We were warned by the local police that you were coming," said Mrs. Dyson. "Would your friend like to come in, too? It's a little cold outside."

"He'll be all right," said Mercer. He could see no sign of an ashtray, and he knew that an hour without a cigarette would be torment for Prothero. "I'm glad they told you what I wanted to talk to you about. It can't have been pleasant news."

"It was a shock," said Mr. Dyson.

"A terrible shock," said Mrs. Dyson.

You're either bloody good actors, or you didn't give a brass button for her, thought Mercer. He said, "Tell me about her."

"Well," said Mr. Dyson, and looked at his wife. She said, "Maureen was a very nice girl. Naturally, you'd expect us to say that, Inspector. Being her parents. But it's true. She was always top of her class in school. And she got a lot of prizes, for good conduct and leadership and things like that. And when she left school, she wasn't like *some* girls we know; she went straight into a job and earned good money at it."

"A job?"

"With a firm of lawyers in the town. Batchelor, Symonds, and Quirk. She was with them for nearly five years. Then she had to go. She couldn't see eye to eye with Mr. Batchelor."

"About anything in particular?"

"Just generally. He was an untidy, unmethodical sort of man, Inspector, and our Maureen was just the opposite. She was neat, and conscientious, too. She never minded going early, or staying late if there was a job to finish. I think she sort of—well—sort of showed him up. That's why he got rid of her."

"That would have been four or five years ago. What did she do next?"

"She joined another lawyers' office. In Stoke. I forget the name, but I could find out if you liked. She was there three years. Then she moved south. We didn't see a lot of her. She came home for Christmas sometimes. Things like that."

"I suppose," said Mr. Dyson, exhibiting the first, very faint, sign of sentiment, "that there's no doubt—I mean, about it being her."

"It's not certain, by any means. But what you told the inspector up here, about her shoes—well, it does make it very likely."

"It's true," said Mrs. Dyson. "And she was sensitive about it. After I'd spoken to the inspector I had a look round up in her room. She left a lot of things there. I found this pair of shoes. The right-hand one's quite different. You can see. It's wider."

"That's really most helpful," said Mercer. "I wonder if I could borrow them."

"I'll give them a clean first."

"Don't bother." He put them into his briefcase. "I don't imagine I'll have to trouble you anymore. There's just one thing. Could you give me the name of her dentist?"

When Mercer came out, he took a deep breath. Porson Street was not an inspiring place, but it had more fresh air in it than the house he had just left.

"How did they take it?" said Prothero.

"They didn't take it at all. They scarcely noticed it. They wrote her off years ago. See if you can find this address. It's a left turn off the main square, behind the town hall."

"It looked a neat little place," said Prothero.

Mercer repressed a shudder. He said, "They put little socks on the legs of the chairs. Tell me, Len, what do you suppose a girl would do who was brought up in a house like that?'

"Get out as quick as she could," said Prothero.

"I expect you're right. What I really meant was, what sort of person would she turn out to be?"

"Could turn out either way. I remember a boy at school. Parson's son. He'd been brought up very strict. By the time he was seventeen you couldn't trust a girl within arm's length of him on either side. This the place?"

"'Maurice Fairbrother. Dental Surgeon.' That looks like it."

Mr. Fairbrother was helpful. He said, "I remember Miss Dyson well. She used to come to me as regular as clockwork. She looked after her teeth as carefully—well, as carefully as she looked after everything else."

"What makes you say that?"

"It does seem a funny thing to say, doesn't it? But she left quite an impression on me. She was a hard sort of girl, even when she was young. Self-possessed, you know. Gave nothing away. We dentists see people's character in undress, as you might say."

"But she had good teeth?"

"Absolutely perfect. And was determined to keep them that way." He was examining a record card. "She had an occasional scrape and clean. And I see that I put a brace on her front teeth when she was ten. She insisted on having it off. Too soon, I thought, but she said it spoiled her appearance."

"*Was* she attractive?"

"She didn't attract me," said Mr. Fairbrother. "But then I don't like my eggs hard boiled."

Batchelor, Symonds, and Quirk occupied premises in the High Street which looked more like a betting shop than the offices of a firm of solicitors. A cheerful girl, in the outer office, who seemed to be going down for the third time in a sea of papers, told them that Mr. Batchelor was out, but should be back shortly.

Mercer and Prothero took time off for coffee.

"Doesn't seem to be much doubt we're onto the right girl now, does it, skipper?"

"No real doubt. There can't be a lot of people reach twenty-five without a filling in their head. If those shoes measure up, I think we can call it a certainty."

"What I can't make out," said Prothero, pouring his coffee into his saucer to cool it, and then blowing on it, "if it *is* her, why did she come back? She packs all up her traps and pushes off up to London—"

"According to Sergeant Rollo."

Prothero poured his coffee back from the saucer into the cup and drank a good deal of it. Then he said, "Ah! According to Dick Rollo. Yes. I see," and said no more.

Mr. Batchelor was still out when they got back to the office. Mercer sat down to wait. Twenty minutes later he arrived in the shape of a small, disorganizing cyclone. Inquired of the girl whether a Mrs. Winlaw had rung. Was told she hadn't. Took Mercer's card, but didn't read it. Asked the girl if she was quite sure Mrs. Winlaw hadn't rung. She was quite sure. Picked up a pile of unopened letters. Tried to look at Mercer's card with the letters in his hand. Dropped the card. Mercer picked it up. Dropped most of the letters. The girl picked them up. Succeeded in reading the card, and said, "Good God. Police. Is one of my clients in trouble? Come inside, Inspector."

In his own office, once he understood what Mercer wanted Mr. Batchelor became a little more composed. He said, "Yes, of course I remember Miss Dyson. She started here as my secretary. Then when old Mr. Quirk retired she took on a number of jobs herself. I suppose you'd have called her a managing clerk by that time. She worked under my general supervision, of course."

"She must have been very useful."

"Oh, very," said Mr. Batchelor. He said it without much enthusiasm.

"Then why did she leave?"

"You're a policeman," said Mr. Batchelor, "and the police don't come into things until they've gone bad. Has Maureen—I mean, is she in trouble?"

"She's dead."

Mr. Batchelor said, "Good God," jumped up, knocked a pile of deeds onto the floor, and picked them up again. The exercise seemed to calm him. He said, "You mean, she's been murdered?"

"As a matter of fact, yes. But why should you suppose I meant that?"

"I don't know. I suppose I assumed that someone— You're not having me on, are you?"

"I'll give you the whole strength of it," said Mercer. He spoke for ten minutes. Mr. Batchelor listened with remarkable patience, jumping up only twice. The first time, he scuttled across to the door and put up the "Engaged" sign. The second time, as Mercer was drawing to a close, he went over to a filing cabinet, unlocked a drawer marked "Personal," and took out a cardboard folder, which he brought back and placed on his desk.

Then he said, quite simply, "I got rid of Miss Dyson because she was blackmailing my clients."

"Ah!" said Mercer softly. "So that's it."

It was as though a window had been opened, as though curtains had been drawn back, throwing a strong shaft of light and understanding into a dark corner.

He sat very still, watching Mr. Batchelor's hands as he untied the tapes of the folder and took out a document.

149

The little solicitor said, "I trust I shan't have to go into any details about this, because it affects other people, and I hoped that it was all dead and buried."

"We'll keep names out of it if we can," said Mercer.

"I'll tell you about the last case. The one I found out about, and that was the reason I got rid of her. She handled a lot of litigation. You know what is meant by a discretion statement, Inspector?"

"Roughly."

"Say a wife is divorcing her husband on the grounds that he has committed adultery. She has clear proof of it. Probably he hasn't troubled to deny it. But she may have gone off the rails herself. It often happens, you know. A woman sees her husband fooling around with another woman. She thinks, what's sauce for the goose is sauce for the gander, if you follow my meaning."

"I follow you exactly," said Mercer. Only half of his mind was attending. The other half was working out the implications of what he had heard.

"That's where a discretion statement comes in. A plaintiff who comes into court asking for divorce must come with clean hands herself. So the wife writes it all down. It's handed to the judge. He's the only person who sees it. After the case is over, it's destroyed."

"And Miss Dyson got hold of it. And blackmailed the wife?"

"Not the wife. The man she'd been involved with. He was happily married. It was a simple indiscretion. He paid the best part of five hundred pounds to keep it quiet."

"And you say that was one of a number of cases."

"It was the only one I knew about when I sacked her, naturally. The facts about the others trickled in later."

"How did she get her hands on this—what did you call it?—discretion statement."

"She stayed working late. She was keen, you see.

She'd have the run of the office. She could look at any paper she wanted. Or listen to phone calls. All the rooms are on one line. You've only got to lift the receiver."

"What beats me," said Mercer, "is how she ever got another job in a lawyer's office.

"Not difficult when it's a woman. She says that up to then she's been living at home looking after her parents. Every job she takes is her first job. The family and the school will give her a reference."

Mercer said, "I suppose that's right," but he said it absent-mindedly. He was thinking about Mr. Weatherman. *That* office would be a good deal better organized and more strictly controlled than the cheerful shambles of Batchelor, Symonds, and Quirk. But all the same, an unscrupulous girl with her wits about her would have plenty of opportunities.

"The fact is," said Mr. Batchelor, "that solicitors do learn a lot of secrets. In ninety-nine cases out of a hundred it's all right, but if you get a bad 'un—"

They had an unsatisfactory lunch in a pub outside Heckmonwith and took the road for the south. It was nearly five o'clock by the time they reached Maidenhead. As they stopped for a cup of tea, Mercer spotted the placard, and bought an evening paper.

The headline said, "WAGE CLERK DIES" and the subheading, "Massive Murder Hunt."

Charles Watson, the wage clerk of Messrs Arkinwrights, the Stepney engineering firm, died early this morning in Guy's Hospital. He and his fellow employee George Radici were the two men who put up such a gallant fight against the six men who attacked them when they were carrying the week's wages to a car. Both men received gunshot wounds, Watson in the head and Radici in both legs. It is feared that he may lose one of them.

151

The Arkinwright factory employs over a thousand men and the weekly wage roll is believed to be between £20,000 and £25,000. The board of Arkinwrights had already announced a reward of £1,000 for information leading to the conviction of the men concerned. When they learned that Watson had died, they immediately raised this to £5,000. Watson leaves a wife and two children. Last night a massive force of police and detectives started to comb cafés, clubs, and garages in the South London area. Chief Superintendent Morrissey, head of the CID in No. 1 District, is in charge of the operation.

15

Oᴜʀ ᴋᴇᴇɴ ʏᴏᴜɴɢ detective," said Sergeant Gwilliam, "hot on the trail of the miscreant, was baffled by a cunning maneuver—"

"What the hell are you talking about?" said Mercer. It was seven o'clock that same evening. He had come straight to the station. Ten hours of driving, coupled with two snatched meals, had not improved his temper.

"The boy shall tell you himself," said Gwilliam.

Detective Massey looked up from the blue report form he was filling up and said, "Last night, at approximately eight o'clock, I was keeping observation—"

"This isn't a police court. Let's have it without the icing. Who were you watching?"

"I was watching Johnno."

"And who the hell told you to do that?"

Even Sergeant Gwilliam was startled by the viciousness in Mercer's voice. Massey was as scarlet as if his face had been slapped. He said, "It's one of my jobs. I was given it before you came here."

"My arrival canceled all standing orders. All right. Tell me about it."

"We've had more than one tip-off that Johnno was doing these transistor and radio jobs. He was seen hanging round the shops just about the time they got bust, and one of Taffy's fingers said one of his friends had seen Johnno offering new stuff for sale in the private bar of the Swan—"

"Third hand. Someone knows someone who says he saw Johnno. What were you supposed to do about it?"

Massey told him what he had done about it. His voice said that he thought he was being unfairly criticized, and if Mercer had had a long day, all right. Understood. But that was no reason to take it out on him.

When he had finished, Mercer went over to one of the closets and got out the set of six-inch and twenty-four inch Ordnance Survey Sheets. He spread out the large-scale map of Slough.

"Show me just where you lost him."

"I think it must have been that one."

"I didn't ask you to think. I asked you to be sure."

"It was that crossroads."

"And when you came out—here—he'd gone?"

"Yes."

"He couldn't have got past you?"

"Not at the speed I was going."

"So he *must* have been calling somewhere in this area." Mercer drew a pencil line round the half dozen streets on the left of the High Street. "*And* what's more, he can't have stopped long. Not if he was already halfway home when you overtook him. Do you know this part of the town, Taffy?"

"I've been there once or twice," said Gwilliam. "I don't know it all that well." He looked at Massey, who shook his head. Mercer rolled the pencil slowly across the map. He seemed to be thinking. Then he said, "Have you got your notes?" Massey stared at him. "The notes you made when you were watching Johnno."

"Oh. Yes."

Mercer studied them. The other two men watched

him in silence. "You were there from half past seven until about half past nine, when Johnno shut up shop?"

"That's right."

"And in that time about twenty cars called for petrol or whatever?"

"Yes."

"What did the drivers do while Johnno was serving them?"

"Most of them sat tight. Some got out and walked about. Two or three went into the kiosk to talk to Johnno while he was getting their change."

"Could you see into it from where you were?"

"No. The glass side is blocked up with advertisements and things."

"Were any of the drivers carrying anything when they went in?"

Massey thought hard about this one. He said, "Do you mean, did anyone leave anything behind with Johnno? I'm sure I should have noticed if they had."

"I meant what I said. Was anyone actually carrying anything in his hand when he went in?"

"I've got an idea that the last driver might have been holding something—it looked like a small suitcase. But he didn't leave it behind. And he wasn't in the kiosk more than ten seconds."

The pencil stopped rolling. Mercer's fingers closed on it. His knuckles showed white for a moment. When he spoke his voice was studiedly normal. He said to Gwilliam, "First thing tomorrow, I want you to take this plan. Get over to Slough, and mark on it any place of business inside this area. Particularly any place that might conceivably stay open until nine or ten at night." To Massey he said, "And a word in your pearl-like ear, my boy. Leave Johnno alone. Understand? Stop watching him. Don't go near him. Leave him alone." Before Massey could say anything he had turned back to Gwilliam. "One other

155

thing. Could you find out who owns the block of flats overlooking the recreation ground?"

"The recreation ground?" Gwilliam was still staring at the map.

"Keep alert, Sergeant. We're no longer in Slough. We're back in Stoneferry. The block of flats overlooking the recreation ground and backing on Westhaugh Road. Can you locate the owner?"

"Now?"

"That's right."

"If there's a porter I could ring him up and ask him."

"Do that. And when you find him tell him to be at the flats in half an hour. That'll give me time to get a bite to eat."

There was a brief silence after he had gone. Then Gwilliam said, "Tom was saying, the other day, he couldn't make the new skipper out at all. When you thought he was thinking about one thing, Tom said, you found he was really thinking about something quite different. I think Tom's wrong. I don't think he really thinks about anything at all. I think he just says the first thing that comes into his head."

Massey said nothing, which was a good deal less than he would have liked to say.

Lionel Talbot, JP, TD, drove home from his office in South Street. He turned right into the High Street, right again past the police station, happening to notice Mercer coming out; then drove across the new bridge, along the first feeder road to the bypass, through the underpass and onto the Laleham Road. The sight of Mercer had temporarily shifted his thoughts away from his own troubles, which had kept him late at the office. These stemmed from two ridiculous building contracts which his late senior partner had let them in for, both of which would cause an uncomfortable loss to the firm of Jocelyn &

Talbot, General Contractors. Unless Weatherman could get him out of them.

He was still thinking about Mercer when he opened the front door and was met and given his evening ration of a single kiss by his wife.

He went into the drawing room, mixed himself a gin and Italian vermouth, warmed his backside in front of the electric log fire, and felt better.

He said, "We shall have to do something about that chap Mercer."

"Mercer?"

"The new CID man."

"Oh, him. What's he been up to?"

"First, he's made a mess of that murder case. Made a wrong identification. Then he pulled in old Hedges, who obviously had nothing to do with it. I mean, it wasn't his daughter they found, so how could it have been him? And when he had him inside he beat him up, I believe. And now Hedges is raising the roof. Can't blame him really. I think I'll have another. It's been a hard day."

"I'll do it. Half and half?"

"That's the girl. A bit more gin than vermouth. Not content with that, he's upsetting his own men. Bob's beginning to hear complaints already."

"Poor old Bob."

"And his latest move—I imagine it's really a sort of smoke screen to hide his own inefficiency—he's trying to throw suspicion on Jack Bull."

"But that's absurd. Jack's as sound as the Rock of Gibraltar."

"Of course he is. He's a damned good chap. And a damned sight better than Inspector Jumped-up Mercer."

"Suspicion of what?"

"Bob said something about driving competitors out of business by crooked methods."

"But that's nonsense. He often says that he's got far too

much work to do and he wishes there was another garage in the place."

"Exactly."

"And I'll tell you something else. At least, I'm not sure that I'm really meant to tell even you, as Pat Clark told me in confidence."

"No secrets between husband and wife."

"Well, then . . ."

Mr. Meakin was waiting in the hall of Bankside Mansions when Mercer got there. He was plainly nervous. He said, "I hope it isn't more trouble with that top-floor pair. Lease or no lease, I'll have them out. I warned them last time, and this time I mean it. Just say the word."

"I'm sorry to disappoint you," said Mercer, "but the matter I've come about concerns the ground-floor flat in your annex. The one overlooking the river."

"Colonel Stanley—"

"And it happened on Friday, November fourteenth, nearly two years ago."

Mr. Meakin said, "Oh." Conducted a mental roll call and said, "Miss Dyson."

"Correct. Were you here when she left?"

"Walked out on us. Leaving five weeks' rent owing."

"Which her employers paid for her."

"They paid the rent. But they didn't settle the dilapidations. That girl was a compulsive smoker. She seems to have left burning cigarettes everywhere. On the mantelpiece, on the tables. She ruined the top of a nice chest of drawers. It cost me forty-five pounds to have the damage put right. If I can find her, I'm going to collect it."

"Tell me about when she left."

"There's not a lot to tell, Inspector. I came, myself, early the following week, to speak to her about the rent. We don't like to let arrears run beyond the month. There were three or four milk bottles outside her door, a pile of newspapers, a box of stuff from the laundry, and a parcel from the cleaners. I thought that justified my going in, so I used my passkey. It was quite clear that she had gone. Drawers and closets were empty and all her personal things were gone—photographs and that sort of stuff."

"Had she emptied the larder?"

"No. Not that there was a great deal in it. Coffee and sugar and breakfast cereals. I gather she took most of her meals out."

"You mentioned a parcel from the cleaners."

"Yes. That was rather surprising. It was a very nice tweed coat and skirt. It must have cost a good deal of money. I suppose she forgot about it."

"Did anyone see her go?"

"Actually see her leave the flat, you mean?"

"Yes."

"I don't thnk so. There's no reason why they should have. It was rather a dirty night, I seem to remember. There wouldn't have been many about, and the back door of her flat opens onto a path which leads through the far end of the recreation ground and straight out into the town. That's where she'd pick up a bus for the station, by the Old Bridge. I believe someone saw her at the station."

"So I'm told," said Mercer. "Was the back door locked?"

Mr. Meakin had to think about that one. Then he said, "Yes. Both doors were locked."

"And the only keys were your master key and the keys she had."

"That's right. I had to get a new set for Colonel Stanley."

"Now let me guess something. When you came in that morning, all the curtains were drawn, tight shut. In the living room and the kitchen *and* the bedroom. Right?"

Mr. Meakin looked at him. There was a hint of worry

in his eyes. "You're right about that. But I can't say it struck me as odd. If she was there that evening, she'd naturally have drawn the curtains."

"Even in her bedroom? When she had no intention of sleeping there?"

"That was a bit odd, perhaps. Tell me, Inspector—I don't wish to appear inquisitive, but is something wrong?"

Mercer said, "Between you and me, Mr. Meakin, I don't think you're ever going to collect that forty-five pounds."

He drove back into the town thinking about it. When he was putting his car away he noticed a light in Jack Bull's first-story flat. The main entrance to the flat was through the shop, but there was an iron staircase leading up from the yard to the back entrance, and that was where the light was. He guessed it was the kitchen. He climbed the stairs and rang the bell. The door was opened by Vikki. She was wearing an apron over her working outfit, and a pair of rubber gloves.

"Why, look who's here," she said. "Come in. Excuse my gloves. I'm just starting the washing up."

Jack Bull sat at the head of the big kitchen table. There was the remains of a supper for two on it. He was smoking a cheroot and looked relaxed and comfortable.

He said, "Surprise! Surprise! What can we do for you, Inspector?"

"I saw your light," said Mercer, "and it reminded me that I hadn't paid my garage bill."

"Why bother? It doesn't amount to a row of beans. Send him a chit at the end of the month, Vikki. Four weeks at five bob a week."

"I don't like running up bills. It makes me nervous." Mercer extracted a sizable wad of five-pound notes from his hip pocket and peeled one off. "I understand that the going rate for a lock-up garage is twenty-five bob a week.

That'll cover a month." He handed the note to Vikki, who tucked it into her apron pocket. She said, "I'll give you a proper receipt in the morning," and showed her small white teeth in a grin.

Bull seemed to be on the point of saying something sharp, then changed his mind. He said, "When you've finished washing up, honey, could you bring us all a nice cup of coffee next door?"

The room next door was a surprise. In front of an open fire were a couple of fat, low-slung leather armchairs which looked as if they had come out of an old-fashioned London club. There was a box of cigars on a table between the chairs. There was a drink cabinet in one corner and a large-screen television set in the other. The pictures on the walls were mostly framed photographs. Regimental groups, with names carefully written in underneath. Pictures of tanks and guns and army vehicles. Pictures of parachutists dropping out of airplanes. One enlarged photograph of a very pretty girl in the uniform of a Wehrmacht nursing sister.

"She was the first thing I saw when I came round from the anesthetic. After the Krauts had had my arm off," said Bull. "I can't tell you how much it cheered me up. Have a cigar?"

Mercer took it. It was a good cigar. He also accepted a glass of whiskey. Vikki brought in three cups of coffee on a tray, drank hers composedly, and said, "Well, if that's all for now, I'll be going."

"Must you?"

"I want to wash my hair tonight."

"O.K.," said Bull. "See you tomorrow."

There was a long silence after she had gone.

"I know what you're thinking," said Bull, "but it isn't so. I wish it was."

Mercer said, "Bad luck."

"She's just about the most extraordinary girl I've ever

met. To look at her, you'd think she was a fold-out from the middle page of *Playboy*, wouldn't you?"

"Something like that."

"How wrong can you be? She does her work in the office better than any girl I've ever had before. In fact she does half of Rainey's work for him, when he's too pissed to do it himself. He says she's a natural mathematician, and he ought to know. He was a senior bloody wrangler or something."

"Useful round the house, too."

"She cooks my supper for me most nights, and washes up. I've got a sort of feeling she's sorry for me. And damn it, I don't *want* her to be sorry for me. All I want her to do is to take her clothes off and get into bed."

"And she won't?"

"No."

"Have you suggested it?"

"Like a worn gramophone record."

"You ever try getting rough with her?"

Bull looked at him out of the corner of his eye and said, "Come, Inspector. That's no way to talk. Anyway, I've only got one arm, and she's probably a black belt a judo and a triple dan at karate."

He hauled himself out of the chair, fetched the whiskey bottle, pulled the cork out with one hand, topped up both glasses, and put it down within easy reach.

"And what do you make of Sinferry, Inspector?"

"You've been here longer than me. You tell me what you make of it."

"It's a bright little, tight little place," said Bull. "No better and no worse than a lot of others, I expect. It's got its fair share of dirt and more than its fair share of phonies. Have you met Lionel Talbot yet?"

"Our revered justice of the peace?"

"Chairman of magistrates, and busted flush. When he's not dispensing justice, he's doing his best to ruin a very sound builders and contractors business, which he inherited from his father and his grandfather before him. You've seen him performing on the bench. He looks just like your commanding officer taking defaulters, doesn't he? Fierce little moustache, eagle eye, voice trained to keep the other ranks in their place. It's all bluff. He's a badly cooked loaf. Hard crust, soggy in the middle."

"Speaking from personal experience?"

"Certainly. If he wasn't soft he wouldn't accept presents from me, would he?"

"It depends on the presents."

"Bloody expensive presents. A color television set, a dozen of Scotch, free service for his car."

"And what do you get out of it?"

"It's always useful to have the law on your side."

"Have you bought Bob Clark as well?"

Bull blinked. Then he grinned, and said, "That's an odd question from his faithful second in command."

"I'm not his second in command," said Mercer. "That's a mistake a lot of people make. He runs the uniformed branch. I run the plainclothes branch. In any station the head of the uniformed branch has one rank up on the head of the CID to give him the impression he's in charge of both. But he isn't."

"You're all part of the same family."

"That's right. And like all the best families, we spend most of our time quarreling. Mind you, we cooperate fast enough if an outsider tries anything. Tell me, what's your honest opinion of Bob?"

"I wouldn't insult him by classing him with Lionel Talbot. Bob's dead honest, personally brave, and a bit stupid. There were a lot of senior officers like him in the army. The only thing they were afraid of was responsibility." When Mercer said nothing, he added, "Since you asked me."

Mercer was sprawled in the low comfortable chair, his

163

legs stretched out, his arms hanging down. One hand held his glass, the other was resting on the carpet, wrist bent, fingers outstretched and quiet. He said, "You're an odd man, Jack."

It was the first time he had used Bull's Christian name.

"Odd! How?"

"So honest in some ways. So crooked in others."

"I must be a more complex character than I thought."

"For years you've been overcharging people who rely on their cars for transport but know damn little about them. I don't suppose you've often gone as far as you did with old Mrs. Tyler. That must have given you a bit of a fright."

Bull laughed. He sounded genuinely amused. He said, "I dropped a clanger there, all right. All the same, that's not crookedness. It's business."

"It's not a criminal offense to overcharge a mug," agreed Mercer. "But to get away with it you had to get rid of your competitors. People your customers could easily go to if they were a bit worried about your estimates and find out that the job could be done for a third of the price. Or perhaps that it didn't need doing at all."

"If I had done everything you say," said Bull, "which I don't admit—"

"Naturally."

"I can tell you this. I shouldn't lose five minutes' sleep over it. When I got back to England after the war, with one arm and no prospects, I did a lot of thinking. I realized that so far I'd been on the wrong tack. I'd been a good little boy. I'd done what I was told. I'd followed the rules. If there was a form to be filled in, I filled it in and signed my name at the bottom. I went with the tide. And I suddenly realized that there were a million other jelly-fish floating in the tide alongside me."

"So you decided to swim against it."

"Not against it. Certainly not. That's a waste of effort. But I thought I might kick out sideways. Get a little off the main track. And it was the right moment to do it. I had my gratuity, you see, and a disablement pension. But mostly, I had friends. A Special Service battalion was a wonderful mixed bag. Saints and sinners. And the ones you got to know, you got to know properly. You sit on a bench next to a man, knowing that in ten minutes' time you're both going to drop through a hole in the floor into darkness and a howling gale, and you really get to know what makes him tick. Believe me, a psychiatrist's couch isn't in it."

Bull refilled their glasses, and said, "I'm talking too much. Tell me something. Why did you really come up tonight? To extract a confession from me about my murky past? You know damn well I'll deny it all tomorrow morning."

"To tell you the truth," said Mercer sleepily, "I don't give a damn for your murky past. Most business is dirty, if you analyze it. When you put it down, in black and white, without trimmings, what does any business amount to? 'I win—you lose.' And all that matters is the money at the end of the day. Sometimes I'm glad I'm just an ordinary, stupid policeman."

"You're the oddest bloody policeman I've ever met," said Bull. "You sit there, drinking my whiskey. Telling me I've been swindling people for years. Telling me I've driven a couple of honest competitors out of business. And then, in the same breath, you tell me you don't care."

"Why should I care? It's all past history, isn't it? And as you say, it's none of it provable."

"If you're not interested in my past, why have you spent such a lot of time looking into it?"

"Because," said Mercer, and there was suddenly no hint of sleepiness in his voice, "I'm more interested in your present, and your future."

Eleven-thirty. Midnight. Half past twelve. One o'clock. Detective Massey got up to stretch his aching limbs, then sat down again. At twenty minutes to two he saw the side door of Bull's shop open, and Mercer come out, and stand for a moment talking to Bull. They were laughing about something. He made a careful note of the time.

16

SONCHUS OERACEUS. The words were emblazoned across two columns of print. Underneath, in one column, there was a photograph of Hedges. He looked like everyone's idea of a jolly old tramp. (You weren't to know that it was the most successful of twelve photographs, in some of which, despite the efforts of a very clever photographer, he had looked like a sex maniac; and in others like a pimp. The camera never lies, but it is possible to be selective among the different statements it makes.)

> Those of our readers [began the article chattily] who are not well acquainted with botanical Latin may not be aware that *Sonchus oleraceus* is also called sow thistle. It is an old English plant, which grows in ditches and disused pastures and other such humble spots. It is remarkable for one thing. The length and tenacity of its roots. In short, it is very hard to remove. And so the authorities have found, to their cost, in the case of Samuel Hedges of The Barge, Easthaugh Island, Stoneferry, in the county of Middlesex. Some years ago the rating authorities tried to shift him. Then the sanitary authorities. Next there was a flank attack fro the Child Welfare. His present assailants are the Metropolitan Police. Superintendent Clark, when questioned about this, said—

"Good God," said Mercer. "Have you been talking to the papers?"

"On the advice of Division," said Clark stiffly. "I had a question-and-answer session with them. It was better than letting them make the whole thing up."

Superintendent Clark had admitted that Hedges had been arrested for assaulting a policeman. What had the policeman been doing? He had been questioning Hedges. What about? The superintendent had sidestepped this one. Had it been anything to do with the discovery of a body on Westhaugh Island? The superintendent had tried to slip this one, too. But had eventually admitted that it might have been not unconnected with it. Was it a fact that the police had now changed their minds and admitted that he had nothing to do with it? It wasn't a question of changing minds. They had never formed any definite conclusion. It had been routine questioning. Did routine questioning usually go on for eight or ten hours and resume on the following morning? And did routine questioning often leave the man being questioned with a cracked rib and bruises all down one side of his body? The superintendent had called this a malicious lie. Hedges had been examined by a police surgeon that same evening, who could, if necessary, testify that Hedges was completely unmarked. Did the police, asked the reporter, always take such curious precautions after a man had been questioned? There was no answer to this. Did it not argue a guilty conscience? No answer.

"You led with your chin on that one," said Mercer.

"You don't seem to appreciate," said Clark, in tones of cold anger, "that what I'm doing, to the best of my ability, is to cover up for you. You were entrusted with the investigation of a murder. You have made what it is charitable to call a complete mess of it. Not only are we no further on than when we started, but you have managed to bring the whole of my force into disrepute in the process."

"I don't think that's strictly true," said Mercer. It was an added offense to Clark that when Mercer argued he argued without heat, as though the matter were theoretical, and hardly concerned him personally.

"For God's sake, of course it's true. Look at that article."

"I didn't mean that. It's not our fault if the press want to turn Sowthistle into a folk hero. They'll drop him as quickly as they've taken him up. I meant about not being any further on. After all, I now know who the murdered girl was. I know how she was murdered, and why. And I know what steps the murderer took to hide his tracks afterward."

Clark stared at him.

"The real trouble," Mercer went on, "is that three different deaths have got sort of mixed up. One murder, one suicide, and one that might be suicide or accident. In a way, it's the murder that's the clearest of the three. The girl concerned was a Miss Maureen Dyson. She used to work for Weatherman, as a litigation clerk. She tried to blackmail one of his clients. And it wasn't the first time she'd tried it, in her short but evil career. Only this time she picked the wrong man. He drove her out in his car one evening, no doubt under the pretext of paying her hush money, took her to a quiet spot near Westhaugh Island, and strangled her. Then he stripped her, and laid her in a grave which I should imagine he had already dug and concealed with branches. It was mid-November and the summer lovebirds would long ago have deserted the island. He had only to shovel back the earth with a spade and pack it down. A good deal later, in the early hours of the following morning, I imagine, when there was no one about, he let himself quietly into Miss Dyson's flat with her key, drew *all* the curtains, turned on the lights, packed up all her stuff into a couple of suitcases, and took them out to his car, which was parked in the byroad which leads to the back end of the recreation ground. I think he had to make more than one trip. He was cool enough to do the job thoroughly. He forgot a few tins in the larder, and it was bad luck that he didn't know that she had a good suit away at the cleaners. When he'd finished he turned all the lights out and let himself out, locking the door behind him. He forgot to open the curtains in the bedroom, but he didn't forget much else. I imagine he weighted the suitcases with rocks and sunk them in the river later on."

Clark considered this in silence. He was not stupid when it came to assessing evidence.

He said, "Go on. What about Sweetie?"

"Father Walcot gave me his version of that. It's largely guesswork, but it's psychologically sound, and it fits in with what we know of her movements. It goes like this. . . ."

At the end of it Clark said, "Then the handbag wasn't put on the island as a plant to mislead us about identity?"

"I thought so at one time. It's still possible. But it's not very likely. Sweetie disappeared in March. Mauree Dyson was murdered in November. A careful man wouldn't hang onto an incriminating object for eight months on the off chance of being able to use it for a murder he hadn't even thought about. And this man was very careful."

"You're jumping the gun. How do you know it was the same man involved in both cases?"

"Assume for a moment that the man who was with Sweetie that night didn't push her. Assume he just saw her fall in. He wasn't to know that she'd been pulled down by the undertow. She might have been floating down the river. What would you have done?"

"Run down the bank. Shouted. Tried to get help."

"You wouldn't have driven quietly home and said nothing to anyone about it, ever."

"Certainly not."

"Well, that's what he did. And in my book it makes him a pretty ruthless sort of bastard. There's no doubt that the man who killed Maureen Dyson was a ruthless sort of bastard, too."

"It's pretty thin."

"Thin, but I fancy it's true," said Mercer. "I'm not greatly worried about it, because I don't think we shall ever prove either of them."

"Then why the hell are you bothering about them?"

There was such a long silence after this that Clark shifted uneasily in his chair and said, "Well?" He saw that the scar on Mercer's face had turned livid. He had noticed this before, as the only outward sign of excitement or tension that Mercer's impassive face would give; a tiny unconscious warning signal that you were trespassing on dangerous ground.

Mercer said, choosing his words with evident care, "Why am I bothered about them, sir? I'm bothered on account of their connection with the third death I mentioned. The only one that's really important, because it's the only one that's unforgivable. I mean the death of Sergeant Rollo!"

"That was suicide."

"Yes, it was suicide."

"Then the only person who needs forgiveness is Sergeant Rollo."

"I wish that was true."

Clark was getting angry again. He said, "For God's sake stop talking riddles. There's no mystery about his death."

"There's no mystery about his death. The mystery is why he agreed to say that he saw Maureen Dyson, with her suitcases packed, on the platform of Stoneferry station, when he must have known it was a lie."

Silence.

Then Clark said, but without much conviction, "He may have made a mistake about the date."

"He didn't. He reported it on November fourteenth. The day we know Maureen disappeared."

"Are you sure?"

"I'm sure," said Mercer patiently. "And so are you. You saw it in the O Book. I found it on your desk."

Silence again. Then Clark said, "Yes, I remember now. Perhaps you're all wrong about what happened to her. There's no direct evidence, after all."

"No."

"Perhaps she did pack up her things herself and go up to London. And came back later and got herself killed."

"Why should she do that?"

"I've no idea. But I'd rather believe that than believe that Dick Rollo was accessory to a murder."

"I don't think it appeared to him like that, at all. I think all he was asked to do was to tell an innocent-sounding lie. By someone he had every reason to oblige. I could make up half a dozen stories that would sound convincing—convincing enough to someone who wanted to be convinced. Let's say Maureen Dyson had gone off with a married man. An old friend of mine. If the hue and cry could be held off—if people could be brought to believe, just for a few days, that she'd gone up to London—it would give me time to sort the tangle out. That's all I want. Right? But, as the days went by, and became weeks, and months, I picture Rollo getting anxious. He couldn't go back on his written report. But I'll tell you something he *did* do. He made two trips up to Missing Persons, personally, to institute inquiries."

"He didn't tell anyone here about that."

"No. He didn't tell anyone. The suspicion was inside him, growing every day. Every police instinct he had told him he'd been conned into something serious. That's why he gave way so easily when the crunch came. Do

172

you think he'd have behaved like that if he hadn't had a guilty conscience? An obvious frame-up! He'd have come storming in here and shouted the house down. But he couldn't do it. He was half rotten already."

"Your imagination does you credit," said Clark bitterly. "There's just one tiny detail you've omitted. Who is this man who watched Sweetie Hedges drown? Who murdered Maureen Dyson and drove Rollo to suicide?"

"I've been accused once," said Mercer, with the half smile which Clark found maddening, "of shooting my mouth off. This time I'd rather be absolutely certain before I start naming names."

"But when you *are* certain, you will tell me."

The silence before Mercer said, "Yes. Of course," was so long that it would have been almost less rude if he had said, "No."

There was a knock on the door. Massey put his head in. When he saw Mercer he started to back out. Clark said, very loudly, "Come in, Massey. Mercer and I have quite finished."

"It's your decision, of course," said Lionel Talbot. "But I think you'll have to investigate. You can't afford to let a situation like that get out of hand."

"No," said Superintendent Clark. "But I wish we had something a little more definite to hang it on."

"Let's sum up. First, he's becoming very friendly with Jack Bull. Nothing wrong with that—in itself. Jack's a good chap. But one wants to keep men like that at a proper distance. Not to spend the whole night boozing with them."

"Agreed."

"Then, when Massey looks like being onto that petrol pump attendant, Johnno, Mercer calls him off, at a rather critical moment."

"I'd say it's pretty clear what Johnno was up to. He was

off to flog the stuff he'd been stealing. Probably to his regular fence. It was bad luck that he lost him. Next time we'd probably have located him *and* we should have had our hands on the receiver."

"That's going to take some explaining away. Let me top your glass up. I'm looking after the house tonight. Maggie's out at her French class. Right. Next, you've had this anonymous letter. Nothing to show where it came from?"

"Nothing at all. Block capitals, written on cheap note-paper. 'If you want to know where Mercer keeps his wad, ask Mr. Moxon at the shop in Cranbourne Street.'"

"Have you done anything about that?"

"We only got the tip-off this evening. We know Moxon's. It's a newspaper and tobacco shop. We've nothing against Moxon. Massey's going over tomorrow to spy out the land."

"Do you think Mercer's taking money on the side?"

"He seems to have enough of it. Whenever he opens his billfold, I'm told, it's bulging with fivers."

"Could be bluff," said Talbot. "I remember a young officer in my regiment who was like that. It turned out that there was one fiver on top and a lot of lavatory paper underneath."

Clark laughed, and then said, "The money side would be the only real proof. He banks with the London and Home Counties. If we could get a sight of his pass sheet it would probably clinch it."

"You'd need a judge's order to make the bank open its books."

"And we shouldn't get it."

"No. All the same, there might be another way. I've known Derek Robbins, the chief cashier, for twenty years. Derek and I play golf most Saturdays. If I told him the whole story, in confidence, he might be prepared to cut a corner for us. He couldn't do it officially, of course.

174

But he might let me have the information."

"Verbally..."

"Of course. He couldn't do it officially. The manager would be bound to be sticky."

"And you could pass it on to me, if it seemed to indicate..."

"Exactly."

Clark said, "What I have to bear in mind the whole time is that I loathe the man's guts. I've got to try not to let it influence me."

"I wouldn't worry about that, Bob. Once one knows the man's a sadistic swine—you know: what you told Pat and she passed on to Maggie."

"In absolute confidence."

"Certainly. But I think it absolves you from any moral scruples at all. What we used to say in the army, if a man's a bad 'un get rid of him at once. By hook or by crook."

"The police force is different from the army," said Clark gloomily.

17

On the same evening that Superintendent Clark had his conversation with Lionel Talbot a number of other meetings and conversations took place.

Venetia had fallen into the habit of looking in at the Angler's Rest shortly after six o'clock every evening. The landlord, an old friend of regatta days, either shook his head, in which case she took herself off, or nodded it, when she walked through the public bar, practically empty at that hour, and into the private bar, where Mercer would be waiting for her.

They would then have not more than two drinks together, and Mercer would drive her, by different routes, to within walking distance of her house. These detours had tended to get longer, and on this occasion had ended under a group of poplar trees, in a side road a mile from Stoneferry, a spot which Mercer had marked down as suitable for the next stage in a seduction which he was enjoying all the more for its slow and stately tempo. Venetia's mixture of inexperience and frankness made her more attractive than any girl he had yet encountered. He had not yet even kissed her.

He was now sitting in the back of the car, comfortably

pressed up against her. He could sense that she was excited about something.

He said, "You remember the night we first went to that pub? When we ran into your brother in the bar. Did he say anything about it afterward?"

"He made one or two snide comments. I don't pay a lot of attention to what Willoughby says."

"Who was the youth with him?"

"I told you. One of the office boys."

"Does he often go out drinking with the office boys?"

Venetia giggled, and said, "With one at a time. This one's the latest. His name's Quentin."

"Really?"

"You needn't worry about it. He's over whatever age it is makes it all right."

"I wasn't worrying," said Mercer. "I was just thinking what singularly innocent old gentlemen our Victorian ancestors were."

"Innocent?"

"Not personally innocent. In spite of their white beards and churchgoing, I imagine their personal habits were unspeakable. I meant the guys like Arnold who set up all that public school stuff, thinking it would be a bulwark of church and empire."

"So it was."

"Maybe. But it was a hotbed of vice, too. A training school in perversion. Can you imagine anything in the world more likely to turn an impressionable youth of eighteen into a raging homo than allowing him to beat, ceremonially and in cold blood, a boy of thirteen who he was probably half in love with already. It's the most infallible sex stimulant known to science. It's the sort of thing prostitutes allow rich, tired old men to do to them in discreet flats off Piccadilly."

"Do they?" asked Venetia. "I didn't know."

There was a long and comfortable silence.

Then she said, "Have you ever beaten anyone? Hard, I mean. To hurt them."

"Why do you ask that?"

"Oh, just something I heard."

"Tell me."

"I didn't believe it."

"Then tell me what you didn't believe."

"That when you were the head policeman in that place in the Persian Gulf, you used to flog people yourself. Men and women."

He could feel that the idea excited her.

"What else did you hear?"

"That once you—well—that you went too far, and the person you were flogging died."

Mercer said nothing, but she could see that he was smiling.

"Is it true?"

"Certainly."

"How—how did you do it?"

"Oh, their wrists were tied together, and attached to a sort of pulley, and drawn up tight. Then they were stripped to the waist, and you beat them across the back."

"What with?"

"With a sort of whippy cane. Who told you about me killing someone?"

"I won't tell you until you've kissed me."

"It's a stiff price to pay, but I'll pay it."

He kissed her gently on the mouth.

"My best friend, Cathy Moorhouse."

"Who told her?"

"Her aunt."

"Who's her aunt?"

"I won't tell you unless you kiss me properly. . . . Beast! That hurt."

"You asked for it."

"I believe my lip's bleeding."

178

"It's an honorable campaign wound. If you were in the American army you could get a Purple Heart for it. Who is Cathy Moorhouse's aunt?"

"Maggie Talbot. Lionel Talbot's wife."

"Ah," said Mercer. He let out a deep breath. It was like a full stop at the end of a long and complicated sentence. His arm slid up her back. He said, "This is where you take off your bra."

"I took it off ages ago."

When Mercer got home, he found Father Philip Walcot waiting for him, curled up in one of his armchairs and smoking a pipe.

The priest said, "I'm sorry to disturb you out of hours. You must be a very busy man."

"You're welcome at any time," said Mercer.

It was nine o'clock. He was wondering what excuses Venetia had dreamed up for missing supper.

"When you came to see me, you asked me about Sweetie Hedges. I told you all I could about her. At the time."

"You've remembered something more?"

"It's not a question of remembering. I had this in my mind. But I hadn't decided, then, to pass it on."

"Why?"

"Because it came to me under the seal of the confessional."

"But you are prepared to tell me now?"

"I've never held it to be a seal which is unbreakable. For instance, if I could save a life by telling some secret which had been entrusted to me, I should not hesitate to do so. More particularly if the revelation could no longer hurt the man who made it." He smiled disarmingly. "After this prologue of trumpets you are going to find the main theme rather tame, I fear. The man who made his confession to me was Detective Sergeant Rollo. He later

179

took his own life. Incidentally, that doesn't speak well for whatever comfort I was able to give him." Father Philip paused.

"Perhaps I can save you some embarrassment," said Mercer. "Did he, by any chance, confess to you that he had told a lie, in the course of duty, and at the instance of a man to whom he was under some sort of financial obligation?"

"Exactly correct."

Mercer leaned forward and added, "I suppose he didn't, by any chance, happen to mention just who he was obliging."

"No."

"Or what the nature of his obligation was."

"He was scrupulous in avoiding implicating anyone else."

"Understandable, but unfortunate."

"He did, however, say that although the lie was originally innocent, he now realized that it was connected with the death of a girl. That is why I thought it right to tell you. Sergeant Rollo is dead. My breach of confidence can do no harm to him. And it might, I thought, help you. But I see that you knew of it already."

"I didn't *know* it. I suspected it. There's a difference. To have positive confirmation is extremely useful, and I'm obliged to you. Tell me, Father, speaking theologically rather than legally: If A deliberately gets B into his debt; and if he then uses his power to force B to tell a lie; and if consciousness of the lie is one of many reasons which causes B to kill himself, would you call A a murderer?"

"I expect the Jesuits could give you a convincing answer to that. It's beyond me. It's certainly not legal murder. A lot of the worst sorts of killings aren't." Father Walcot uncoiled himself and got up to go. He reached the door before he said, "I nearly forgot. Dolly Grey says you're to watch out."

"Dolly Grey?"

"She's one of the oldest members of my congregation. A dear old soul, who lives across the road from you. She makes a sort of living by letting out rooms. She says that about a fortnight ago a very sinister man took her front room."

"Did she say in what particular way he was sinister?"

"According to Dolly, he was very large."

"That can't have been all."

"And very rough."

"You mean he didn't shave."

"I think by rough she meant the opposite of smooth in appearance and manner."

"I see."

"But her chief criticism was that he didn't seem to have anything to do. He seems to spend most of his time sitting near the window, watching this house. That's why she thought I ought to warn you."

Mercer considered the matter. Then he said, "Tell Dolly that I am very grateful for her information. It's co-operation of this sort between members of the public and the police force which makes our job the pleasure it is."

"If I say it in that tone of voice she'll think you're laughing at her."

"No, no. I really am very grateful."

Evan Pugh was known to his friends as "Dutch" Pugh, not from any connection with Holland, but because he preferred to pay for his own drinks and to let his friends pay for theirs. In the company in which he moved this was considered antisocial, and he was not a popular character, though respected for his handling of the short length of rubber tubing loaded with lead which he carried in a special pocket on the left-hand side inside his coat.

The last person on whom he had used it was still in hospital, unable to speak or see.

As he came out of the bar of the Duke of Cumberland public house, and stood for a moment to accustom his eyes to the dark, someone cannoned into him, nearly knocking him off balance. Pugh swung round, with a selection of obscenity, and advised the man who had bumped into him to watch his step, to mind where he was going, and generally to behave himself.

"Take it easy, cock," said the man. "The pavement doesn't belong to you, does it?"

"Oh, it doesn't, doesn't it?" said Pugh. A couple of shuffling steps brought him within hitting distance. He could see the man more clearly now. He was big, but Pugh had cut down bigger men than he. The fingers of his right hand closed round the rubber grip of his favorite weapon. At this moment something hit him on the back of the neck. It hit him so hard that he had no clear impression of what happened next, but when the inside of his head stopped swinging round inside his skull and he had blinked his eyes open, he realized that he was sitting in the front seat of an old sedan, beside the driver.

As he shifted in his seat, a bland voice from the back of the car said, "I shouldn't do anything you'd regret, Dutchy."

Pugh twisted his head. As the car passed under a street lamp he could see that there were two men in the back. They were both large, and were both smiling. The man who had spoken said, "He's in a delicate state. Shook up. I wouldn't advise him to do anything violent. Would you, Charlie?"

The second man agreed. He said he wouldn't advise it, either. They were like two Harley Street surgeons discussing a difficult case.

Pugh sat still. A purveyor of force, he respected superior force when he ran into it.

182

After about ten minutes the car swung into the courtyard of a big, undistinguished office building and drew up opposite the back entrance. A voice from the rear invited Pugh to dismount. He opened the side door of the car and slid out. For a moment there was no one near him, and he contemplated the possibility of making a bolt for it. As his feet touched the ground, the firm earth rolled under him. He realized that he was in no condition to fight or fly, and followed the men into the building. They went up two flights of uncarpeted stairs, along a corridor, past a few thousand similar doors, and then through a pair of swinging doors which shut off the end of the passage.

The words painted in black on the glass of the left-hand door said MINISTRY OF AGRICULTURE and on the right-hand door, SOFT FRUIT DIVISION. In the room at the end were two men. The one who was sitting on the edge of the table, swinging a leg, he recognized as Chief Superintendent Morrissey, CID head of No. 1 District. The other, seated behind the desk, was a stranger. He looked young enough to be Morrissey's son. He had blue eyes, light hair, and a complexion so delicate that one imagined he would blush very easily. His name was John Anderson, and when Vidall died and Morrissey was promoted he was destined to become one of the most feared gang-breakers in England.

Morrissey said, "Sit down, Pugh."

Pugh said, "You've got no right to do this to me. That man hit me. It's unlawful. What am I supposed to have done? I haven't heard no charge yet."

"No difficulty about a charge, if you insist. Carrying an offensive weapon."

Pugh's hand went to his coat. The cosh was no longer there. One of the men who had brought him in laid the length of rubber tubing gently on the table beside Morrissey. "That's right, sir. In his inside pocket."

"Resisting arrest?"

"That's true, too, sir. Took a definite swing at me, didn't he, Charlie?"

"He certainly did."

"Driving a stolen car, too."

"That's a lie. I never had no stolen car. I never had no car at all. What are you talking about?"

"The car you came here in. Stolen twenty-four hours ago. Covered with your fingerprints."

Pugh started to say something, and stopped. The floor had started rocking again. Morrissey said, "Sit down, Pugh. All right, you two, I'll deal with this. Now you listen to me, Pugh, or Taylor, or whatever you call yourself. We've been watching you. You've been working at the Hexagon Garage, haven't you?"

"So what! It's a job, isn't it?"

"How much do they pay you?"

"That's my business."

Morrissey lumbered to his feet, came across until he was standing over Pugh, and said, "I'm not a very patient man. If I have any more lip from you, you're going to be in dead trouble."

"Twenty pounds a week."

"All right. And how much do the Crows pay you on the side? How much did they pay you for that job you did down in Stoneferry?"

Nearly three hours later, Morrissey said, "All right, you can go now," and Pugh clambered to his feet. He was a badly puzzled man. He had been questioned by the police before, but never quite in that way. He had told them very little. But they seemed to have told him quite a lot. If they knew about Stoneferry, it was a fair bet they knew about other things. That was important. It would have to be passed on at once. When he reached the ground floor, there was no one about. The back door was open. The car had gone. The streets round the office were quiet and empty under their neon lights. He had no idea where he was, except that his instinct told him he was still south of the river. He padded off down the street.

From their second-story window the two policemen watched him go.

"Do you think he'll fall for it?" said Anderson. "I thought you laid it on a bit thick."

"He's got a thick head," said Morrissey.

"He has that," agreed Anderson. "I'd say he was still concussed, too."

"If you want my guess, he'll go into the first telephone booth he finds, and ring Paul Crow."

When the telephone rang, the man rolled over in bed, cursed, turned on the bedside light, and sat up. He was middle-aged, thick but not fat, and had a white face and black hair streaked at the edges with gray. The girl in bed beside him muttered something and he said, "Shut up, and go to sleep." And into the telephone, "Yes, what is it?" As the thick voice at the other end rumbled on, the man's face remained impassive. A very close observer might have noticed a slight tightening of the mouth, a wariness in the eyes. He said, "What was that name again? The new man at Stoneferry. Mercer! All right. Go on." Later he said, "Just where are you? A telephone box in Paxton Street, S.E. Right. Stay where you are. I'm sending a car for you." He rang off, dialed a number, and spoke to someone he called Mo. His instructions were clear and categorical. As he rang off the girl said, "Do you have to do business in the middle of the night?"

"I do business when I like, sweetness. And I make love when I like."

He pulled her toward him. The girl said, "For God's sake! You're insatiable."

Calling Cards 201 774 0020 9816

809 774 8784 Aaroon Benjamin

tomorrow morn

18

On the following morning, too, a lot of things happened.

A photograph of a man coming out of a garage was sent by Telephoto to the Isle of Wight. A police officer took it to a terrace of small houses overlooking the sea, near Ryde, and showed it to a man who was spending a fortnight in one of them with his aunt. The man's left arm was in a sling, and there was a heavy bandage round his wrist.

He examined the photograph carefully and said, "Yes, that's Taylor, all right. He looks a bit older, but I'd recognize him anywhere. Do I have to make a statement about it, or something? Because I'm not keen on getting involved."

The policeman said he didn't know anything about that. All he'd been told to do was to get a positive identification.

Other photographs were being examined that morning.

A middle-aged man, who was wearing a blue suit and a bowler hat but still carried the stamp of past military service about him, was shown into the new Defense Ministry building in Whitehall and taken, after a minimum of delay, to a big room with a skylight on the sixth floor.

Here he met a corporal from the Records Section of the 1939–45 war, who had laid out a number of photographs on a table. He said, "Would you start on these, Mr. Sykes? If you don't have any luck we've got a lot more, but these are the most likely ones."

Some of the photographs were formal groups. Some were informal snapshots. Each of them had a reference number and a letter on them.

"I didn't know you went in for this sort of thing," said Sykes.

"Very useful, sir. You'd be surprised how many men we've traced through them. Men who served under another name. Or changed their names when they left the army. They couldn't change their faces."

"That's me!" said Sykes. "I wish I was as thin as that now."

A few minutes later he said, "I think this is the one you want."

It was a group of men dressed in service overalls, with the light-blue insignia of the Para Corps sewn over the breast pocket. Some of them were squatting on the ground, others were standing behind them. Their faces were upturned and serious. It looked as though they were listening to a briefing.

"That one must have been taken when we were at Lakenheath, getting ready for operations at Arnhem. That's Jack Bull, all right. One of the best. He collected a Spandau burst in his arm, and it had to be taken off."

There was another man in the room, in plain clothes, young and fresh-faced, who spoke with a Scots accent. He said, "Can you put a name to any of the others, Major?"

"At one time I could have done you the lot," said Sykes. "But a quarter of a century is a hell of a long time."

"We could let you have a nominal roll of the unit if it would help," said the corporal.

The Scotsman said, "It'd be better if he made the identification himself. We can check up on the roll later."

"Is there anyone you're particularly interested in?"

"Yes. The man on Bull's right."

"Oh, well, no difficulty about that. He really *was* a character. I often wondered what had become of him in peacetime. . . ."

Mercer dialed a number, and breathed a sigh of relief when it was a woman's voice that answered.

He said, "Is that you, Mrs. Prior? Mercer here."

"Mercer?"

"Detective Inspector Mercer."

"Oh."

The drop in temperature was perceptible even over the telephone line.

"Something has come up. I wanted a word with you about it."

"You promised me you'd leave us alone."

"I know I did. I'm not trying to involve you in anything. But there's just one piece of information I *must* have. It's not really something I could discuss on the telephone."

"I don't think—"

"You remember that teashop. The room at the back is perfectly private."

"I'm not sure—"

"I could come out to your house, but the trouble is my car would certainly be recognized."

"No—no. Don't come out here."

A voice in the background said, "Who is it, dear?

Who's that on the telephone?"

"It's the laundry. There's been some muddle over the sheets. I'll have to go and sort it out." And to Mercer, "Very well."

"As quick as you can."

Twenty minutes later, he was stirring a cup of coffee and pacifying an angry Mrs. Prior.

"We're getting near the end of the track now," he said. "And if everything goes as I hope it will, two of the people who'll get what's coming to them are the men who assaulted your husband."

"I hope so," said Mrs. Prior, through thin lips. "I most certainly hope so."

Looking at her, it occurred to Mercer that, if they had consulted Mrs. Prior, the theorists who maintained that punishment should be reformative and not retributive might have been considerably shaken in their views.

"What are you smiling at?"

"Nothing," said Mercer. "Just a thought. Look, what I wanted to know was this. When you had that lawsuit brought against you by the motorist whose car Taylor—his real name's Pugh, by the way—was supposed to have repaired, what exactly happened?"

"How do you mean, what happened?"

"Let's take it in steps. First a writ was served, right? Then you must have had a number of conferences with Weatherman."

"We saw him the first time. After that it was mostly dealt with by his litigation department."

"Meaning who?"

"There was an elderly man, rather deaf. I think his name was Pollock. But most of the work was done by a young woman. She seemed to know her stuff all right. I didn't like her much."

"Would her name have been Maureen Dyson?"

"Yes. That's right. I remember the reference on all the

189

letters was M.D. I'd nothing against her. I think she worked very hard. It was just her manner. I don't think Mr. Weatherman liked her much, either. I remember at the last conference we had before the case was due to come to court, she actually suggested that the whole thing might have been a put-up job, and Mr. Weatherman shut her up pretty sharply."

"Now why would he do that?"

"He said it was pointless bringing vague accusations like that if we couldn't support them. He said it would put the court against us, and drag out the proceedings and make them much more expensive. Actually, it was after that conference we decided to settle."

Mercer leaned forward, his elbows on the table. He said, "This is vitally important. I want you to tell me everything you can remember about that last conference. Who said what to who, and why."

"Oh, dear," said Mrs. Prior. "I'll do my best." As she talked, a thick skim of milk formed over two untasted cups of coffee.

John Anderson said, "We were on target there, all right. His old company commander identified Jack Bull."

"A bull's eye, in fact," said Morrissey. He was given to making bad puns when he was pleased.

"And guess who was sitting right next to him."

"You tell me. I can see you're happy about it."

"It was Paul Crow."

"Ah," said Morrissey softly. "Yes. That explains a lot, doesn't it? Dear old Paul. We knew he had a service background, but we could never trace it. What name was he using?"

"Barker. Ron Barker."

Morrissey had unlocked the steel filing cabinet behind him and was looking through a bulging cardboard folder.

"You've asked the army to send us copies of everything they've got?"

"They're sending a messenger down with it. I picked up something else this morning. It came from Ernie Milton. He says that the field squad is being mobilized, for action this evening, he thinks. And outside London. Mo Fenton would be in charge."

"Ernie's information is usually reliable." Morrissey was rummaging through the contents of the folder, which seemed to contain a large assortment of typewritten documents, photographs, blue and buff forms, and newspaper clippings. "It was Ernie who put us onto Stoneferry in the first place, I seem to remember." He found the paper he was looking for. "Getting on for a year ago."

"That is so," said Anderson. He repressed a sigh. Every time Morrissey looked through one of his files it took him ten minutes to put it together again in proper chronological order. "It looks as if that fly you cast over Pugh has been snapped up. Incidentally, if tonight's party is not a success, he'll be in trouble himself."

"Pugh's troubles are over," said Morrissey. "He was picked up this morning on the Great West Road. He'd been run over by a very heavy lorry. More than once. It was lucky they found some papers in his pocket. They confirmed the identification from fingerprints. There wasn't a lot of his face left."

Mercer called on Mr. Weatherman that afternoon. Knowing the ways of solicitors, he had telephoned first, and been given a grudging appointment for three o'clock. When he arrived at the office in Fore Street, the receptionist apologized for keeping him waiting. She said confidingly, "Mr. Weatherman's busy with Mrs. Hall. She's our head cashier. There's been some muddle over accounts. Papers getting lost. You know how these things happen."

Mercer said he knew how those things happened.

It was nearly half past three when a buzzer sounded, and he was invited to go in. He met Mrs. Hall coming down. She was frowning, and there was a slight flush over her prominent cheekbones. She recognized Mercer, and gave him a smile.

Mr. Weatherman apologized briefly for keeping Mercer waiting and motioned him to a chair. This, Mercer noted, was placed directly in front of the desk, which stood in the bay window. The effect of this was that Mr. Weatherman could study his face, while his own remained obscure. He said, "I gather you've been dealing with an office crisis."

Mr. Weatherman said, "A minor one. Some accountancy records seem to have gone astray. I'm sure Mrs. Hall will be able to deal with it."

"Yes indeed. I remember you telling me what an efficient person she was."

"Quite so. Now what can I do for you, Inspector?" He didn't actually add, "I'm a very busy man."

Mercer smiled politely. He said, "It's strange how many of the jobs in offices which used to be male preserves are now carried out by women."

Mr. Weatherman said nothing, and his expression was hidden. But Mercer saw that he had raised his chin very slightly and seemed to be busy rearranging the pencils on his desk. He went on, at the same leisurely pace. "I believe I am right in saying that toward the end of her time here, your litigation department was practically run by Miss Dyson."

"Until his retirement, and death, last year the litigation department of this firm was run by Mr. Pollock."

Mr. Weatherman's voice was cold.

"He was, I believe, over seventy. It would have been natural for him to have passed on a good deal of the responsibility to a younger colleague."

192

"Do you mind telling me exactly what you want, Inspector?"

If Mercer noted the icy hostility in Mr. Weatherman's voice he was apparently unperturbed by it. He continued in the same unhurried way. "What I want is what policemen are always eager to have. Information."

Mr. Weatherman had nothing to say to this.

"I understand that a conference took place here in connection with the Prior garage case. Mr. Pollock was not present, but no doubt he was—ah—controlling matters from the background. But Miss Dyson *was* at the meeting and she made a suggestion. She suggested that, possibly, the whole matter had been rigged. That it was a put-up job. I don't know if she went as far as to suggest *who* had rigged the job, but there was one obvious candidate, the owner of the only remaining garage in Stoneferry, Mr. Bull."

Mr. Weatherman was not only silent; he was completely motionless. He had slightly turned his head and Mercer had the impression of a black profile against the gray of the window.

"I understand, however, that this suggestion of Miss Dyson's did not find favor with you, and was not followed up. Is that so?"

Mr. Weatherman said, "Your ignorance of the law seems to be equaled only by your gaucheness. You must be aware that I am quite unable, even if I wished, to answer questions about my clients' affairs."

"It wasn't really their affairs I was asking about," said Mercer mildly. "It was your own reactions. Did it never occur to you to wonder *why* Miss Dyson made such a suggestion? And, if it was based on information, *how* she had got that information." He paused, and added, "Of course, Mr. Bull was your client, too, wasn't he?"

"I am not without influence in this town," said Mr. Weatherman. "Unless you leave this office at once, I shall telephone Superintendent Clark."

"You can do better than that," said Mercer. "Why not ring up the Chairman of Magistrates, Lionel Talbot? You act for him, too, I believe."

Massey had not found the watching easy. There was, on this occasion, no conveniently vacant building over the way. His own aged sports car would, he realized, be too conspicuous. In the end he had parked it round the corner, and managed to keep the tobacconist's shop under observation by making occasional trips on foot down the road.

Mercer had arrived at dusk. Fortunately he arrived when Massey was at the far end of the road. He had stayed in the shop for about fifteen minutes. As soon as he had driven off, Massey had moved in.

The proprietor was behind the counter, sorting out a late batch of evening papers. Massey saw a man in early middle age, with a brown and cheerful face. His shirt sleeves were rolled up to show a pair of thick forearms with an army insignia tattooed on each. He said, "And what can I do for you, sir?"

Massey had been considering his tactics. He was, he knew, on delicate ground. He had decided to be official, but friendly. He produced his identification card, and said, "I'm a police officer. It's been reported to us that the man who has just left is in the habit of coming here regularly, in the evenings. You understand that you're under no obligation to answer any questions, but if you can help us, and trouble does arise, we can probably help you."

Massey was rather pleased with his speech. He had, he thought, put the situation neatly. The proprietor seemed to be weighing things up. He said, "From what he told me, the other gentleman is a police officer, too."

"That's correct. But I'm afraid that proceedings are

pending against him. Disciplinary proceedings, you understand. These things happen from time to time. Mostly they're kept very quiet."

"Yes, I understand that," said the proprietor.

"And the names of people who help us can usually be kept out of the record altogether."

The proprietor said, "Ah." He appeared to be arriving at some sort of decision. Massey prayed that no one would come into the shop.

"You understand, I only did it to oblige."

"Did what?"

"Took in letters for him. And let him use my telephone. Little things like that."

"Nothing else?"

The man hesitated. Massey noticed his glance shifting toward the old iron safe, under the shelf behind the counter. He had an inspiration.

"You didn't look after anything for him, did you?"

"Well, yes," said the man. "There was a package. He said he didn't trust the people he was staying with, you see."

"Did you know what was in it?"

"I never asked. Why should I?"

"Of course not. Could I see it?"

"I couldn't let you do that. Not without his permission."

"I only want to look at it. I'm not going to take it away."

The proprietor hesitated. Then he opened a drawer and took out a ring of keys. With the largest of them he unlocked the safe, and after what seemed to Massey to be interminable deliberation drew out a sealed manila envelope and laid it on the counter.

Massey picked it up.

"I don't think you ought to open it. Not without him being here," said the proprietor anxiously.

"That's all right," said Massey. He ripped open the flap. A wad of new one-pound notes slid out onto the counter.

"Well, that's that," said Lionel Talbot. "You've got it both ways. First, we know from Derek Robbins that three deposits of fifty pounds each have been made in Mercer's bank account. And the first one was made the morning after he'd spent the evening talking to Jack Bull at that public house."

"Yes."

"Now we know that he's got at least one other cache that he visits secretly."

"I suppose I shall have to make an official report."

"You'd be failing in your duty if you didn't," said Talbot. He said it with considerable satisfaction.

19

"WHAT THE HELL'S up with everyone this morning?" said Gwilliam.

Prothero said, "In what way?"

"When I came in, when Tovey-luvvy saw me, he had a grin all over his stupid face. Like he'd won the Treble Chance or something."

"Funny you should say that," said Prothero. "I got the same idea. Nothing pleases the bluebottles like we're in a right mess up here. What do you think?"

Sergeant Gwilliam lowered his massive form onto a small chair, which squeaked in protest, and disposed himself to consider the matter. He said, "Bob Clark's got his knife into the skipper. But there's nothing new about that. They've been cat and dog ever since he arrived."

"Nor the skipper doesn't strain a gut trying to be matey, neither."

"He's not too easy to get on with," agreed Gwilliam. "I grant you that."

"And Bob's getting old. He's got an eye on that sunny day when they hand him his first pension check, and he can stay in bed as long as he likes next morning. You know why our crime figures are so low? For the last few years, if there's been any doubt, Bob's idea has been don't count it as a crime. That way, he's got a nice quiet little manor. Then Mercer comes along, and bingo! Before he knows where he is, he's up shit creek without a paddle. You've got to be sorry for the old sod, really. Did you see this? It was in the papers last night."

It was an imaginative effort by the cartoonist. It showed Sowthistle, with a black patch over one eye and a cocked hat on his head, booting a black-coated civil servant carrying a briefcase labeled "Ministry of Interference" off the deck of his barge and into the river. The caption underneath said, "The Nelson Spirit."

"It beats me," said Gwilliam. "Here's this old toe rag, living in a pigsty, making money by flogging dirt, pissed as a newt most days by lunch time, and the way people carry on about him he might be Saint George for Merry England."

"Here comes the boy scout," said Prothero. "Maybe he can tell us what's up."

Detective Massey was looking serious. He said, "What's up about what?"

"Taffy and me both got the idea that our chums in blue were sitting downstairs rubbing their hands together like they'd heard we'd dropped a great big clanger. What about it?"

"I did hear," said Massey, "off the record, that Mercer was in some sort of trouble."

The other two looked at him.

"You never really hit it off with the skipper, did you?" said Gwilliam.

"He's been picking on me ever since he got here," said Massey. "Not that it signifies. Because he's on his way out."

"Then you do know something," said Prothero.

"Out with it, laddie," said Gwilliam.

"Well—" Massey stopped as the door opened and Mercer came in. He stood for a moment, viewing his three subordinates. All had fallen strangely silent and seemed to be absorbed in their work. Mercer grinned. Then he tiptoed across the room to his desk, humming the opening bars of a funeral march. Lowering his voice almost to a whisper, he said, "Who are we in mourning for, eh?"

Gwilliam said, "We heard Bob died—of laughing. He saw that cartoon in the papers last night."

"That," said Mercer. "I saw it. Not very funny really. Did you get what I wanted in Slough, Taffy?"

"I'm not sure if it's what you wanted, but I got something." Gwilliam unrolled the map on the table. "There's not a lot of places in that area would be open at nine o'clock at night. There's two pubs and one drink shop with a late license, but I don't suppose Johnno went all that way to fetch back a bottle of booze, do you?"

Mercer shook his head.

"Then there's a workingman's club. On the corner there. That was open. All the other side of the street is offices and suchlike. All tight shut."

"And that block along the other side?"

"That's the Southern Counties Safe Deposit."

"Which was also shut?"

"Yes and no. You couldn't get in, but there was a night safe. If you had anything to deposit, you labeled it and pushed it down the slot, and the management would look after it for you until you could stow it away in your box, I imagine."

Mercer said, "That'd be the sort of arrangement." He swung round on Massey. "When you were watching that night, did you get the number of the car? The last one that came in before Johnno shut up shop."

"No. I'm afraid I didn't."

"Why not?"

"I was watching Johnno. Not the customers."

"You've forgotten the rules, lad. When on observation, never assume what's important and what isn't. Write it *all* down. Didn't they teach you that?"

"I suppose so," muttered Massey. He didn't look up from the form he was filling in. Mercer watched him for a few seconds in silence, then said to Gwilliam, "If anyone should want me—by any chance—I'm going over to Slough. I should be back in about an hour."

"There's a message from Brattle at the boathouse. You could look him up on your way."

"All right," said Mercer. "I'll do that, too. Let's say an hour and a quarter." He moved out, and closed the door softly.

"He knows," said Prothero.

"And he doesn't care," said Gwilliam.

Massey said nothing. He seemed to have got the form wrong. He tore it up and dropped the pieces inthe wastepaper basket.

Mr. Brattle was sitting in an old chair outside his boathouse. He waved a hand at Mercer, who took it as an invitation to make himself at home, and squatted on top of an upturned dinghy.

"I found something out for you, son," he said. "It's probably not important, but you never can tell. I once read in a book that when you're investigating a crime, any little detail can be the vital link in the chain."

"I must introduce you to Detective Massey," said Mercer. "You could teach him a thing or two."

"I do a lot of reading in the winter, when I've got the boats cleaned up and put away. I don't care for this modern stuff."

"I don't read a lot myself," said Mercer.

It was a perfect autumn day. The sunlight was gilding the leaves of the poplars, already yellowed by the turn of the year.

"You don't know what you're missing." Mr. Brattle

gazed fondly at the river. Scarcely a breath of wind troubled the smooth brown surface of the water that slid past at their feet. The river was so low that the sluice gate had been shut and the roar of the weir had sunk to a distant mumbling. A family of swans advanced in line astern along the far bank. The father and mother were followed by four bobbity cygnets. They had lost their brown baby plumage and were beginning to have the look of youngsters sneering at the apron strings. Fifty yards away, on their side of the river, a solitary fisherman reeled in his line, jerked the red float upstream, and let it go. The silence was so complete that they could hear the *plop* of the float as it hit the water.

"Eighteen eighty-seven," said Mr. Brattle. "The year of the old Queen's Golden Jubilee. That was when my grandfather opened his boathouse. The girls used to wear bustles and carry parasols and the men wore straw hats. Do you remember that book about the three men who took a trip on the river with a dog? It was well known in its day."

Mercer racked his brain but could recall no such book. He realized it was going to spoil Mr. Brattle's story if he said so, and nodded his head.

"The man who wrote it used to hire his boat from my grandfather. Very humorous, so I'm told. When my grandfather died, my father took over. Then me. I had the one son, but he was killed in the war."

Mercer looked at the old man, and decided that he wasn't asking for sympathy. He was stating facts.

"Even if he had come back, I don't know that he'd have fancied this job. He had ambitions."

"He didn't know what was good for him, then."

"If you ever thought of retiring from the police force, you might consider it yourself."

Mercer said, "Don't be surprised if I take you up on that," and got up. Mr. Brattle said, "Damned if I didn't nearly forget what I got you down here to tell you. Mrs. Prior said you were asking about that boat. Diesel-powered twenty-footer. I asked one or two of my friends down the river. She comes from Lock's at Teddington. One of the residents has her on hire for the season. Man of the name of Fenton."

"Mo Fenton," said Mercer softly. The scar showed red.

"My friend did say that he had a bit of a reputation. Maybe nothing to it. You know the way people talk. Anyway, he didn't like him much."

"If Fenton's the man I'm thinking of," said Mercer, "you can tell your friend from me, he's dead right."

The fisherman seemed to have caught something. It looked like a fair-sized chub or dace, maybe a barbel.

Mr. Nevinson, the manager of the Southern Counties Safe Deposit, received Mercer in his office. *Received* seemed the appropriate word. Mr. Nevinson, in early middle age, had acquired that regal air which comes upon a man who has a job which suits him, is secure in it, and can see an untroubled road stretching ahead of him to retirement.

He invited Mercer to be seated, contemplated offering him a cigarette out of the silver box on his desk, and decided against it. He said, "Well, now, Inspector. What can I do for you?"

"It's good of you to see me at such short notice," said Mercer.

Mr. Nevinson inclined his head. He thought it was good of him, too.

"I realize that a relationship of confidence exists between you and your clients." Mercer was choosing his words with care. *Clients* was a lot more dignified than *customers*.

"Certainly," said Mr. Nevinson. "At Southern Coun-

202

ties we endeavor to observe exactly the same rules that govern our banking institutions."

Right, thought Mercer. *And those same rules can be a real pain in the neck to hard-working policemen.* He said, "I appreciate your position. You look after a lot of money and valuables for people, and they've got to have confidence in you. I see that. And that's why I'm only going to ask you questions it won't embarrass you to answer. First, can you simply tell me if you have a client of the name of Jack Bull, from Stoneferry?" As Mr. Nevinson hesitated, Mercer said, "I could, of course, find out for myself, by putting a man permanently outside the door to see if Bull or any of his employees turned up, but that'd take time, and I haven't much time to spare."

Mr. Nevinson weighed the possibility of indescretion against the embarrassment of having a policeman scrutinizing his customers, and said, "Yes. I don't think there could be any objection to my answering that question. Mr. Bull of the Stoneferry Garage is one of our oldest clients. When I came here twenty years ago he was renting a strongbox. He now has a small strong room."

"Can you tell me when he changed over?"

"The exact date, you mean?"

"Approximately."

"As I recollect, three or four years ago."

"If *I* were a client, and wanted to rent a safe, how much would it cost me?"

Mr. Nevinson extracted a brochure from his desk, smoothed the pages, and said, "It would depend on the cubic capacity of the receptacle. A medium-sized strongbox, eighteen inches square by two foot deep, would cost you forty-five pounds a year to rent. A strong room is a good deal more expensive, of course. The smallest would cost you two hundred fifty pounds a year."

"I see," said Mercer.

If Bull was renting even a small strong room it was

costing him nearly a fiver a week. It seemed a lot of money for a garage proprietor. A lot of space, too.

He said, "I imagine you keep a duplicate key for each safe and strong room. Or is it one master key for the lot?"

"Neither, Inspector."

"I don't follow you."

"Each lock is unique. And there is only one key in existence for each. That is held, of course, by the renter. We could not contemplate any other system. If we held a key, the responsibility on us would far outweigh the occasional convenience."

"But what happens if the renter loses the key?"

"It happens very rarely."

"But it must happen sometimes."

"Yes," said Mr. Nevinson. "Well—I don't suppose there's any harm in your knowing this, but the information is, of course, extremely confidential. I keep, in my safe, a set of templates which can be fixed to the exterior face of the locked door. They enable us to locate, with minute accuracy, the position of the metal rivets on the *inside* of the door which hold the locking mechanism in position. We can then punch out the rivets from this side. The whole operation costs the renter twenty-five pounds. You'd be surprised how carefully that makes him look after his key."

"If you've got no key to the safes, how does the night service operate?"

"Very simply. All depositors have code numbers. They mark night deposits with that number and we keep them for them, in a central strong room, of which *we* hold the key. When the depositor pays us his next visit, he can himself transfer his property to his private safe."

Mercer thought about it. Then he said, "Could you get one of your staff to show me the strong rooms? Tell him I'm a prospective customer."

"I'll show you round myself," said Mr. Nevinson.

He walked across to the paneling and opened a door. Behind it was a steel grille.

"You've got to realize," he said, "that above ground everything is quite normal. We have bars on the ground-floor windows and an alarm on the front door, but so do a lot of office buildings." He pushed the grille, which swung back ponderously on its roller-bearing hinges. "It's only below ground that we begin to be something out of the ordinary. After you."

A flight of stone steps led down into a basement. Mr. Nevinson touched a switch and the neon strip lighting came on, showing a long line of numbered, green-painted steel boxes on either side of a central corridor. There were further sections of boxes arranged in bays behind the corridor.

"Fireproof paint," said Mr. Nevinson, "and the boxes themselves are waterproof. The floor you're standing on is steel latticework. There's a subbasement below this which holds the strong rooms. The whole subterranean area is hermetically sealed and surrounded by a water jacket. In the unlikely event of a fire starting down here, we would shutter off the air-conditioning vents and flood the whole place, ceiling high in five minutes. Just a matter of turning two wheels in my office."

"You mean that we're in a sealed box, surrounded by water?"

"That's right. It really is rather ingenious. The water jacket stops anyone trying to tunnel in from outside. They could of course try getting through the ceiling, or the floor, but they are alternate steel and specially hardened concrete. I don't say they couldn't do it. Modern tools will cut anything. But it would take a very long time. This way."

They went down the second flight of stairs into the subbasement. This was arranged on a similar plan except that the doors were larger, and completely filled the central corridor.

"Twenty strong rooms on each side. The two very large ones at the end are used by the banks. They are *much* more secure than their own."

"And the smaller ones belong to private renters?"

"That's right."

Mercer wondered which of the green-painted doors concealed Jack Bull's secrets. He would have liked to ask, but felt that he had trespassed far enough on Mr. Nevinson's patience. They climbed back to his office.

"I take it there is another entrance?"

"Certainly. There is the main entrance to the vaults. That's the one the renters use. My head guard, Sergeant Beale, has one key. I have another. To open it, you need to use both."

"And this door?"

"The same. When it is finally shut for the night you need both our keys to open it."

When Mercer got out into the street he made for the nearest telephone box and rang up Stoneferry station. Tom Rye answered him.

Mercer said, "In case anyone is wondering where I am, tell them I've been having a conducted tour round a safe deposit. It took longer than I anticipated, but it was very interesting. I now propose to have some lunch. After lunch I've got a date with a Mr. Michael Robertson."

Rye said, "O.K. There's no particular panic on here at the moment." And then, "Did you say Michael Robertson?"

"That's right," said Mercer. "Michael Robertson."

20

THE EARLY afternoon post delivered two trade catalogues and a small buff envelope to Bull's Garage. Jack Bull was alone in the office when they arrived. Vikki had telephoned to say that she was feeling under the weather and wouldn't be turning up for work that day.

Opening letters was one of the more difficult jobs for a one-armed man, but Bull managed it, as deftly as he had taught himself to get over most difficulties.

He read the catalogues first, marking one or two items that interested him. Then he opened the buff envelope.

Ten minutes later he was storming down the High Street and into Fore Street. The receptionist at Weathermans said she wasn't sure if Mr. Weatherman was free. Had Mr. Bull an appointment?

"I haven't got an appointment," said Bull. "But I'm going to see Mr. Weatherman even if it means turning out the person who's with him. Tell him that, will you?"

The receptionist was frightened. She found angry men alarming. She picked up the telephone, and said, as calmly as she could bring herself to do, "Oh, Mr. Weatherman, I have Mr. Bull here for you. He says it's *very* urgent."

There was a slight pause, and then Mr. Weatherman's

dry voice said, "If it's very urgent, of course I must see him. Ask him to come up."

Mr. Weatherman smoothed out the buff-colored letter which Bull had slammed down on his desk and read it through carefully. Then he adjusted his glasses and read it again.

He said, "This is very surprising."

"Surprising," said Bull, in a choked voice. "It's a bloody impertinence. What the hell does it mean?"

"It means that the Inland Revenue authorities have come to the conclusion, on the basis of certain evidence which has come into their possession, that you have been understating your taxable income for the last six years by approximately three thousand pounds a year. This is, they agree, only a rough estimate. They have accordingly raised a provisional assessment on you, to tax and surtax, based on a figure of eighteen thousand pounds. They invite your comments, and point out the procedure for appeal. I take it you have only just received this?"

"A quarter of an hour ago."

"And that you haven't done anything about it?"

"Like hell I haven't. I rang up the Charlie whose reference is on that letter and told him he could stuff it up his arse."

"I don't think that was wise," said Mr. Weatherman.

"What do you mean, wise? What the hell did you expect me to do? Write him out a check for the full amount?"

"The procedures for appeal are well established."

Bull, who had been standing, now sat down. He also lowered his voice. He said, "I think we'd better understand one another. *You* know perfectly well that I've been fiddling my tax returns for years. You've been helping me to do it. And taking a thick cut for your pains. So don't start talking about the procedure for appeals. If anything comes out, everything comes out. You're a professional man. You've got a bloody sight more to lose in this case than I have."

"Are you threatening me?"

"Certainly I'm threatening you. And when I said everything, I meant everything. Like that little job you did for me over Prior's garage. I expect the Law Society would be interested to know that you acted for the poor old sod but never told him you were taking money from me, under the counter, to make sure he went down."

Mr. Weatherman's face had been a mottled red when Bull began speaking. By the time he finished it had lost most of its color. He said, "If you were to say . . . anything like that, I'd take you through every court in the land for libel."

"Even if I could prove it was true?"

"You couldn't."

"I most certainly could. You remember that girl you had working here? Called Maureen Dyson. She was a smart operator. Did you know she'd tapped your office telephone? And not only tapped it, but recorded some of the interesting conversations we had. And taken a photograph of that harmless little bit of paper you made me sign and locked away in your safe. Only like the stupid old berk you are, you left the key of the safe in your desk drawer. She had the whole thing lined up. She sent me copies of one or two of the transcriptions and documents. I've still got them. They're very convincing. There was just one thing I couldn't understand. Why the hell did she try it on me and not you? You'd have paid up. Wouldn't you? . . . Wouldn't you?"

"Please keep your voice down. What did you do?"

"I told her to take a running jump at herself. The only person who could make trouble for *me* would be old Henry Prior, and I doubted if he'd have the guts. But you—it'd be different for you, wouldn't it? You'd be finished. You'd be struck off the whatsits. You'd be flat bust.

209

Why didn't she put the screws on you!"

When Mr. Weatherman said nothing, he added, thoughtfully, "Or did she?"

Mr. Weatherman's face was now an unhealthy grayish white. He said, in a voice which was a parody of his normal pedantic tones, "I can assure you that she never said a word to me about it. I can equally assure you that I shall never repeat a word of what you have just told me."

"Right," said Bull. "Now we understand each other. So perhaps we can get down to business. What does this letter mean? And what do we do about it?"

"It means that the Revenue have some evidence that you have been understating your income." Mr. Weatherman was speaking slowly, drawing a breath after every few words, as though he had surfaced after an unexpectedly deep dive. "Very often they take this sort of action because a man is observed to be living beyond the income he has declared. That can hardly be the case here. You have a substantial income, and you have always behaved discreetly."

"Right. So what do they mean by 'evidence'?"

"It must, I think, be documentary evidence of some kind. I have all the papers here which deal with your declared income—"

"And I've got a few books and papers in my office," said Bull with a grin, "which deal with my undeclared income."

"They'd need a sight of both lists to bring a charge home." Mr. Weatherman lifted the receiver on his internal telephone and dialed a number. "We'll go through our records here first. Oh, Miss Atkins, would you ask Mrs. Hall to bring up the folders containing Mr. Bull's tax returns. She's what? Oh, I see. Well, then, perhaps you could bring them up yourself." He replaced the receiver and said, "My invaluable Mrs. Hall is away sick this morning. It's the first day she's missed since she's

210

been here. Never mind; Miss Atkins will produce them for us."

But that, it appeared, was just what Miss Atkins could not do. When she appeared in the room three minutes later she was flustered, and empty-handed. She said, "I've looked in Mrs. Hall's filing cabinet, Mr. Weatherman. I know she kept Mr. Bull's tax returns and papers there, in two folders, because she looked after them herself. They aren't there."

"Are you sure?"

"Quite sure, Mr. Weatherman. I know just where she kept them. I saw them there only last week. Do you think she might have taken them home to work on them? She did that sometimes."

"It would be against our rules for any member of the staff to remove confidential papers from the office. However, it's a possibility, I suppose. Have you her telephone number?"

Miss Atkins produced the number and Mr. Weatherman dialed it. They could hear the telephone ringing. It rang for a long time. Mr. Weatherman replaced the receiver. He said, "When Mrs. Hall informed the office that she was not coming in today, who took the message?"

"I did."

"How did the message arrive?"

"She telephoned. Just after I got here. She said she had a bad migraine, was going to take a couple of pills and go to bed."

"She has a small furnished flat, I believe."

"That's right."

"If the telephone is in the living room, and she is asleep—very fast asleep—in her bedroom, it is, I suppose, possible that she would not hear the telephone."

"Would you like me to go round and make sure that she's all right?"

"I was just going to suggest it," said Mr. Weatherman smoothly.

When Miss Atkins had taken herself off, Bull said, "What's she playing at? Don't tell me you've got *another* blackmailer on your staff."

"I think it highly unlikely. Mrs. Hall is a most respectable and reliable sort of woman. But even if she has removed the taxation folders with some ulterior motive, it still makes little sense. It's true that there are working papers there, which we should not normally show to the inspector. But to make anything out of them, he would have to compare them with the records of actual receipts which you maintain."

"And if my records didn't happen to be available . . ."

Mr. Weatherman considered the point. He had recovered his self-possession and now seemed to be the dominant partner. He said, "I don't think it would be convincing to say that there were *no* records. After all, we would have had to get the figures from you in the first place. And *all* businesses keep accounts. Cash receipts, expenditure, bank statements, and that sort of thing."

"My bank statements won't show them much. I encourage my customers to pay cash. Any spare cash goes into my safe deposit."

"Are there any books at all?"

"I keep a private cash record. For my own use."

"In what form?"

"In an ordinary cash book. There are three or four of them, covering the last few years."

"Where?"

"In my safe."

"Who has a key?"

"I've got one. Rainey's got the other."

"Are you sure you can trust him? The last time he was round here, I thought he was going to pieces."

"I don't trust him. But he won't step out of line. I could send him to jail longer than he could send me."

"All the same, I think those books had better go. Take them out of the safe, and put them in a cabinet, along with any other records. Then organize an accidental fire."

Bull looked thoughtful. He said, "I could do that, I suppose. But I'll tell you something. A book's a bloody difficult thing to burn."

"You don't have to destroy the books," said Weatherman impatiently. "All you need is a convincing fire. Then we tell the Revenue the books have been destroyed. Produce a few ashes. The onus will be on them to prove you're lying. They'll have a job to do that."

When Bull got back to the garage he found three customers waiting impatiently, and served them himself. He remembered that it was Johnno's afternoon off. As he crossed the yard he could hear the sound of someone working in the repair shed at the back, but the yard itself was deserted. He picked up a big handful of oil cotton waste and walked across to the wooden annex at the far end of the shed which Rainey used as an office.

The cashier was there. He was lying back in his chair, his mouth wide open, snoring. His face was red and sweating, and the small room stank of whiskey.

Bull stood looking down at him, smiling. It would serve him right, he thought, if he organized the fire and left Rainey in the middle of it. Then a further thought occurred to him. If the cashier had come back, demonstrably drunk, after lunch, wasn't it very plausible that *he* should have started the fire. He could easily have kicked over the single-bar electric fire. It was a rickety affair, and he had warned him more than once to be careful of it. With a little care and scene-setting it could be made to look very convincing. He, Bull, coming back, would find the office ablaze, would dash gallantly in, and secure considerable kudos for rescuing his sottish cashier. But by that time the fire would be too well away to stop.

There was a small wooden cabinet, which was used for stationery. The incriminating records could go in there, with the door wide open, as it would be, of course, if Rainey was working on them.

Bull moved softly across to the safe in the corner, unlocked it, and swung back the door. After that he stood, for a full ten seconds, staring into the interior. Then he stepped back and started to search the room. There were very few places to look. He already knew the truth.

He grabbed Rainey by the hair and banged his head down onto the table. Then he took him by the collar and shook him. When he was certain that he was awake, he said, "What the hell have you done with the cash books?"

Rainey stared at him. A bruise was forming on his forehead with a trickle of blood in the middle of it and tears were running down his cheeks, but the drink was temporarily out of him.

He said, "Last time I used them, I put them back in the safe."

"They're not there. Who's had your key?"

"My key?" He clapped his hand to his pocket, but it was shaking so much that it took several attempts to find what he wanted. Then he drew out a ring of keys.

"It's still there," he said.

"Of course it's there," snarled Bull. "I didn't imagine you'd swallowed it. Who have you lent it to?"

"No one. I haven't lent it to anyone."

"Have you been out and left the safe open?"

Rainey was trying to think. He said, "Yesterday evening. I slipped out for ten minutes. To buy some cigarettes."

"And left the safe open?"

"Yes." Seeing the look on Bull's face, he added hastily, "But it was all right. Vikki was here."

Bull hit him. It was a wicked, swinging punch, intended to hurt. It caught Rainey under the heart, and put him flat on his back, where he lay moaning and gasping. Then he rolled onto his side and was sick.

21

I$_T$ WAS a quarter to six before Mercer, having concluded his business with the well-known Mr. Michael Robertson, finally got back to Stoneferry.

The fine weather of the morning had given way to cloud. It looked as though they would have rain before midnight.

He drove straight out to Mr. Moxon's shop, going openly and without any of the precautions he had observed on his earlier visits.

Mr. Moxon said, "They told me you might be looking in. I got a message for you. Two messages actually. I wrote them down just as they came."

He passed across two pages torn from a notepad. The first was headed "Time of message, 1135 hrs." Mr. Moxon had been a signaler in an artillery regiment and preserved his orderly habits. "May and June withdrawn at 2000 hrs. last night. July standing by. Message ends."

The second sheet, headed "1515 hrs." said, "July will give the red light by telephone for tonight."

Mercer read them, folded them up, and put them in his wallet. He said, "If there's any money for me, I'd better have it."

Mr. Moxon opened his safe and produced a manila

envelope. It was open at one end and the sight of it seemed to put him in mind of something.

He said, "That young feller you said might be looking in—he looked in."

"I suppose it was him opened this envelope."

"That's a fact. I told him he wasn't to, but he did."

"He's a headstrong lad," said Mercer. He was counting the money.

"He had an identification card. I suppose he *was* a policeman."

"He thinks he is," said Mercer. "By the way, he didn't help himself to any, did he?"

"Certainly not. I watched him close."

"No. It's all right. I thought there was one missing. Two notes got stuck together." He peeled one off and handed it across. "That's this week's rent. There may not be any more. But thanks for what you've done, Albert. By the way, I'd better take that other parcel you've been looking after."

Mr. Moxon produced, from under the counter, a white cardboard shoebox, tied with string. From the way he handled it, it was fairly heavy. Mercer said, "Well, thanks again," and went out into the street, dumped the box in the back of his car, and drove off. There seemed to be no watchers. He had not expected any.

He parked his car carefully in the small yard behind the station, facing outward. Medmenham's car was the only one there. Then he walked into the station, said, "Good evening," to Station Sergeant Rix, who nodded but did not reply, and went upstairs. Prothero was alone in the CID room, completing a careful plan of an accident which had taken place the day before. Mercer said, "Hullo, Len. Any excitements while I've been gone?"

"Quiet as a dean's dinner party," said Prothero. "The old man went up to London early this afternoon. He hasn't come back yet, as far as I know."

217

"His car's not in the yard," agreed Mercer. He dumped the shoebox on the table. "Since no one seems to want me, I think I'll go and get myself a drink. Who's on duty tonight?"

"Tom's on divisional call. He's getting his supper. He'll be back here at seven. Is something up?"

Mercer said, "What makes you think that?"

"There's a sort of atmosphere about the place. I don't get it."

"What you want to do," said Mercer seriously, "is go home and get a good night's sleep."

The public bar of the Angler's Rest was empty except for two old regulars, who were sitting in the corner watching their first pints of the evening as though they might vanish if they took their eyes off them. Mercer ordered himself a double whiskey and carried it through to the private bar. This was empty. The landlord had just lit the fire, which was crackling into a blaze. Mercer took a long pull at his drink, put it on the table, lowered himself into a chair, and stretched his feet toward the warmth. The only noise was the ticking of the clock in its mahogany case next to the stuffed pike. Mercer's big frame sank lower into the chair. A small coal fell from the fire and tinkled against the iron guard.

It was black night, and he was walking down a street. The street lamps were few and a long way apart. The shadows between them were full of shapes. Shapes which moved and shifted but made no sound. All that he could hear was the noise of his own footsteps rapping on the pavement. They kept time disconcertingly with the beating of his own heart. He woke with a start, to find someone standing over him.

It took him a moment to realize that it was Willoughby Slade, that Willoughby was at least half sober, and very angry.

He said, "What the hell have you done with my sister?"

Mercer blinked, and looked at the clock. It showed twenty-five to nine. "Good God!" he said. "I must have been asleep for over an hour."

"Stop fooling about," said Willoughby. "I want to know where Venetia is."

"Search me," said Mercer. And, as Willoughby took a step closer, "Why should you think I'd done anything with her?"

"Because, as you bloody well know, and as everyone in this town bloody well knows by now, she's been out with you almost every bloody evening for the last week, and it's bloody well got to stop."

Mercer shifted in his chair so that the palm of his right hand was on the floor and most of his weight was taken on his stiff right arm. He said, "She's over the age of consent. She's a girl. I'm a chap. Someone ought to explain the system to you. It's fun when you get the hang of it."

As Willoughby swung at him, Mercer rolled out of the chair, pivoting on his right arm. The blow caught him on the shoulder and did no harm and the chair got in the way of any second blow. By the time Willoughby had got round it, Mercer was on his feet. Willoughby came in, using his fists like a public school boxing champion. Mercer did a half knee bend, after the style of a Russian dancer, shot out his left leg, and kicked Willoughby hard on the ankle bone. Willoughby got his legs crossed and fell over, hitting the back of his head on the table and toppling Mercer's almost untouched glass of whiskey.

Mercer leaned forward, rescued the whiskey, picked the boy up by the lapels of his coat, and slung him into the chair. He then pulled his head back by the hair, held the drink to his lips, said "Open your mouth," and tipped it down his throat.

Willoughby sputtered, and sat up. He was still dazed.

Mercer said, "Never box against someone who knows how to fight. Now just listen to me. I don't know where your sister is. I haven't seen her this evening. She's probably home by now. Keep her there. That's not advice, it's an order. *Keep her home tonight, and stay with her.*"

When he got back to the station he found Tom Rye in the CID room. Tom said, "There's been a message for you. I couldn't make out who it was from. Sounded like July. Do you know a Mr. July?"

"I might. What was the message?"

"He just said that nothing had started yet, but you were to stand by. Does that make sense?"

"Sort of," said Mercer.

He was untying the string round the shoebox and now took out what looked like a pair of climber's shoes. They were made of heavy leather with rubber studs underneath.

"You planning to play football?"

"Party games."

"Don't you think you might let me in on this?"

Mercer considered the matter seriously. Then he said, "I'd like to, Tom. If I let anyone in on it, you'd be first choice. The fact is, I'm expecting an invitation to a party. It's the sort of party where steel toecaps are going to be more use than a white tie and tails. If I could bring a guest, I'd bring you like a shot, but tonight is strictly by invitation only."

Rye said, "You're a close-mouthed bastard. I suppose one day we're going to find out what all this is about. By the way, Bob's back."

"Did he come down here?"

"No. He seems to have gone straight home."

"Any messages for the troops?"

"He said he'd see you in the morning."

It was past ten o'clock when the telephone rang. Rye

took the call. He said, "It's your friend July again. He thinks you ought to be moving."

"Tell him I'm on my way," said Mercer. He went down the back stairs to the courtyard, climbed into his car, and switched on the ignition. The heavy shoes were going to make driving difficult, and he was experimenting cautiously with the clutch when he realized that he was not alone in the car.

An arm slid softly round his neck from behind, and Venetia said, "It's been a long wait, Bill, but here you are at last."

22

"WHAT THE HELL do you think you're doing?" said Mercer.

"Waiting for you."

"Why here, for God's sake?"

"I went to the pub. Willoughby was propping up the public bar. He'd have seen me if I'd gone in."

"Would that have mattered?"

"He's been in such a foul temper about us. He'd have made a row."

"He did," said Mercer. "Look, Venetia, you've got to get out and go and stay home. Right now."

"That's a nice way to talk. I should have thought the least you could do was drive me there."

Mercer looked down at his watch. He said, "I haven't got time. Don't argue. Do what I say. Just this once."

"I'm damned if I will. I've been waiting for an hour. My feet are blocks of ice. You can drive me home and keep your next girl friend waiting for five minutes."

"It isn't a girl. It's a job."

"I should have thought it was the same thing with you."

"Do you want me to throw you out?"

"If you touch me, I'm going to scream. And I warn

you, I *can* scream. I've won prizes for it."

"All right," said Mercer, in tones of sudden cold anger. "You can come to the party. Only don't sit in the back. Come in front with me."

"Oh, yes," said Venetia, "and when I get out, you'll drive off and leave me."

"Then climb over the bloody seat."

As he spoke, Mercer was engaging gear. He nosed the car out into the High Street. Venetia settled in the seat beside him, and slid an arm through his.

"That's better, Bill," she said.

"There's one condition."

"What's that?"

"When the party starts, you do *exactly* what I tell you. And keep on doing it."

"Certainly, your majesty. Where are we going? And what sort of party is it?"

"It's at my house. It's a sort of housewarming. Fasten your seat belt."

"It's not worth it for such a short trip."

Mercer brought the car to a halt, and said, in the same cold, serious voice, "You're breaking the rules already. On this party you're to do what I tell you, remember? If you don't, I really am going to throw you out."

Venetia looked at him. She was still angry, but a less comfortable feeling was beginning to take over. She said, "All right, Bill. If that's one of the rules." She fastened the seat belt. "Aren't you going to use yours?"

"As it happens," said Mercer, "in my case mobility is more important than security."

As he pulled away from the curb, he leaned across her and pressed a switch on the dashboard. A blue light showed, and began to flicker, on-off-on-off, in regular rhythm.

"What's that?" she said.

Mercer said nothing. The glow from the dashboard

223

light was playing tricks with his expression. There was nothing comfortable in it.

As they passed under the railway arch, Mercer flicked on his headlights, and flicked them off again quickly when he saw that there was no one there.

Cray Avenue was a cul-de-sac, with a short side road at its far end which ran back to the railway embankment and stopped there. As he turned into the avenue, Mercer flicked on his lights again. There were three men waiting on the pavement in front of his house. No car visible. He guessed it was tucked away round the corner at the end.

He said to Venetia, "Hold tight. Here it comes," swung the car across the road and up onto the pavement, stood on the brakes, and cut the engine. Then he opened the offside door, squeezed through it, and slammed it shut. He was now standing in the sharp angle made by the car and the garden wall.

There was a moment of complete silence. Then the three men came across the road. The leader was a big man with a nose like the prow of a ship. His silvery gray hair was smoothly brushed. Grizzled sideburns came down almost to the angle of his chin. There were tufts of hair on his high-colored cheeks. The dignified, almost benevolent face sat oddly on an anthropoid body. The arms were unnaturally long, and the large hands hung almost level with his knees as he walked.

He said, "It looks as if these people have had a bit of trouble with their car. Better help them out, Sam."

Mercer said nothing.

Sam said, "Perhaps he doesn't want to be helped." He was working his way round to the back of the car, where there was a narrow gap between it and the wall. The third man, who was smaller than the other two and had red hair and a face like a sick fox, moved to the left, but was blocked by the hood of the car.

The big man said, "Have him out, lads."

Sam came in through the gap. Mercer, with one hand on the top of the low garden wall, kicked him hard on the knee. Venetia heard the kneecap go with a crack. Pivoting on the wall, Mercer turned in time to meet Sick Fox, who had hurled himself across the hood of the car. Mercer caught his hair with his left hand and hit him with his gloved right hand, holding him and pulling him onto the punches. Then he let him go and he tumbled back onto the roadway.

Mercer said, "Are you coming in yourself, Mo, or do you leave all the fighting to the boys?"

"I do what I have to," said Mo Fenton. His church-warden's face was thoughtful. Sick Fox had picked himself up. He said, "I could get into the garden behind him, Mo. We'd have the bastard fixed, then."

Mo whistled, and the black snout of a car showed round the far corner. The driver and another man jumped out and came running.

Mo said to the driver, "You help Sam back to the car. Take it easy. His knee's busted. When you get him there, stay with him. Mick, you can lend a hand here." He spoke in a level conversational tone.

"A pleasure," said Mick. He looked like a big school-boy, ready to go in to bat at a crisis in the innings. "How do we get the bugger out?"

"We don't," said Mo. "We invite him to step out."

"Do you think he'll oblige?"

"I think so," said Mo. He opened the near-side door, and looked down at Venetia. She had managed to undo the seat belt, but seemed too paralyzed to move further.

Mo dipped his hand into his top pocket, took out an old-fashioned cutthroat razor with a black handle, and flicked the blade open. He said to Mercer, "Either you come out, or I start cutting bits off your girl friend and throw them over to you."

"You're dead wrong," said Mercer. "She's not my girl

friend. She's a stupid little bint who insisted on coming for the ride. If she gets hurt, it's her fault."

"I don't think you can mean that," said Mo. He was holding the door open with his left hand and looking down curiously at the girl. Venetia was leaning forward as far away from him as she could. His right hand moved. She gave a little scream. The razor had traveled down the sleeve of her coat, slicing it through, barely touching the skin.

She threw herself sideways across the car, but her legs were blocked by the steering column and the gear lever. As the top part of her body shifted, the dashboard of the car came into sudden view.

Mo said, "The bastard. He's got a flasher going. All out, quick!"

Mercer put his arm into the car and touched the horn. A lot of things started to happen at once.

The front door of the house behind him flung open and a man came pounding down the path. He was out through the gate in time to collar Mick round the waist and the two men rolled across the road, and carried on with their fight in the gutter on the far side.

There was a car coming fast down the main road, its lights full on, its police siren blaring. By this time the black car was moving. Mo Fenton and Sick Fox tumbled aboard.

The police car swung round the corner, its headlights picking out the scene in sharp black and white. Mick and his opponent had rolled out of the gutter and onto the pavement. Mick was underneath. The police car was blocking the middle of the road. The driver of the black car had only one chance, and he took it. He drove onto the pavement. Mick's opponent saw it coming and rolled into the open gateway. Mick had no time to move. He gave one scream as the car went over him. The rear wheels bumped over the body, the driver threw the car to the left, missed the lamppost by inches, made a racing turn at the corner, and was gone.

John Anderson, in the seat beside the driver of the police car, was talking urgently into his wireless set.

"Where the hell's the second car got to?" said Mercer.

"It's behind us. I've sent it after them."

As he spoke a police car went past the end of the road.

"He won't catch them," said Mercer. "That driver was Kowalski. He's Grand Prix. If the two of you had got here together, ten seconds earlier, you could have blocked the entrance. That's what I was holding them for."

"I'm sorry," said Anderson. "How are you, Milner?"

The newcomer had picked himself up out of the gateway. He said, "I'm all right, sir. Better than that poor bugger."

He was looking down at what had once been a man. The car had gone over Mick's head. Anderson turned back and started talking into his wireless set again. He seemed to be setting up roadblocks.

Mercer walked back to his own car. A tousle-haired figure in a raincoat was standing beside it. He recognized Father Walcot.

He said, "I got her arm tied up. It's not a deep gash. Then she passed out."

Mercer said, "Thank you, Father. As soon as they've cleared this shambles, I'll drive her home."

He sounded deadly tired.

23

THE MEETING to which Bob Clark had been summoned after lunch that day took place in an office on the third floor of a building which seemed to be occupied by the Statistics Department of the Board of Trade. It had a fine view over the Thames, though it needed an effort of the imagination to identify this gray, swollen, dangerous stretch of water with the friendly river he had left behind him at Stoneferry.

If the location of the meeting was a surprise, even more surprising were the people assembled there. He had supposed that a disciplinary complaint would be dealt with at division, by Chief Superintendent Watterson, or at District by Commander Blakemore, with the senior corresponding CID officer in attendance. And if the hearing had been at district headquarters, it would have been logical enough for Morrissey to be there, as indeed he was, ponderous and unsmiling on one side of the table. The man next to him he thought he recognized as Deputy Commander Laidlaw, founder and head of the Regional Crime Squads; and what *he* had to do with the matter was a mystery. But it was the sight of the third man which took the matter out of the realms of surprise and produced what was almost a shock. This was a man of

Oriental appearance, as feared for his tongue as he was respected for his ability. Deputy Commissioner Arthur Lovell, number two in the Metropolitan Police hierarchy, tipped for the top post when the present commissioner retired.

It was Lovell who opened the proceedings.

He said, "Sit down, Superintendent. I never like taking a working policeman away from his manor, but your report on Detective Chief Inspector Mercer contained matters which we thought ought to be discussed at once, at the highest possible level. There are, I understand, four grounds of complaint against him."

He glanced down at the paper on the table, but it was no more than the gesture of a barrister who has already mastered his brief. "First that he has been receiving regular and unexplained payments into his account at the local bank. How did you find that out, by the way?"

Clark explained how he had found out.

Lovell said, "I suppose no system of security is proof against that sort of disloyalty. However, it's not our business. Your second point also deals with money. You have discovered that additional payments, in cash, are reaching Mercer at an accommodation address?"

"To be fair," said Clark, "we only traced one lot of money, but we know he was making regular visits to this shop. And taking good care not to be followed."

"But you managed to follow him?"

"We got a tip-off about it."

On the other side of the table, Morrissey showed his teeth in what might have been a grin. It was a momentary flicker of expression, then his heavy white face was impassive again.

"The third ground of complaint is that he was too friendly with a local character called Bull, a garage owner. He had long evening sessions with him, I understand. Drank with him in pubs until all hours. Inciden-

229

tally breaking licensing regulations."

Clark nodded.

"And arising out of that, he got his subordinates to lay off what looked like a promising line of investigation which might have involved one of this man's employees? And this seemed to you evidence that he was prepared to do favors for Bull."

Clark nodded again. The indictment had been fairly put. Taken together the four counts added up to something. He had been right to report it.

"Wasn't there a fifth item?" said Morrissey. His face was perfectly straight now. "Something about flogging natives."

Clark said, stiffly, "That was no part of my report. But it is true that it had become known in the area that he had been dismissed from a previous post for brutality."

Morrissey started to say something, but a tiny movement of Lovell's hand checked him. The Deputy Commissioner said, "I am going to ask Commander Laidlaw to put you in possession of certain facts, Superintendent, so that you see both sides of the picture."

Laidlaw said, "I think a lot of things will fall into place if I tell you that Mercer is not on the regular establishment at all. He is a member of Number Three Regional Crime Squad. As you know, our squads have no exact territorial boundaries. We investigate groups of criminals, and areas of crime. One of our constant preoccupations is with wage snatching. It's particularly serious because it's organized, lucrative, and brutal. It was to counter it that the banks and the police evolved Dibox. It's a very simple system. All new notes issued to a bank are marked with a symbol. It can only be read under oblique light. It indicates the date, the bank, and the branch of origin. Here's how it works. Suppose there was a big wage snatch on Monday. On Tuesday Mr. A puts down a deposit on a new car. The money is paid into the bank in new notes.

They check the Dibox mark, and are able to identify the notes as part of a batch paid out to the victim of the recent wage snatch. Then the finger is on Mr. A for that job. Apart from this the chances are he might never have been suspected. Now his head is on the block. He can be followed. His contacts noted. All other payments he makes in cash in the following weeks are checked. We pulled off one or two quite spectacular jobs by this method. Then, as was bound to happen sooner or later, the smart boys put two and two together. And they came to one obvious conclusion. That a fairly long period must be allowed to elapse before stolen notes were put back into circulation. You see the point? The Dibox system only works if it works quickly. After a few months there are too many notes in circulation which were drawn from that particular branch on that particular day. Possession of one of them ceases to mean anything. But there was a drawback to that, too. The boys involved in a job usually want their money on the nail. The answer, for the big organized outfits, was to set up 'stockings.' The proceeds of today's wage snatch were put into the top of the stocking, and the boys were paid out in notes which came from the bottom. Plain so far, Superintendent?"

Clark said, "Yes, sir. But I don't see—"

"You will," said Morrissey.

"Now it's easy enough to talk about setting up a stocking. But it's not so easy in practice. It had to be somewhere completely safe, and reasonably large. It also had to be accessible. No one wants to hang onto hot cash a moment longer than he need. The Crows found the perfect answer. Paul Crow, who became boss when his cousin Abel stopped two barrels of a shotgun with his stomach last year, had an old friend of Para Corps days. Jack Bull. Incidentally, Mercer stumbled on the connection at one of those late-night Bull-sessions you were talking about, Superintendent."

Clark said, "I see."

"Bull was the ideal man for the job. He had a garage within easy driving distance of the West End, which stayed open late. As soon as the money got there, the pump attendant, Johnno, motored it over to Slough and cached it in the safe deposit. Nothing suspicious about it. They might have been banking their own money. I believe one of your men watched him doing it."

"I believe he did," said Clark.

"The only drawback, from Paul Crow's point of view, was that the system entailed trusting Bull. And Paul isn't a man who trusts anybody. An old friendship from army days was fine, too. But it didn't go far enough. Fortunately fate dealt him a couple of aces. When Bull set up in Stoneferry he wanted to get rid of his two main rivals. You know how he did it?"

Clark said, "Mercer told me what he suspected."

"Well, it was Paul Crow who worked the oracle for him. He supplied the hot cars which the police found at one of the garages, and the mechanic who wrecked the other one. After that he reckoned he had Bull where he wanted him."

"How did you get onto Bull?"

"As soon as the boys knew we were hunting for stockings we got dozens of tip-offs. One of them happened to be Bull. We had no particular reason to concentrate on him until we got a cross-bearing. Sergeant Rollo . . ."

Sergeant Rollo. It was something Mercer had said to him. The one death which was important, because it was the one which was unforgivable.

"We were very unhappy about that. He'd already put in a number of adverse reports on Bull, suggesting that he was swindling his customers. But without any definite proof. Then this happened. It looked to us like a put-up job. But not a simple job. An elaborate, professional job. From which we deduced that Bull had a big-time backer.

So that was when we decided to investigate him a bit further. About six months ago we put in two of our people. Mrs. Hall, who's an inspector in the Women's Police, and Vikki Severn, who was an assistant in the Fraud Squad before she joined us. They're both trained accountants. We had no difficulty in placing them where we wanted them. People with good qualifications who only ask for a modest wage don't get turned down. They confirmed our view that Bull was crooked. He was swindling his customers and defrauding the Revenue. Quite systematically, with the help of his solicitor. That's when we decided to send Mercer in. We took a few precautions. We put a bodyguard in with him. He lodged in the house opposite. And we made special arrangements about his pay. We've had too many cases where a man has been put on the spot by having money paid into his bank account. Easy to do, difficult to refute. So we opened a very special account at the local bank for him."

"A lobster pot," said Morrissey. "Easy to get into, impossible to get out of."

"In this particular account, money could be paid in. But the only person who had authority to draw on it was the Receiver of Metropolitan Police."

"Highly satisfactory," said Morrissey. "Any unclaimed money goes to the Police Orphanage."

"If he couldn't draw money from his own bank account—" said Clark. Then he stopped, and said, "Oh, yes. I see. That was the reason for Moxon's shop."

"Moxon was his paymaster, and his line of communication."

"If you had told me some of this before," said Clark, and he found it difficult to keep the stiffness out of his voice, "wouldn't it have saved a lot of misunderstanding?"

"That's a legitimate comment," said Lovell. "And every time we send a man in we have to make the same decision. Maximum cooperation or maximum security. It isn't an easy decision. If it's a short assignment, we usually say nothing. The man's in and out again, and no harm done. If it's likely to last longer—and we'd no idea this would come to a head so quickly—then there's more reason for letting the local man know, but more chance of it slipping out. In this case, we left the decision to Mercer."

"I see," said Clark. "And he decided that I wasn't to be told."

"He decided to test the security-mindedness of the person chiefly concerned," said Morrissey with a grin.

"Need we go into this?" said Lovell.

Clark stared at him, his face going red.

"I'm not certain what that last remark meant," he said, "but if it concerns me, I think I ought to hear it."

"You're not going to like it," said Morrissey. "What he did was, he had us put a paragraph in his confidential report. The one that went to you. About flogging natives. It was a load of rubbish."

Lovell said smoothly, "The object of this discussion was to put Superintendent Clark in the picture. I think we've done that?"

The other two men nodded. Clark was beyond speech.

"What we are going to have to think about is the future. The immediate future. As I said, this matter has come to a head more quickly than we had expected. Commander Laidlaw will explain what we are planning to do, and the sort of cooperation he's going to need."

"We're going to need all we can get," said Laidlaw. He was smiling, the atmosphere seemed to have become easier. "I believe it was President Kruger who said that the only easy way of killing a turtle was to get it to stick its head out. That's what we're planning to do. We think that a minor attack will go in on Mercer personally. We've let them know that he's closing in on Bull, and their natural reaction will be to put him out. We're ready for that, and they'll get more than they bargained for. But it's not the main effort. It's what you might call, in military parlance, a platoon attack. We're going to offer them a bait which will bring the whole lot out, fighting." He looked at his watch. "In fact, the opening rounds of the barrage will be going down in about an hour's time."

It was exactly half past three when the routine of Mr. Justice Arbuthnot's court was disturbed. The case was a complex one, concerning the rights of neighboring buildings to mutual support, and counsel for the defendant had concluded the examination of the principal expert witness. The judge ruled a neat line under his notes and turned to the plaintiff's counsel, inviting him to open his cross-examination.

Counsel said, "I have been asked to give way, my lord. And I think I must do so."

Two new figures had entered the courtroom. Mr. Justice Arbuthnot recognized, with some surprise, the attorney general and his leading treasury junior.

The attorney general said, "My learned friend, Mr. Lavery, has very kindly agreed, if your lordship consents, to defer the opening of his cross-examination, which will, I understand, be a lengthy one, until tomorrow. This would enable me to make a short, but extremely urgent, ex parte application on behalf of the Crown."

Mr. Lavery bowed. The judge said, "Very well." There was a bustling of silk gowns as counsel left the court, followed by solicitors and underlings. The few spectators at the back sat tight. An urgent application by the Crown sounded more exciting than rights of mutual support.

"I have been instructed in this matter by the Commissioners of Inland Revenue. They have raised a provisional assessment of a very substantial amount—eighteen thousand pounds in the first assessment, but the figure may, in the event, prove to be considerably greater. The taxpayer, a garage owner of Stoneferry on Thames, Mr. Bull, is apparently resisting the assessment. I need not repeat the precise terms of his refusal, which he made verbally and of which I have a note. It is remarkably offensive. But I can assure you that he has denied liability in categorical terms.

"The dispute will come before the court in due course, and it will be alleged that systematic and fraudulent evasion is involved. Meanwhile, however, it has come to our knowledge—and this will be one of the principal allegations in the case—that the taxpayer has been making regular deposits of money, over a considerable period, in a safe deposit at Slough. The Revenue asks for an injunction preventing the taxpayer from having access to this safe deposit until the matter has been decided."

The judge pondered. He said, "It seems an extreme step, Mr. Attorney General, to deprive a citizen of access to his own money. Particularly since, your application being ex parte, he is not here to argue against it."

"I appreciate that, my lord. In the circumstances I would only ask for an injunction effective for seven days. This will afford ample time for the taxpayer to be represented and to put any counterarguments before your lordship."

Mr. Justice Arbuthnot said, "Very well."

At the back of the court, Superintendent Morrissey breathed a sigh of relief.

24

"I SUPPOSE we've got to make the best of it," said Clark.

"You won't have to put up with me for long," said Mercer. "A week at the most, would be my guess. You know they're promoting Tom Rye. He was lined up for this job anyway. I've just kept him out of it for a month."

"It seems more like a year," said Clark. It was a back-handed offer of peace, but Mercer accepted it gladly enough. "I hear you had some trouble last night," Clark added.

"Not as much trouble as we'd planned for, I'm afraid. They left one man behind, very dead. And one of them won't walk for a few months."

"What's the next move?"

"They'll fight that injunction, no holds barred. They're not short of money. They'll put leading counsel up next week, and I think they'll probably win. The judge wasn't at all anxious to give us even a temporary stop."

"And after that?"

"Bull will try to move the money somewhere else. We'll have to play it as it comes."

"Suppose he ignores the court order, and shifts it now?"

"He's not going to hear about it until later today. By

that time I shall have fixed the safe deposit. I'm going over there right away."

The receptionist at the Southern Counties Safe Deposit depressed a red switch in the gadget on her table and said, "Detective Inspector Mercer is in the waiting room for you, sir."

"What does he want now?" said Mr. Nevinson irritably.

"He said his business was urgent."

"No doubt. It hasn't perhaps occurred to him that other people might be busy, too."

"There's another gentleman with him."

"Another policeman?"

The receptionist hesitated. The truth is that she had been impressed by the second man, a military type of early middle age with a red-brown face and formidable eyebrows, tufts of graying hair which stood out horizontally over a pair of angry brown eyes.

"I think he might be, sir."

"Did he have a name?"

"It's a Mr. Michael Robertson, sir. Do you know him?"

Mr. Nevinson said, "Oh, yes. Please show them up at once."

The chief constable came straight to the point. He said, "Show Mr. Nevinson the office copy of the injunction, Mercer."

Mr. Nevinson read it carefully. He said, "It's effective for a week, I see. After that, I imagine I cannot refuse Bull access to his own strong room."

"It's not what happens after the end of the week that's bothering us. It's what might happen now."

"I'm afraid I don't follow you," said Mr. Nevinson. "Naturally, any application for access during the next seven days will be refused."

Mercer said, "I'm not sure if you quite understand the

sort of people we're up against. The money in that strong room doesn't belong to Bull. It represents the proceeds of half a dozen highly successful robberies by a powerful, violent, and very well organized group of criminals."

Mr. Nevinson's face went first red, then white. He said, "I can assure you—"

"It goes without saying that you knew nothing about it," said the chief constable. "The point is that the men it belongs to will stop at nothing to get it back. I'll go further. They *must* get it back. If they don't, they're finished."

"What do you want me to do?"

Mercer said, "Last time I was here, you were explaining to me the steps you took if a key was lost. You had some system of knocking out the lock."

"Yes. We can do that. It takes a bit of time."

"How quickly could you remove the existing lock and put in a new one?"

"If I gave the orders now, the old lock could be drilled out in about three hours. A new one could be put on in two."

"Then," said the chief constable, his eyebrows coming together with an almost audible click, "give the orders right away."

Mercer went next to call on Superintendent Ferraby of the Slough police. There he made arrangements for a twenty-four-hour watch to be kept on the safe deposit. Two squad cars were to be available on immediate call, with two more from Stoneferry.

"If we want anything heavier," said the chief constable, "we'll have to get soldiers from Windsor. I'll do it if I have to, but I don't like calling out the army. Bad for public relations."

"Do you think it might be necessary?" said Superintendent Ferraby, trying to keep the surprise out of his voice.

"I'm not taking any chances. And I'm going to give

239

you the necessary authority, in writing, now, to arm the crews of the standby cars. Pick the men yourself. And don't issue a gun to anyone who doesn't hold a Firearms Proficiency Certificate; we don't want them shooting each other."

Mercer was back in Stoneferry by midday, and at a quarter past twelve he was letting himself in at the front door of Messrs. Weathermans' offices in Fore Street. The young lady behind the reception desk seemed worried about something. Her worry increased when she understood that Mercer wanted to see Mr. Weatherman.

She said, "I'm sure I don't know if he can see you."

"Suppose you were to ring through and find out?"

"It might be a bit difficult. You couldn't come back this afternoon, I suppose?"

"It's rather urgent," said Mercer. "Has something happened?"

The girl looked even more worried. Then she said, "We had Mr. Bull here, about half an hour ago. He was in a terrible state. I don't know what it was all about. I could hear him shouting from down here."

"He must have been shouting very loudly."

"Oh, he was. When Mr. Bull came down he looked terrible and Mr. Weatherman told me he wasn't seeing any clients this morning. I had to put off Colonel Watterson. I don't like to interrupt him."

"Quite right," said Mercer. "It's always better to obey instructions. But there's nothing to prevent *me* from interrupting him, is there?"

The girl started to say something, but Mercer was already halfway up the stairs. He went into Mr. Weatherman's room without knocking. The solicitor was seated behind his desk. He looked up as the door opened and Mercer thought he had never seen a face in which fear and anger made a more ugly mixture.

Mercer said, "You know what I've come for?"

Mr. Weatherman said nothing.

Mercer said, "You're to give instructions to your partners, and your staff, that no papers are to be taken out of this office until further notice. And you are to hand over your passport to me."

There was a long silence.

Then Mr. Weatherman said, "I presume that you imagine you have some right to make such an outrageous request."

"Whether I have the right or not isn't important. I can offer you an alternative. I have a warrant for your arrest on charges of criminal conspiracy and fraud. And I have a warrant to search this office. If you don't do as I say without further argument, I shall execute those warrants."

There was another long silence. Mr. Weatherman said, "I have no alternative."

"None at all. And may I say that of all the people involved in this matter, I have least sympathy for you. I can get along with ordinary crooks, but a crook in striped trousers turns my stomach."

On his way out of the office half an hour later, Mercer ran into Willoughby Slade. The young man looked embarrassed, but resolute. He said, "I say." Mercer said, "Hullo." Willoughby said, "I gather—I mean—My sister told me that you tried to discourage her from coming out with you last night."

"I tried to throw her out. But she wouldn't be thrown. How is she this morning?"

"She's all right. She's pretty angry with you. I can't quite make out why."

"Girls aren't logical," said Mercer.

He spent the rest of the day at the station. There was a lot to do. Sergeant Gwilliam went over to Slough in the afternoon, and reported that the lock on Bull's strong room was proving difficult to shift. Also, that he had

241

made contact with his opposite number in the Slough force, Sergeant Harraway, who thought that Stoneferry were getting the breeze up about nothing.

Mercer said, "Tell him to read Confidential Information File thirty-six stroke sixty-nine. There'll be a copy at his headquarters station."

At half past three, and again at four o'clock, Bull telephoned the station and was told that Mercer was in conference.

At five o'clock Gwilliam came through again. He said that the lock had responded to treatment and the new one was now going on. And Sergeant Harraway had read CIF 36/69 and had changed his mind.

At seven o'clock the conference in Superintendent Clark's room broke up. He said to Mercer, "Well, that's all we can do for the moment. I suggest we have two of the four of us on call on alternate nights for the next few weeks."

Mercer nodded. It was, he thought, the first time since he had arrived at Stoneferry, that Bob Clark had referred to the uniform branch and the CID in the same breath as "we" and "us."

"Medmenham and you stand by tonight. Rye and I will take tomorrow. There's no need to hang round here. Have a line put through to your digs when you leave and have your cars on stand by with a driver."

When Clark got home himself he found Lionel Talbot drinking his sherry and chatting with his wife. When Pat had departed to see to the dinner, Talbot said, "How did it go?"

Clark stared at him. Then he said, "Oh, that. Yes, well, it seems we were on the wrong tack."

"The wrong tack?"

"I'm afraid I can't say any more."

"If it's confidential," said Talbot stiffly, "I can't, of course, press you."

242

He finished his sherry and got to his feet. At the front door Clark said, "And incidentally, I should tip off that cashier friend of yours, Derek Robbins, that he may be looking for another job."

Pat, who had come out into the hall, said, "What's wrong with Lionel? He looked a bit huffed."

"He'll get over it," said Clark. "What about that dinner you were promising me? I only had a sandwich for lunch and I'm ravenous."

"Come and get it."

Halfway through the first course they heard the telephone ring from the drawing room.

"Take no notice," said Pat. "Pretend you're not here. If it's important they'll ring again."

But Clark was already in the drawing room.

It was Mercer on the line. He said, "We've had a message from Slough. It was Mrs. Nevinson. Her husband's the manager of the safe deposit. He hasn't come home!"

25

"WE'LL BE OVER right away," said Clark. "Please alert the crews."

"They're standing by," said Mercer. "Might I suggest we fix a preliminary rendezvous at one of the local stations? The Windsor Road substation is nearest to the safe deposit."

"Why not go straight there?"

Mercer said, in the slow way which never failed to irritate Clark, "If they've picked up Mr. Nevinson, it's clear they're already in the building. They'll have used the key to his private back door and got into his office. But that's only the start. They can't open the grille, which leads from his office down to the basement strong rooms, until they've got hold of the head guard, Beale."

"Better warn him."

"I spoke to Ferraby. He's sent a man round. But I rather hope he gets there too late."

"You hope—"

"Where I want them is down in that basement. They can't do a lot when they do get there. Because we changed the lock on Bull's strong room this afternoon, and I've got the only key."

"All right, all right," said Clark. "You've made your point. Let's get cracking."

At the Windsor Road substation they found Superintendent Ferraby holding a council of war. There was one civilian present. He was wearing white shorts, gym shoes, a jersey, and a club sweater. This was young Mr. Jenner, the assistant manager of the safe deposit, who had been hauled off a squash court in the middle of a game and had not been given time to change. He seemed more excited than alarmed.

"Have you got hold of that guard yet?" said Clark.

"We tried to. No reply, and no one at the house. One of his neighbors says he thought he noticed a big car—one he hadn't seen before—outside the house. That was about seven o'clock. When he looked again the car was gone."

Clark happened to glance round at this moment. The smile on Mercer's face disturbed him.

"If they've got Beale," said Ferraby, "they've got both keys. That gets them into the basement. Right?"

Young Mr. Jenner nodded.

"When they get there, they'll find that Bull's key no longer fits the lock. Let's suppose they've brought along the necessary equipment. How long to cut open the strong-room door?"

"We had to do it once, with a blowtorch," said Jenner. "It took us all of two hours."

Clark said, "For God's sake! They've had nearly an hour already." He was fidgeting with anxiety. "What are we waiting for?"

"There's a snag," said Superintendent Ferraby. He was a big, solid West Country man. "You know we had a man in observation on the place. Constable Pike."

"I'd forgotten."

"As soon as we got the message from Mrs. Nevinson, we sent a man down to contact Pike. He couldn't find him. But he found his motorcycle. In a passage between the two office blocks opposite the safe deposit. It was lying on its side, and was damaged. He thought that Pike had noticed something, and had started back to report."

"You think they're holding him as a hostage?"

"That's what I'm thinking," said Ferraby. "And that's what I'm hoping."

"Hoping?"

"There's an alternative, isn't there?"

There was a short silence, while they thought about it. Superintendent Clark made an impatient noise in the back of his throat. Mercer said, "I agree. Anyone who gets between the Crows and what's in that strong room is going to have to be quick and lucky, if he wants to come out on his feet."

Clark said, "We shan't solve anything by talking. And time's going past."

"Before we go any further," said Ferraby, "let's get one thing straight. We're on my territory, and I'm in charge."

"Of course," said Clark hastily.

"Then here's what we're going to do. We'll bring all our men, and all yours, to this point." He demonstrated on the street map. "We'll leave the cars in Canal Street, and come in on foot. We'll have one portable radio with us, netted to the car. We'll try the simple approach first. Mr. Jenner has supplied us with a key of the main door. If we can get inside the building, that's a big step forward. After that we play it by ear. If anyone has any suggestions, let's have them now."

He looked politely towards Superintendent Clark, but he had nothing to say.

Mercer peered cautiously round the corner of the Southern Counties Safe Deposit. Ahead of him was a short, completely deserted, and silent stretch of street. On the far side were the two office buildings, divided by the alley in which Constable Pike's motorcycle had been discovered. On the near side loomed the bulk of the safe deposit building. The overhead lamps threw a cold blue light down on the scene.

The two superintendents were standing beside him, talking in low tones. Behind them, he could hear an occasional click as a policeman handled a rifle. He hoped they knew how to use them.

The whispered conference behind him reached a conclusion.

"I'll go first," said Ferraby, "with Sergeant Harraway."

"I'll come with you," said Clark. "If you don't mind."

Ferraby looked, for a moment, as if he was going to say no. Then he nodded abruptly. "Keep as close as possible to the building. If they've got men upstairs, they won't be able to sight us too clearly."

Mercer said, "If there is a covering party, I guess it'll be in the office building opposite."

"What makes you think that?"

"It would be the natural place to put it."

"We can't guard against every possibility," growled Clark. "Let's get going."

"At least have some of our men covering those windows."

Ferraby said, "That's sensible," and gave the orders. Two men moved up behind them. "All set? Then let's go."

He walked forward, followed by Sergeant Harraway. They had covered half a dozen yards when the shotguns opened up. Ferraby was hit at once. Clark ran forward, grabbed him, and started to drag him back into shelter. By this time their own rifleman were firing back. They were making good practice at the office windows. Mercer ran out to give Clark a hand. As he started he saw Clark go down. Sergeant Harraway had got hold of Ferraby and was helping him round the corner. Mercer, assisted by

247

Sergeant Gwilliam, dragged Clark back into shelter.

The shooting stopped as suddenly as it had started.

Mercer stood looking down at the two men on the pavement. Ferraby seemed to have collected a blast of shot in his legs. His trousers were black with blood, and his face was distorted by pain. Clark was unconscious. His right shoulder was a mess where the jacket was torn away. There were other, probably more serious, wounds lower down. The dragging along the pavement hadn't done him a lot of good.

Mercer realized that he was the senior police officer on the spot, and that a lot of people were looking to him for orders.

He took a deep slow breath to steady himself, and said to Sergeant Harraway, "Get on the radio, sergeant, and whistle up an ambulance. Then post men with rifles at both ends of this street. They can get to the other end quite safely if they circle round behind the office block. Next, do the same in the street at the back. There's a private entrance there, which they'll very likely try to use. I want it covered from both sides. If anyone does try to get out, don't argue. Shoot."

Sergeant Harraway said, "They won't need telling."

When he had detailed the men and sent them off, Mercer said, "Next thing, could you move up two spotlights. Put one at the end of each street, focused on the door, but not switched on. That's in case it occurs to them to shoot out the street lights, and make a run for it in the dark."

"Can do," said Sergeant Harraway, and disappeared.

"Now could someone with a bit of local knowledge tell me where I can get hold of a ladder?"

One of the Slough policemen said, "There's a window cleaners not far from here. He's got one of those metal expanding jobs on top of his van."

"Get over there," said Mercer.

The ladder arrived at the same moment as the chief constable, who said, "Just put me in the picture, would you?" And when Mercer had finished, "You say there are men giving covering fire from the office block. We'd better clear them out first."

"If we've got enough men to do it," said Mercer, "it's worth a try. But I doubt if they're still there. These men aren't heroes. They're strictly smash and grab, shoot and scarper. The better plan would be to locate their getaway cars. They'll be parked somewhere handy."

"We've got plenty of men to cover both jobs. What next?"

"It's only the ground-floor windows of this building that are barred. We can get in at any of these side windows at first- or second-floor level. If they've left any men on guard in the upper stories of the safe deposit, we can flush them out easily enough. Mr. Jenner here can come with us. He knows the lie of the land."

"And then?"

"If we don't find anyone upstairs, we know exactly where they'll be. In the subbasement, busy cutting open Bull's strongroom door. They're the people we want."

The chief constable considered the matter for a long minute. It was not the plan which he mistrusted. What was worrying him was the look on Mercer's face.

He said, "Will they have heard the firing?"

"They wouldn't hear it themselves. They're two stories down, underneath a three-foot concrete and steel floor. If they've left a link man in the upper part of the building, he might have warned them. Unless he's run away, too. Like I said, they're not heroes. In fact the only real cards they've got to play now are Nevinson, Beale, and Pike. When it comes to the pinch, they'll try to use them as hostages."

The chief constable considered the matter. He said, "Take it as far as you can. But no unnecessary heroics.

While you're operating inside, we'll clean up out here."
He looked at his watch. "I've got some heavy stuff coming
from Windsor. It should be here very shortly. Meanwhile, I'll keep the top brass off your neck."

Mercer looked round. There certainly seemed to be a
lot more senior officers on the spot than there had been
five minutes before.

The ladder was now in place. He went up it carefully.

Mercer had a poor head for heights, but a ledge under
the first-floor window gave him something to put his knee
on while he wrapped a scarf round his hand and broke
the glass. Then he opened the catch and slid forward into
the darkness of the room. It was, as far as he could see,
an office, and it was empty.

He tiptoed across, eased the door open, and peered
out. A blue night light showed a length of passage, also
empty. There was no sound of any sort from inside the
building. Then a black shape moved at the far end of the
passage. Mercer's grip on the doorjamb tightened, and
relaxed as the light was reflected from a pair of green eyes
turned in his direction. He said, "Good hunting, puss."

The room behind him was filling up steadily. Mercer
gave his orders in a low voice. "Six of you go with Mr.
Jenner. He'll show you which rooms to search. No
shooting if you can help. It's the party below we're after.
And Jenner—let me impress on you that you're a guide.
Not the spearhead of a forlorn hope."

Mr. Jenner said, "I can look after myself." He sounded
aggrieved.

"I don't doubt it," said Mercer, "but we don't want
civilian casualties. They come heavier on the rates than
policemen. One of you stop here, as contact man to pass
reports. Gwilliam and Prothero, come with me."

He moved off down the passage, and located a flight of
stairs which took him to the ground floor. Here the passage was carpeted. The manager's office, he knew, was at

the far end. There was an interior window giving onto the corridor at head height. A light was shining through it, diffused by the frosted glass. The three men stopped to listen. There was someone in the room. They could hear a curious muffled sound, halfway between a whine and a snuffle.

Mercer touched Gwilliam's sleeve, and as the big Welshman bent forward, breathed in his ear, "See if you can find two tables and a lightish wooden chair. Should be something in one of the offices. Quick and quiet as you can."

While they were gone Mercer bent his head to listen. The noise inside the office worried him. It reminded him of something, but he couldn't place it.

Gwilliam loomed up. He was carrying a typist's desk. Mercer positioned it carefully opposite the right-hand side of the window, and about a foot away from it. When Prothero arrived with a second desk he put that opposite the left-hand side of the window, close up against the wall. By this time Gwilliam was back again. He had a wooden chair, a heavy affair with arms. It was bigger than Mercer had intended, but Gwilliam looked as if he could handle it. He whispered to him, "Get up on that table. Take the chair by the legs. When I give the signal, smash the window. I don't mean knock out a pane of glass. I mean smash it. Frame and all."

Gwilliam nodded to show that he understood. Mercer climbed onto the left-hand table, took the police automatic out of his shoulder holster, and held it loosely in his right hand, with his left hand raised and his eye on the window.

Then he brought his left hand down. The chair flailed round in a semicircle and the window dissolved inward in a cascade of broken glass and fractured wood. And Mercer saw Jack Bull.

He had just come up the stairs from the basement,

and was closing the door. He had his back to the room, and the crash made him jump round. For one frozen second they faced each other. Then, as Bull's right hand moved up with a gun in it, Mercer shot him. The heavy bullet caught him in the face, just above the mouth. He spun round under the impact, and dropped. As he fell, the left sleeve of his jacket jerked out of his pocket and fell across the back of his head, as though he was trying to protect himself with an arm that was no longer there.

Mercer said, "Break down the door." He had to shout above the reverberation of the shot, which had deafened them.

Gwilliam jumped down, motioned Prothero to stand aside, and swung the sole of his foot, once, twice, three times against the door, below the handle. The door was a solid piece of wood, but the repeated drive was too much for the lock, which came away with a crack. The three men tumbled into the room.

The noise which had puzzled them was explained. Mr. Nevinson had been lashed to a chair with electric cord. He was sobbing gently. His right ear was a mess of charred and bloodstained skin and flesh.

"For God's sake," said Mercer. "Get him untied and see if you can do something for him." He moved across to the door in the paneling, stepping over Bull's body as he did so. The door was ajar. Still holding his gun, he edged it open with his foot and looked in. The steel grille was open, too. There was no sign of it being forced. That made it certain they had Beale.

A sound from the passage made him jump round. It was the chief constable who came in, followed by a middle-aged man who looked like a soldier in plain clothes. They stared down at the body of Bull, sprawled on the carpet, and then at Gwilliam, who was trying, unsuccessfully, to force some brandy from a flask down Mr. Nevinson's throat. The room reeked of blood, exploded cordite, and the sickly smell of burned flesh.

The chief constable said, "We've found their cars. And we've cleaned up their supports. The ones that hadn't had time to run away. I'm sorry about Superintendent Clark."

Mercer said, "Is he . . . ?"

"Yes. He's dead." He was looking steadily at Mercer when he spoke. "That makes one on each side, Inspector. I'd like it to stop there if possible."

Mercer said thickly, "It may not be possible."

"What's your plan now?"

"If they didn't have Beale and Constable Pike with them, I'd go straight down and rush them. If they've got their minds on the job they're doing down there, we might jump them without too much trouble."

"Won't they have heard the shot?"

"I rather doubt it," said Mercer. "There are two floors between us. And if they did hear it, they could have assumed it was their own side giving covering fire."

The chief constable said, "What do you think, Colonel?"

The colonel said, "I don't think we've got any weapons which would be effective against the sort of construction there is in this building. Might the best plan be to cut off the electricity and rush them in the dark?"

"I'm afraid it might provoke just the sort of blood bath I'm anxious to avoid. What do you think, Inspector?"

The scar on Mercer's face showed like a red slash. He said, "I don't think they'd put up much of a fight. I'm for trying it."

"Starve them out or rush them," said the colonel. "I can't see any other way."

Sergeant Gwilliam said, "Excuse me, sir. But I think this gentleman has something he wants to say."

They all turned to look at Mr. Nevinson. He was a pathetic parody of his important and orderly self, but a light was observable in his eyes. He said, speaking very slowly, "I told you, Inspector. You remember. In case of fire."

"Of course," said Mercer. "Where are they?"

"Closet in the corner."

Mercer raced across and opened it. Inside were two heavy brass wheels, each with a metal tag attached. A chain through the spokes was padlocked. There was a key in a circular glass case inside the door. Mercer poked the barrel of his pistol through the glass, picked out the key, opened the padlock, and slid off the chain.

Then he examined the tags. The left-hand one said "Shutters." Mercer rotated it as far as it would go.

The chief constable said, "You seem to know what you're doing. But perhaps you would explain."

"This wheel shuts off the air intake into the cellars. They are now sealed."

"You think shortage of air will drive them out?"

"I expect it would," said Mercer. "In time. But this will bring them up a damned sight quicker." He indicated the second wheel. "This one opens the water jacket. It's a fire precaution. It will fill both cellars to the top in ten minutes. I suggest we flood the bottom cellar first. We could then tell them that unless they came out, *with* their hostages intact, we propose to fill the top cellar, too."

"Do you know," said the chief constable, "I think that's an extremely sound idea. Start turning."

One by one they came up. Constable Pike first, his face drained and the blood still welling from a bruise on his forehead, supported by Beale, unharmed and surprisingly cheerful; followed by six of the Crows, soaked, sullen, contemptuous, aggressive, impassive. Last of all came Mo Fenton. He had taken off his coat to work on the door of the strong room, and lost it in the first inrush of the water. His shirtsleeves were rolled above his elbows, showing his great forearms covered with reddish-gray hair.

"I've special instructions from Commander Laidlaw about this man, sir," said Mercer. "I'm to talk to him alone."

"Better search him first," said the chief constable. There was no weapon on him. Mercer led the way to a room opposite, turned on the light, and shut the door behind them.

"I know what you want," said Mo. "You want Paul Crow. And I can give him to you. But first I want to know what I get out of it."

Mercer was standing beside him. His shoulders were slouched, he had his right hand in his jacket pocket, and he looked relaxed and a bit tired.

"We're not interested in Paul Crow anymore," he said. "After tonight, he's a dead duck. He's not only lost his best men, and most of his money. He's lost his magic. People won't believe in him anymore. Very soon, someone will decide to take his crown away. They'll take it with a sawed-off double-barreled shotgun at close range."

"You could be right," said Mo. "If you don't want Paul, what do you want?"

"You," said Mercer. His right hand came out of his pocket. Mo saw the glint of steel and ducked too late. The armored knuckles caught him full in the middle of the face.

26

"I KNOCKED OUT three teeth, split both lips, broke his nose, and fractured his cheekbone in two places. And I've never felt happier about anything in my life."

"You got into a lot of trouble over it," said Venetia.

"Of course I did. They couldn't possibly overlook it. That's why I'm going back to the Middle East. Bahrein this time." Mercer grinned reminiscently. "Defense counsel tried to make capital out of it on behalf of his poor, ill-treated client. When the jury heard that Mo had burned off Nevinson's ear with a cigarette lighter, trying to extract from him a master key which didn't exist, they somehow lost interest in *his* little troubles."

"Keep out here," said Venetia. "If you get too close to the bank you'll lose your pole in the mud."

She was sprawled on the cushions of the punt, trailing one brown hand in the water, and watching Mercer, who was punting with considerable skill and assurance.

"All the same," she said, "it was silly to hit him. He was bound to get a long sentence, on account of the superintendent being killed."

"You wouldn't understand," said Mercer. He rubbed one finger down the scarred side of his face. "How do you think I got this?"

"I've often wondered."

"Mo did it. While two of his men held me. For various reasons there wasn't much I could do about it at the time. But I couldn't let him get away with it. It would have been bad for morale."

"I don't suppose his morale will be up to much for the next fourteen years."

"I wasn't thinking of his morale. I was thinking of mine. All the same, the biggest kick I got out of the whole trial was seeing Weatherman go down for seven years."

"He wasn't a very nice person," agreed Venetia. "A good lawyer though."

"Will the firm survive?"

"I think so. Willoughby's having to work really hard for the first time in his life."

"It'll do him a power of good."

"They've lost a lot of clients, of course. But they've got quite a few new ones. People will always go to a solicitor if they think he can fiddle their taxes for them."

They slid on in silence for a few minutes. It was early summer and there were no other boats on the river.

Mercer said, "I meant to congratulate you on Robert."

"Thank you."

"Just the right husband for you. Clean-living, upright, and industrious."

"Now you're being beastly."

"No. I mean it. Did you tell him about us?"

"Naturally. I didn't want him to imagine I was entirely inexperienced."

"What did he say?"

"He said, 'Oh!'"

Mercer laughed so much he nearly dropped the punt pole.

Venetia said, "I suppose when you get to Bahrein you'll turn Mohammedan, and have four wives."

257

"It would be nice in some ways. But terribly expensive."

"As I probably shan't see you again, there's one thing I wanted to ask you." Having said this, Venetia was silent for so long that Mercer said, "I can't bear the suspense. What is it?"

"It's impertinent. And nothing to do with me. But *why* did you shoot Jack Bull?"

"He'd have shot me if I hadn't."

"Couldn't you have disabled him?"

"It's only in cowboy films that the sheriff shoots the gun out of the bad man's hand."

"I think you're ducking the question."

"Yes," said Mercer. "I'm ducking the question." He rested on the pole for a moment, holding the boat into the current, and staring back into the past; only six months gone, but already a world away. "I think," he said, "that I shot him because I realized that prison would kill him, but it would take a lot longer to do it. You can't think out elaborate reasons when you've only got a split second to make up your mind. But I think that's why I shot him."

"You were fond of him?"

"Yes. I liked him a lot. We were the same sort of people, really. We had the same sort of outlook on life. But he made a mistake. When he came back from the war, with one arm and not much money, he decided to go against the herd. It was a perfectly conscious decision. And it was a mistake."

"How do you know all this?"

"He told me about it, one evening when we were drinking together. He didn't put it in so many words, but I knew exactly what he meant, because I very nearly did the same thing myself once."

"And why didn't you?"

"I worked out that it was easier, and a lot safer, to go

along with the herd and take up any easy pickings on the way."

"You make it sound as if the only difference between honesty and dishonesty is the safety factor."

"You could be right."

"I think it's a disgusting philosophy," said Venetia. "Bull was a crook. And his friends were crooks. He swindled old ladies. And he was a murderer. Wasn't he?"

They were level with Westhaugh Island now and they could see the spit of gravel where the body of Maureen Dyson had been laid.

"Yes," said Mercer. "He certainly killed Maureen Dyson. Who was a most unpleasant little girl and no loss to the community. I doubt if we should have been able to prove it. Although I think there *was* a witness, who either saw him digging the grave the night before, or saw him putting Maureen into it."

"I suppose that was Sowthistle?"

"I think so. It would account for all the muddled stories he told. I don't think he'd have made a very convincing prosecution witness, though. He was scared stiff of Bull."

"Do you think Bull killed Sweetie, too?"

"No. I'm quite certain that was an accident."

"How can you be sure?"

"Because he was very fond of her."

"You can't know that."

"If he hadn't been fond of her, do you think he'd have made a will leaving her everything he had?"

"Did he do that? I didn't know."

"They found it when they were searching through Weatherman's papers. He made it four years ago. What's more, he didn't change it after she was dead."

"Is it a lot?"

"When the garage has been sold up, and everything got in, it will come to about forty thousand pounds, and

259

unless they can prove that any of it came from his dealings with the Crows—which I don't think they can—it will all go to Sweetie's next of kin."

"Who is?"

"Her father."

"Sowthistle?"

"That's right."

"What on earth will Sowthistle do with forty thousand pounds?" said Venetia.

"The imagination," said Mercer, "absolutely boggles."